MCR

The PIG WHO SAVED the WORLD

About the author:

Gryllus the Pig enjoys fine dining, power napping,
and going to any lengths necessary to avoid physical danger.

About the translator:

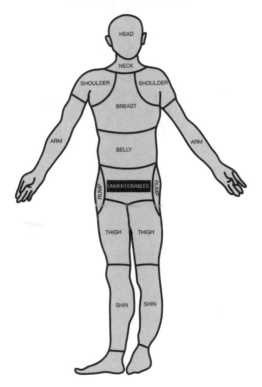

Other books by Paul Shipton

BUG MULDOON: THE GARDEN OF FEAR
THE MIGHTY SKINK
THE PIG SCROLLS

The PIG WHO SAVED the WORLD

by Gryllus the Pig

translated by

Paul Shipton

CANDLEWICK PRESS
CAMBRIDGE, MASSACHUSETTS

Copyright © 2006 by Paul Shipton

First U.S. edition 2007

Library of Congress Cataloging-in-Publication Data is available.

Library of Congress Catalog Number pending.

ISBN 978-0-7636-3446-9

2 4 6 8 10 9 7 5 3 1

Printed in the United States of America

This book was typeset in Perpetua.

Candlewick Press
2067 Massachusetts Avenue
Cambridge, MA 02140

visit us at www.candlewick.com

For Art and Judy

LEGAL DISCLAIMER

Inside this book you may find the ultimate meaning of life. The publisher and translator can accept no responsibility for head injuries caused by the sudden rush of ancient secret wisdom into unprepared modern brain stems.

BOOK I

The past is another country (except the people there still speak Greek and you can drink the water).

"So, what's it like being back, then?"

I placed a tentative hoof onto the rocky ground of Aeaea, unsure how to respond to Sibyl's question. Excitement and nerves were arm wrestling in my heart, and it was a toss-up which would win. It's not easy putting a jumble of feelings like that into words. Luckily the gods have blessed me with an uncanny ability to find the perfect turn of phrase:

"A little freaky."

You could hardly blame me. The island of Aeaea was the only place in the civilized world where I might be turned from a pig back into the fine figure of a man I had once been. It was hard to think about anything else. Throughout the voyage here, I had lovingly built up a mental picture of my new life as a reinstated member of the human race. I'd find myself a nice little island and open up a pie shop, and then I'd lead a nice quiet life with absolutely no dangerous adventures.

Hold on a sec—you *do* know I was a pig, right? When I said that I put a hoof on dry land, that wasn't some fancy-pants poetic metaphor. It was a real hoof on the end of a real pig's leg, namely mine.

Don't go thinking I was just any old pig, either. I was the one-and-only PIG WHO SAVED THE WORLD! (For full details, go and ask your village storyteller to recite the first set of *Pig Scrolls*. Then, if you want to send me a postcard as a thank-you for your continued existence, go right ahead.)

Homer clambered off the ship next. The young poet waded gingerly ashore, holding his sandals in one hand and the hem of his tunic in the other. He gave the wooded interior of the island a wide-eyed stare, no doubt cooking up some la-di-da poetic description of the trees that lined the beach and how foreboding they looked.

Admittedly, there *was* something a bit unnerving about the darkness through those trees.

"So . . . where's Circe's palace?" Homer asked breathlessly.

"Through the dark, creepy forest, then turn right at the nightmarish dead tree stump."

Sibyl was still on board, waiting to confirm plans with Captain Simios, who was currently yelling lots of nautical instructions to the crew. They hopped to it, dropping anchor and tying knots and doing many other things of a technical, maritime nature that I won't describe here, not because I don't understand them; I just don't want to take up valuable scroll-time going into unnecessary detail. So that went well.

While she waited, Sibyl called down to me and Homer: "You should gather some of that plant you told us about, Gryllus. What was it? Moly. We'll need some, and we should leave some with Captain Simios too. Just in case things don't go according to plan."

I responded with the no-nonsense nod of a can-do pig. We *were* on the island of Circe the enchantress, after all, and there's no telling what someone like that will do. Though she wasn't one of the actual Olympians, Circe *was* a divine immortal; she was capable of powerful magic, and she wasn't afraid to use it. A little green plant called moly was the only thing that could protect a person against her powers, so it made sense to stock up.

"Shake a leg, Homer," I said. The pimply teenage epic poet followed me up the beach to the outer edge of the woods. We had to go in a little way past the tree line, but we kept the ship in sight at all times.

"Here's some." I thrust my snout at a clump, and the young poet knelt and pulled the plant up.

"How do you know this stuff works, anyway?" the pale lad asked.

"It was the god Hermes," I explained. "He came and told my old captain, Odysseus, all about it."

The usual spark ignited in Homer's eyes. He got this way whenever there was talk of immortal gods and legendary heroes. If you ask me, that boy needed to get out more.

"Then what?" the epic poet urged me.

I did my best to put him off with a few monosyllabic grunts, but the memories of my first visit to this island came crashing back.

Of course, I had been human when I first trod these shores—a member of Odysseus's crew. We had been on our way back to Ithaca from the Trojan War when we landed here, lost and in need of fresh supplies. Our heroic leader organized a party to explore the island's interior. I could still picture the captain's rugged face as he growled, "Might as well take Gryllus."

I manfully ignored the groans from the rest of the scouting party.

3

(*Hurtful as they were, these came as no surprise. I had always been more of a heroic outsider than a team player, more lone wolf than social animal. Or, in the words of my first-grade teacher, I "didn't play well with others."*) So that's how I ended up tramping to the middle of the island, even though my military record specifically said that I was excused from such duties on account of flat feet.

It was a long, hard walk. But just as I was urging the group to listen to reason and turn back, the land leveled off and we stepped into a clearing. We found ourselves gazing at a sumptuous palace set back in tastefully maintained grounds, and there were wild animals everywhere — bears, lions, stags, that sort of thing — all just wandering around. The beasts made a lot of noise when they spotted us, but none attacked.

That's when Circe emerged from the front door. She swept back her raven hair and smiled. It wasn't so much a "Come in; why don't I get out some chocolate chip cookies and put the kettle on?" sort of smile. More of a "Looky, looky, here comes fresh meat" sort of smile.

The leader of our group started prattling on, invoking the rites of hospitality observed throughout the civilized world. Circe smiled and nodded, but I don't think she was listening to a word. Then she raised this big wooden staff in her hand and pointed it right at us like a loaded bow.

I tried to dodge, but it was no good. A bolt of light shot out of the staff and wrapped itself around us. I was on fire, as if every last bit of me were being changed and mixed and smushed. It felt like being deep-fried.

It wasn't just me, either. The panicked squeals of my comrades filled my ears—filled my piggy ears, that is. Yes, Circe had turned us all into pigs!

Well, unless Zeus has seen fit to bounce a thunderbolt off your head, you know the rest—how Odysseus, armed with his bag of moly, came to the rescue. How, once she realized that the captain was immune to her spells, Circe agreed to turn the other crew members back into humans. And how, while all this was going on, I hid, having chosen to remain a pig at that time.

"Here's what I don't understand." Homer was cradling enough of the plant in his arms to serve moly salad to a small army. We were making our way back to the ship. "Why? Why did Circe turn you all into pigs?"

"Who knows? Perhaps her mom and dad didn't let her keep a pet when she was little."

Back at the ship, Sibyl had disembarked and was telling Simios that we'd return before darkness. The grizzled captain jerked a thumb back at the crew and said something along the lines of "Oshur de ladz'll len jan, eh?"—which I *think* was an offer to have some of the crewmen accompany us and help. (The captain's thick Corinthian accent was a formidable barrier to communication. When you also threw in his fondness for seafaring lingo, I was left taking random guesses at what he was going on about.)

Sibyl shook her head in apparent understanding. "Thanks, Captain, but I don't think anyone can really help with this."

WHAT? One of my core beliefs in life is *never, EVER turn down an offer of assistance*. But before I could voice my concerns, the captain fixed his salty old sea dog's stare on me.

"Eh, dinna liv tall upta scurra, reet og," he said (possibly).

As usual, I fell back on the same answer I'd used throughout the voyage whenever the captain addressed me: "What's that? Oh, terrific, Captain!"

The seaman's eyes darkened beneath bushy gray eyebrows. I hoped he hadn't just told me that his dear old mother had perished on these very shores.

Sibyl quickly defused any tension by having Homer pass up a bundle of moly to Captain Simios and the rest of the crew.

The priestess turned to me. "Right, then. Are you ready?"

A tremor of anxiety trotted through me, but I reminded myself that anxiety had no place in one to whom the entire Cosmos owed a hearty vote of thanks. I squinted up and in a cool, heroic fashion drawled, "Sibyl . . . I was born ready."

At least that's what I would have said if a gust of wind hadn't blown sand into my eyes. Blinking rapidly, I stepped into a rock pool, where a crab seized the opportunity to nip me on the ham hocks. I had to make do with a startled howl, but it was still sort of cool and heroic—just not in the traditional way—and I think they got the gist.

BOOK II

Magical powers are no guarantee of a tidy house.

OK, here's what was supposed to happen:

We'd march at a sprightly pace up to Circe's palace, taking the opportunity to get a little fresh air and exercise along the way. We'd arrive to a warm, completely unmysterious welcome from the enchantress—perhaps something along the lines of "Hello, Gryllus. Back for a little retransformation, are you?" Then she'd add, "Oh, and by the way, thanks ever so much for saving the entire Cosmos. Very decent of you."

Cue lots of magical stuff involving mystical staffs and multicolored light shows and open-mouthed gasps of wonder, etc., etc. And then, once I was human again, it'd be time for a bang-up feast, with steaming hot pies all around and several pints of honey wine to wash it all down. Brilliant!

And that's what *would* have happened if there were any fairness in this Cosmos. I mean, is that too much to ask for?

Apparently—and the theologians among you can take note—it *is*. For one thing, the hike to the center of the island was much harder than I'd remembered. Sibyl was the only one who lived up to that whole "marching at a sprightly pace" idea. At least I wasn't the only one struggling. Homer had clearly spent too much time thinking up rhymes and not enough time building up his leg muscles at the local gymnasium.

As we trudged along, my mind grappled with weighty matters. This was hardly surprising. After all, had I not looked down on the Earth from the Chariot of the Sun itself? Not a lot of pigs can say that. OK, not a lot of pigs can say anything—but my point is, this sort of experience will get even a pig-of-action like me thinking about the meaning of it all.

Philosophy, that's what they call it. *The love of wisdom.*

Well, I love a lot of things, most of them involving pastry. However, I had decided lately to make room in my ample heart for wisdom as well. Seeing as how I had saved the Cosmos, I was determined also to understand the *point* of the Cosmos.

Sibyl noticed the look of intense philosophical thought on my face.

"What's up, Gryllus?" she asked. "Got indigestion again? I've told you time and again: *breakfast is NOT a competitive event.*"

"No, no. I was just thinking . . ." I cleared my throat. "Life's a bit like this, really. You know, sort of an uphill struggle, through the woods, and . . . and you're not even sure what you'll find when you get to the top, and you try to avoid all the stinging nettles but you still get stung, so there's an itchy rash up the back of your legs and, and . . ."

If I could just focus, I felt I might nudge my brain toward some important truth about this thing we call life. Unfortunately, the brainbox was digging its heels in.

"Know what I mean?" I ended weakly.

As a teenage poet, Homer was no stranger to fumbling attempts to define life and its meaning. He tried to nod his head in sympathy while at the same time shaking it in confusion. The result was an unusual bobbling motion.

However, a former priestess like Sibyl, more used to the practicalities of temple work, was having none of it.

"Don't think so hard, Gryllus," she advised. "This wouldn't be a good time for your head to go *pop,* now would it?" (Astonishingly, this was Sibyl trying to be friendly. The timetable at the temple in Delphi must not have devoted much time to developing interpersonal skills.)

Still, no time to dwell on such matters, because the unbroken sunlight up ahead told us we had reached the plateau at the island's center. We were almost at the palace of Circe. Within minutes I would be resuming my true human form.

Sibyl entered the clearing first, and right away she let out a gasp. I found out why when I nosed my way past the trees.

When I had been here the last time, Circe's palace looked pretty impressive. Admittedly, not as grand as the marble palaces of Mount Olympus (which I saw not long after *I saved the entire Cosmos,* in case you didn't know), but definitely a nice starter home for the minor deity on the go.

Not anymore. Where once the adjectives *magnificent* and *sumptuous* had jumped to mind, they were now elbowed aside by tougher words like *ruined* and *dilapidated.* One whole wing had collapsed into rubble. The rest of the place looked in need of a lick of paint and several decades' worth of tender loving care. No animals wandered across the unkempt lawn now. As we neared the building, we soon realized there was no Circe in residence either.

"*Not* how you remember it, I assume?" said Sibyl. She spoke softly, but her voice seemed loud in the silence that lay over the entire place, not like a nice warm blanket of silence but more like a funeral shroud or something equally creepy.

"Hell-oooo, Circe!" I shouted. "Are you here, your mystical enchantressness?"

"It's too quiet," said Homer as he stepped carefully over a pile of rocks. "It feels . . . ominous. I don't like it."

"I don't blame you," commented Sibyl. She was already gathering kindling and twigs, which she expertly propped together into a cone shape in the shelter of a low stone wall.

She sparked a flame with her flint, and soon we were looking into the yellow-blue flames of a small fire.

"O gray-eyed Athena," Sibyl called in invocation as she sprinkled a secret blend of herbs and spices (all from her trusty backpack) onto the flames, "we humbly ask your assistance."

Sibyl had been a priestess in the temple of Apollo, but recently she had formed a closer bond with his sister, the goddess Athena.

However, the gray-eyed goddess did not appear now. Instead, a rasping, disembodied voice rose from the flames: "The deity you have invoked is not available to take your prayer at the present time," it groaned. "At the sound of the moan, leave a brief message stating the purpose of your entreaty and giving details of the offering you intend to make." This was followed by a ghastly moan and then an expectant hiss.

Sibyl's only response was to kill the flames with a handful of dust.

"Who was *that*?" asked Homer.

"Not a *who*, a *what*," explained Sibyl. "Hephaestus, the Smith of the Gods, created an automaton that would pass on messages to the Olympians when they were otherwise occupied."

I nodded knowledgeably. "Like when they're on the toi—"

"When they're busy doing ANYTHING else," snapped Sibyl. (She had become a lot friendlier of late, but here was a glimpse of the old Sibyl—the one about as friendly as an alligator with an attitude problem and a full set of choppers.)

"Sorry," she muttered.

"Why didn't you leave a message?" Homer asked.

Sibyl's eyes took in the desolate ruins around us. "Because I've got a bad feeling about this place and I would like to talk to one of the Olympians *right now*." The slight wobble in the former priestess's voice didn't do much to set my mind at rest. Sibyl's old temple job had involved predicting the future— when *she* had a bad feeling, it was worth paying attention.

"I'm going to see if there's a temple somewhere in the palace," she said. "That might get a stronger signal through so that I can make contact with the Olympians. In the meantime, why don't the two of you just . . . er, just have a rest. Don't do anything, OK? Don't *touch* anything."

Young Homer nodded sheepishly. Me, I nodded piggily— I don't need to be asked twice to do nothing.

After Sibyl had disappeared inside the palace, I scanned the area for somewhere more comfortable for a bit of a well-earned rest.

"This way," I instructed the young poet. "The moss looks nice and springy over here."

"Shouldn't we wait right here?" Homer cried. "Sibyl said not to do anything. . . ."

I shook my head. "Homer, Homer, Homer," I said, the seasoned hero imparting hard-won wisdom to yet another small-town kid with big dreams. "I think I can be trusted to make a few decisions for myself, don't you?"

An answer was too slow in coming for my liking, so I added, "Look, we're just going to sit down! We can do nothing just as well over there!"

Though not completely convinced, the epic poet followed. I slumped down on the moss. I have always been able to think things through more clearly when horizontal—something to do with the flow of blood to my larger-than-average brain.

"OW!" said a small, muffled voice.

"Er, Gryllus? I think your . . . rear end just said something," said Homer in bewildered alarm.

It was true—the voice *had* come from my other end (the one not traditionally associated with the gift of speech)!

This was an odd development, no question, and dozens of thoughts tumbled through my mind about what it might mean in terms of my day-to-day life. I'm well known for looking on the bright side, but I could think of few situations in which having a talking bottom appeared to provide much of an advantage.

BOOK III

A mysterious stranger tells his tale
(and when I say mysterious . . .).

"Getting a bit of a headache down here," continued the mysterious voice from my nether regions. "Be a pal and get off, would you?"

Something stirred underneath me. That's when I realized that it wasn't, in fact, my rear end speaking—thank the gods! No, it was something *underneath* my rear end. I leaped up sharpish.

There on the ground was a grasshopper—a bit battered

but not in too bad a condition, considering that a not-quite-petite adult hog had just used it as a sofa.

"Cripes!" chirped the crumpled insect. "No offense, old chum, but has your personal physician ever raised the topic of dieting?"

I sighed heavily at the sight of another talking creature. "Let me guess . . . you used to be human, but Circe transformed you, right?" I stifled a yawn and gave Homer a knowing look. "Been there, done that, bought the commemorative toga."

"Well, you're half right, I'll give you that," answered the grasshopper chirpily. "Circe didn't have anything to do with it, but I *was* human, all right, years ago." His exoskeleton straightened with pride. "I used to be a prince," he chirped, adding unnecessarily, "not a grasshopper. Sort of a demotion really, but one mustn't grumble, that's what I always say." He hopped forward gamely. "The name's Tithonus, but most people call me Hoppy for some reason."

Homer craned forward, sensing fresh material for an epic poem.

"What happened to you?" he urged the six-legged minibeast.

"I was not only a prince, but I was also widely considered to be quite the catch—according to some, I was the most handsome and eligible young bachelor in the kingdom," continued Hoppy the tiny grasshopper.

"Oh, yes?"

"That wasn't just my opinion, you understand," the grasshopper added hastily, in case we thought he was being a bit boastful for a tiny invertebrate. "Everyone said so, even the peasants and the city rabble. And especially the young ladies of the kingdom. . . ." For a split second, I thought one of his glittering black eyes winked. "And I'll tell you who else thought so . . . Eos!"

"You mean the rosy-fingered, saffron-robed Goddess of the Dawn?" asked Homer.

"I say! Fancy yourself a poet, do you?" commented the grasshopper, springing around to address my companion. "Good for you! Don't you pay attention to what the other boys say; they're only jealous. You keep on writing those hexameters, that's what I say."

"So *was* it Eos?" I grunted.

"The one and only!" replied Hoppy. "She took a shine to my rugged good looks, apparently. And, naturally enough, I took a shine back to her, too. After all, I'm only human . . . or at least, I was back then. Well, one thing led to another — in the usual manner of these things — and before you knew it, the two of us were what you might call an *item*."

"You're telling us you . . . went out with the Goddess of the Dawn?" I made no attempt to stifle the disbelief in my voice. "As in, the Goddess of the Dawn was your girlfriend?"

"Oh, yes, indeed!" replied the small insect merrily. "And we made a lovely couple, if I do say so myself."

"What went wrong, then?" I pressed him. "Why aren't you on Olympus now, slugging ambrosia?"

The grasshopper's multifaceted eyes glittered as he lowered his head.

"Ah well, things were peachy keen to begin with. But time has a rotten habit of slipping by, and young Hoppy wasn't getting any younger. Eos started to worry, what with me being mortal and all. So off she went to ask old Zeus to grant me immortality. A grand idea, you might think? But here's what the King of the Gods went and did. He granted me immortality all right . . . he just didn't bother to grant me everlasting youth to go with it."

For an instant, I detected a new quality in Hoppy's chirpy little voice: a sharp, bitter edge. The grasshopper's lower lip wobbled for a moment, or at least those weird mandible things did.

"It wasn't too bad for a while," he continued, once again chirpy, "but of course I kept on getting older and older. Before long my hair turned white as snow — what little of it was left, that is. And wrinkles! My face was covered in them."

"People say wrinkles make faces look more interesting," Homer offered.

"You don't see too many interesting-looking raisins though, do you?" I said.

Hoppy went on. "My joints began to creak, and my hips ached in damp weather. I took to having afternoon naps, and I grew inexplicably interested in acquiring little knickknacks to put on the mantelpiece."

"What terrible illness afflicted you?" asked Homer gravely.

"It's called old age," answered Hoppy, "and there's rather a lot of it about, I fear. But don't forget, I was immortal. No one-way ticket to the Underworld for old Hoppy! No, I just kept on getting older and older, not to mention weaker and weaker — and littler and littler. I was actually shrinking.

"It seems there wasn't much Eos could do, apart from tuck me away in a back room and make sure I got everything I needed, which was mostly sleep and lots of mushy food. Before long, I was too small even for the bed, and her servants popped me into a basket in the corner.

"I just went on withering and withering until finally . . . well, finally I turned into this."

"So . . . did Eos transform you?" asked Homer.

"Couldn't tell you," replied the grasshopper. "Maybe she did in an attempt to help me. Maybe old Hoppy was destined to shrivel down to this all along. Either way, I've been like this for an awfully long time."

I contemplated the terrible fate of living as an insect for all eternity.

"Still," I commented, "at least you've got your health."

The grasshopper made no immediate reply. At last he spoke. "And what, may I ask, has brought you to the island of Aeaea?"

"A big ship," answered Homer, looking puzzled.

"I believe our six-legged friend is referring to the chain of events that led us to this fateful moment," I said. Homer's face reddened as I went on. "It's a long story. As you probably know, the Cosmos was recently in terrible danger. Well, let's just say, it was saved by a certain talking pig not a million miles from here."

Hoppy said nothing.

"Me!" I clarified. "It was saved by me!"

"Really?" said Hoppy conversationally.

"Yes, REALLY!"

"It's true," Homer chimed in, "he did. And then we came here—in our big ship—so that Circe could transform him back to his true shape." The young poet leaned in over the insect. "Is that why you're here, too? So that Circe can change you back to the way you used to be?"

Hoppy's silent gaze bounced back and forth between Homer and me. "I strongly suspect it's too late for me to change now," the insect said at last. "No, I came here seeking Circe's help in another matter. I recently had a falling-out with an old acquaintance of mine by the name of Sisyphus. I'm afraid he has treated me rather poorly, and I had hoped that Circe might help me to exact revenge of sorts. You see, he's —"

"I'm sorry," I interrupted, "but we really don't want to get involved in petty squabbles between a couple of insects."

"Sisyphus is no insect!" exclaimed Hoppy. "He's a man, and not a very nice one." The insect looked at the ruins all around us. "I rather fear that his people have found Circe first. She is probably now on the island of Crete with him."

"*Crete?* What's she doing on Crete?" My geography was not exactly up to scratch, but I knew that the island of Crete was a long way from here.

"Er, Gryllus . . ." said Homer, looking up nervously. "I think maybe we'd better continue this conversation somewhere else, somewhere a bit more . . ."

"Not now!" I snapped. I was too anxious to learn what had happened to Circe; she was, after all, the only person who could change me back into my true form. "Why *Crete* of all places? And why —"

Before things could be made any clearer, a shadow from above crossed us. Then a large white shape fell out of the skies. It landed right on top of Hoppy in a flurry of feathers and stabbing bill. I just had time to make out what it was —

a pelican — before it raised its head and flew off again, leaving behind a patch of nothing. It didn't go far before landing on a half-ruined pillar, where it watched us with a bored yellow eye.

"It ate him!" cried Homer.

"Get it!" I yelled. The young poet hitched up his tunic and took off after the pelican. The seabird didn't seem troubled as the poet flapped and gasped toward it.

Just then I spotted something moving in the trampled grass in front of me. The grasshopper!

"It's all right, Homer. Come back!" I shouted in relief. "It *didn't* get him! I've got Hoppy right here!" As Homer slowed to a doubtful halt, I looked down to make sure our tiny new acquaintance had not been hurt: "Are you OK then, Hoppy?"

The little grasshopper stared back at me with the look of sheer, dumb incomprehension usually associated with lower animal orders and professional wrestlers. Probably in shock.

"I don't think that's Tithonus!" Homer shouted, still out of breath.

"Who?"

"Hoppy! I don't think that's Hoppy!"

"Of course it is!" I scoffed. "He's probably too scared to speak in case it attracts the pelican again. Right, Hoppy?"

Once again, Hoppy the grasshopper held his tongue, in a manner of speaking. (Do grasshoppers have tongues? You don't see them licking many ice-cream cones.)

The know-it-all young poet still didn't look convinced, so I said to Hoppy, "Listen, take a hop forward, will you? Just to show our skeptical friend that you understand what I'm saying."

Sure enough, the grasshopper bounded forward.

"See?"

Homer still wasn't going for it. "But, Gryllus," he objected, "isn't that what any grasshopper would do? Hop? It doesn't prove it can understand you. We should . . . I don't know . . . ask it to turn left or hop backward or something."

"Oh, for gods' sake!" I huffed. "Did you hear that, Hoppy? Do us a favor and take a hop back the other way now, will you?"

The grasshopper took another leap forward.

"Oh gods!" I gasped. "You know what this means? . . . He can't hear us! That pelican's squawk must have damaged his sensitive little ears!"

Homer had a funny look on his face, sort of tense and red.

Suddenly a tiny voice piped up in the distance. "Help!" It was Hoppy, only here's the odd thing: the voice seemed to be coming from the pelican!

Huh? I looked down in confusion at the little insect near my front hooves. Why was Hoppy throwing his voice from here to over there?

"Help!" the tiny cry sounded once more. This time the pelican's bill opened a little more. Before it snapped shut again, I spotted something in there. Something sort of . . . insect-y.

Something really rather *grasshopper-ish*.

I glared down at the real bug in front of me. "You're not Hoppy at all," I spat, "you creepy little impostor!" The treacherous insect hopped away before I could treat it to the full weight of a pig's foot on its head.

I brought Homer up to speed. "The real Hoppy is in that pelican's bill!"

"I know!" exclaimed the poet crossly.

"Well, why didn't you *say* something? Great Zeus on a zebra, I can't be expected to work out absolutely *everything*!"

The pelican's unblinking yellow eye was still trained on us.

"So what are you waiting for?" I yelled at Homer. "GET IT!"

If I'd asked him to whip up a vivid, cliché-free description of the seabird, he'd have done it, quick as a wink. What he *couldn't* do was the simple task of trotting over, jumping up, and grabbing that flying rat by one of its webbed feet.

As soon as Homer came near, the pelican simply unfurled its wings and flew unhurriedly to a higher perch.

"Chuck something at it!" I instructed. "Make it drop him!"

I looked around for a handy-size rock that the poet could throw. There wasn't one—but there was a staff propped up against the inner part of a half-destroyed wall.

"Throw this!" I cried.

Homer picked up the staff in both hands and looked down at it uncertainly.

"I . . . I think this is Circe's staff," he said gravely.

He was right. The last time I had seen that staff, it was in the hands of the enchantress herself. It was easy to recognize because of the various symbols carved along its shaft. I'm no big reader, but I was willing to bet those mystical runes didn't say *Made in Corfu*.

A single thought hammered relentlessly through my skull:

only Circe could transform me back to my true shape, and only Hoppy seemed to know what had happened to Circe. Which all added up to one simple fact—we couldn't let that stinking pelican fly off with the grasshopper!

"Throw it!" I roared at Homer.

This jolted the poet into action. Alas, the lad was no athlete. He elected not to hurl the staff like a top Olympic javelin thrower. Nor did he swing the staff around and around, finally releasing it so that it zoomed through the air like a spinning disc. Instead, he chose to jerk his arms forward in the startled manner of one who has just spotted a wasp crawling up his sleeve. He accompanied this with a panicked yelp.

The staff did go in the general direction of the pelican, but it clearly wasn't going to make the distance. I knew this, Homer knew it—even the *pelican* knew it, judging from the way its wings didn't even twitch.

Sure enough, the staff fell short and hit the ground. But then an explosion of orange erupted from one end of it and a beam of light shot out. It only just missed the pelican, which let out a fearful squawk.

My eyes followed the beam of light as it arced over the trees, back in the direction we had come from. It was quite a sight, and I would have watched it a little longer, but I was distracted by something crossing my line of vision. The pelican! Flying! Away! And presumably with Hoppy still in its enormous bill!

With a couple of powerful flaps it rose higher into the air. "Stop!"

But in next to no time the seabird was above the treetops,

and then it was heading out toward the ocean. There was nothing to do but watch it go.

I couldn't believe our rotten luck. Captain Odysseus always said it does no good laying blame when Fate deals you a poor hand. Me, I prefer a different management style, one in which the right words of constructive criticism can help people see where they went wrong. I shot a poisonous look at Homer. "Way to go, Plato*!" I spat.

Homer was giving me the look that sulky teenage epic poets seem to specialize in—as if it were *my* fault or something—when Sibyl's voice barked out from behind us: "Just WHAT is going on here?"

I whirled around. Under other circumstances, I might have noticed how drawn the former priestess's features were.

"Well?" she demanded.

Seeing the flustered look on Homer's pimply face, I knew it was up to me to give the essential information.

"OK, it all started when we heard my bottom talking . . ."

Sibyl raised one eyebrow. "So what else is new?"

* Translator's Note: As one of the ancient world's top brains, the name *Plato* was a byword for great intelligence. A modern equivalent might be *Einstein,* as in the following exchange:

    Person 1: Oops, I appear to have spilled milk all over my new Sunday-best pants.

    Person 2: Excellent work, *Einstein.*

    Person 1: But my name is ———, ** not Einstein.

    Person 2: Whatever. You still smell like milk.

** This name has been removed for legal reasons. But you know who you are.

BOOK IV

Sooner or later everything changes, and it's not often for the better.

We told Sibyl all about Hoppy, and her grim expression grew ever grimmer. He eyes widened in silent alarm when I came to the name Hoppy had mentioned: Sisyphus. As she listened, she held the staff of Circe, now spent of all its magic, in both hands.

"What about you?" Homer asked. "Did you find a temple in the palace?"

Sibyl nodded distractedly. "There was a little one over on the west wing."

"And did you manage to get a message through to the gods?"

Sibyl was back to her old habit of biting her bottom lip in thought. "Not exactly."

"What does *that* mean?" I asked.

Sibyl looked up and grimaced. "It means we're going to Crete, I suppose," she said wearily.

This news came like a slap in the face with a wet fish. This day was most definitely *not* going according to plan. I had expected to be leaving this afternoon walking tall, on two feet, ready to start my new life. Now, annoyingly, it seemed that our journey was not yet over. I would have to wait a while longer before I was human again.

"How far away is Crete, anyway?" I asked glumly. It wasn't a rhetorical question—I really would have liked an answer— but my companions remained silent.

We made our way back to the ship with heavy feet and hooves, respectively, each of us lost in private thoughts. We still hadn't broken our silence when we reached the beach, where our ship lay at anchor.

One of the crew members—a hairy little bloke I couldn't remember seeing before—was swinging in the rigging. After what we had found at Circe's palace, his air of carefree abandon seemed out of place—a bit like a children's entertainer doing the hokey-pokey at the reading of a will.

Sibyl froze. "Er, Gryllus," the former prophetess began with one of those unnerving tones you'd rather not hear, "you *did* give the crew some of that moly plant, didn't you? To protect them from Circe's magic?"

"Do you think I'm *completely* useless?" I grunted. "Of course I did!"

The same little crewman was now executing a backflip off the crow's nest. As Olympic gymnastics go, it was easily worth a solid 9.9 for level of difficulty and technical precision, but Sibyl wasn't impressed.

"Gryllus . . . show me some moly, will you?"

I pointed my snout back at a clump of the broad-leafed plant. "There," I said impatiently. "And there! Look, it's all over the place. . . . But quite frankly, is this is the right time for a discussion of island flora? I think not."

The former prophetess looked suddenly tired. "This isn't moly, Gryllus," she said through clenched teeth, bending down to pluck up a leaf. "For your information, this is a dock leaf, which will come in handy if anyone gets a nettle sting, but, to the best of my knowledge, it isn't much use in warding off magical enchantments."

I glared at the plant that had tricked me with its apparent moliness. Well, looking at *that* was better than looking at the crewman, who was now swinging from the crow's nest by his prehensile tail.

By now we could hear the whoops and calls and shrieks of the rest of the crew, who were also sounding distinctly *monkey-ish.*

"It's not my fault!" I blurted in response to Sibyl's unvoiced accusation. "I'm not a botanist, am I? One plant looks just like another!"

On board, the baboon formerly known as Captain Simios was picking fleas off the first mate's head. Other crew members scampered up the mast and leaped from yardarm to rigging and back again, howling and hooting. Do I have to spell it out in simple Greek? The. Crew. Were. Monkeys.

"Must have been that blast from Circe's staff," commented Homer, proving himself an ideal candidate for the post of Poet Laureate of the Gob-Smackingly Obvious.

"It might be OK," I ventured. "I mean, we'd have no chance if they were tortoises or guinea pigs. But monkeys, they've got nimble little hands, haven't they? Just look at them scooting up the rigging. . . ."

Sibyl marched across the gangplank with the determined step of someone with nothing to lose. The monkeys let loose a chorus of aggressive calls at this invasion of their territory, but the prophetess strode up to the former captain.

"Nod if you can understand me," she began.

The captain flattened his ears and bared huge canine teeth. "Agh, agh, AGH!" he declared, a guttural noise that vibrated up from his hairy chest in an impressive display of I'm-not-sure-what.

This outburst seemed to be directed at me, so I responded the only way I knew how: "Oh, really, Captain? That's terrific!"

BOOK V

The tale of Sisyphus is not the most relaxing bedtime story ever.

As things turned out, the mere fact that they were monkeys didn't stop the captain and his crew from sailing the ship. Admittedly, they weren't too keen on the idea at first—at least that's the conclusion I drew from all the explosive grunting and furious prancing around. But Sibyl carefully explained that they would have to take us to Crete if they ever hoped to be turned back into their human forms. This got them to ease off on all the shrieking. Then Sibyl promised she'd get them a sack of nuts and raisins at our next port of call, and that sealed the deal. The monkeys would take us to Crete!

And I'll tell you something: those little primates did a grand job. They got the ship ready in next to no time, and then we were off. Their sea shanties were a little less melodious now, I'll grant you—but then again, it wasn't as if they'd *ever* wowed anyone with their close harmonies. (And, on the plus side, I no longer had to listen to cries of "Avast behind!" whenever I walked down the deck—seafaring types can be so cruel.)

It was hard to tell what the crew themselves made of their new position in the great Chain of Being. Unlike yours truly, the effects of Circe's magic had left them unable to speak, although they gave every impression of understanding what was said to them, more or less.

With this in mind, I did my best to remain chatty—which is why I found myself commiserating with a heavyset rhesus monkey who was mopping the deck that evening:

"Still, it's not all bad being an animal, is it?" I began cheerily, one mammal to another. The primate let out a warning grunt. "I mean, look at you. At least you've got a full head of hair again, haven't you? It's what I always say, every cloud—"

The rhesus picked this of all moments to smash the mop. He leaped up and down, howling and baring his teeth and jabbing the jagged ends of the wood in my direction.

"Yes, well, I can see you've got lots on your plate," I said hastily, "so I'll just be moving along."

This seemed like a good moment to head up to the other end of the ship, the pointy bit at the front. I found Sibyl and Homer sitting there. They were hunched over in serious discussion about something or other. As I neared them, I overheard Sibyl say the name "Sisyphus."

"What's that?" I asked. "You're talking about that bloke Hoppy mentioned, right? What about him?"

Sibyl looked up as if I'd caught her scarfing the last pie. "Er, no . . ." she stammered. "I was talking about my SISTER. . . . She's always making a FUSS, that sissy of mine."

"You haven't *got* a sister," I said accusingly.

Sibyl looked to Homer for help, but the young poet had none to offer.

"OK," the prophetess sighed at last. "I didn't want to trouble you unduly, Gryllus, until we had completed more of the voyage. But, yes, we were talking about Sisyphus."

"Who is he, anyway?" I asked, plunking myself down. "Hoppy said he wasn't very nice."

"That's one way of putting it," said Sibyl. "King Sisyphus was one of the most evil men ever to walk the Earth." She treated me to one of her best disappointed-teacher looks. "You mean, you've never heard of him?"

"I was out sick the day we did evil kings at school."

Sibyl rolled her eyes. "When he was alive, Sisyphus was a wealthy king, but he angered the gods with his evil ways. So, after he died, he was sent to a special area of the Underworld. Some people know it as Tartarus; others just call it the Punishment Zone. It's the place where evildoers are punished in the afterlife for their crimes in this world. Sisyphus's penalty was a particularly terrible one. He had to roll an enormous boulder up a hill."

"What happened when he reached the top of the hill?"

"The boulder rolled back down again."

"And then what?"

"And then he'd have to push it up again . . . and again . . . and again, forever and ever."

"What's the point of that, then?" I grunted.

"Precisely!" said Sibyl.

I looked out across the wine-dark sea and contemplated the terrible fate of evil King Sisyphus.

"You know . . . life's a bit like that," I said at last. "When you think about it . . ."

Sibyl looked as if she had swallowed the wrong way. "Oh yes? How do you mean exactly? That life's a bit like doing the same pointless task, again and again and again?"

"No, I mean . . ." My thoughts were back in the general proximity of greatness. "You've always got to be on the lookout for things like giant boulders rolling down the great hill of life. Because, let's face it, if one of them rolled over you, you'd soon know about it. Squash you flat as a pancake, a whopping great boulder like that. Just try playing the lyre after one of them's done a number on you."

The former priestess was tapping an impatient foot on the deck. "So, let me get this straight, Gryllus. Your philosophy of life is that one should always avoid giant boulders?"

"Yeah . . ." I nodded slowly. "But only when they're rolling toward you. The stationary ones are all right. . . ."

"Yes, well, I think we're straying off the point here. You asked about Sisyphus," said Sibyl. (It's a sad truth in this life that some brains are simply too narrow to accommodate the big ideas.) "The thing is, it seems that your little insect friend was right—Sisyphus is no longer in the Underworld."

"So?"

"Perhaps you'd better let him hear the message," said Homer. The young poet's face was even paler than usual, and that's saying something.

Sibyl quickly built and lit a fire in the copper bowl she always kept in her backpack.

"You know when I went looking for a temple at Circe's palace?" she said. "This is what I heard when I tried to call the gods."

When the flame was burning strongly enough, she sprinkled the same herbs and spices onto it. As it had done before, a single voice rose from the fire, but this one was very different.

"Hello? Hello? Is this thing on?" said a reedy voice from within the fire. Then it went on more confidently: "Greetings, fellow mortals. Sisyphus here! I'm afraid the gods are feeling tired today, so they're having a bit of a snooze. Actually, you might say they're my prisoners." The voice sounded as if it were constantly on the verge of laughter, and at this point it did erupt into a high and hysterical giggle. "So anyway, there's not much point sending up your prayers because there's no one to hear them. Imagine that—there's no one watching you from Mount Olympus. So just . . . go and do whatever you want."

For a few seconds all we could hear was the crackle and hiss of the fire, then Sisyphus's voice sounded again, more quietly now, saying, "Is it off now? It's so hard to tell with this contraption." And then all was silence.

Sibyl killed the flames, and her anxious eyes met mine. I became suddenly and uncomfortably aware of the relentless lurching of the ship beneath my hooves.

"What does it mean?" I said, knowing that very probably I would not like the answer.

The giant snowball of Sibyl's anxiety crashed down on an innocent bystander's head: mine.

"It means that we've got more to do on Crete than just find Circe and get you changed back," Sibyl replied. "If Sisyphus has somehow managed to capture the Olympian gods, it means the whole of the Cosmos is in danger."

My heart plummeted like a free-falling, heart-shaped object. I didn't speak for a long time, until:

"What, *again?*"

BOOK VI

The future isn't looking all that bright.

It took me ages to get to sleep. As I lay in my cabin, unpleasant thoughts flitted around my mind like a flock of razor-winged Stymphalian birds, and let me tell you, that isn't quite as relaxing as counting fluffy baa-lambs jumping over a fence.

This whole situation just didn't seem fair. Was it too much to ask that the Cosmos keep itself out of trouble for once? I mean, what was the point of having gods anyway, if they couldn't take care of this sort of thing? OK, so I was the pig who had saved the world. . . . Did that mean I had to be the one to help save it AGAIN? Surely some other up-and-coming wannabe hero deserved a shot at that honor.

Coming at the problem rationally, I couldn't help thinking that it made more sense simply to drop me off on an island one stop before Crete. I could wait there—selflessly denying myself the chance of further glory—while Sibyl sorted everything out and rescued the gods. (Let's face it, that sort of thing was more up her alley.) Then I could finish the last leg of the journey, go and see Circe, and be changed back to human form. This seemed like a pretty sensible plan to me. And even if this best-case scenario didn't come about for whatever reason . . . well, surely it was better to be a live pig than a dead man. Right?

The same jittery thoughts crowded back to flutter and caw around in my mind when I woke the next morning and looked out across open water. They were still flapping around as I made my way to the front of the ship. Unusually, Sibyl hadn't emerged from her cabin yet, but Homer was up and about. The young poet was bent over a scroll, no doubt working away on a new poem.

He looked up, blinking, and wrinkled his nose as I approached. Guilt stabbed at my heart. Would my traveling companions see the good sense in my not accompanying them to Crete? I knew this lad looked up to me as a wise mentor. Both he and Sibyl revered me as a cool-headed hero. If I told them that, all things considered, I'd rather not go and help rescue the gods, would they look on it as a betrayal of sorts? Would they think I was letting them down?

WOULD I be letting them down?

It isn't always easy to broach the most important topics — they're just too big to launch into right away — so I took refuge in small talk and just said, "What's your new poem about, then?"

Homer automatically covered his work with a defensive arm. He thought the question over before saying warily, "It's an epic cycle about the Underworld."

"Oh. Not a comedy, then?"

"No . . . I've just got to the part where I describe Typhon."

"What, Typhon the fishmonger and street entertainer from Cos Harbor?"

Homer blinked uncertainly. "No . . . Typhon the dreaded monster that has lain buried under half a mountain in the bowels of the Underworld ever since Zeus defeated it in battle, eons ago."

"Not the one who can juggle five pickled herrings, then?"

Homer cleared his throat and began to recite:

"In the bowels of Tartarus lies a beast
Big as one hundred triremes, at least.
Its name is Typhon and it's really, really scary —
Imprisoned by Zeus, with his chin so hairy."

He looked up anxiously. "What do you think?"

"Honest opinion?" I sucked in air meaningfully. "Well . . . it shows promise, for a first draft, by a novice, written under difficult conditions, while at sea. I don't like the sound of this Typhon *thingamajig* . . ."

Homer blinked in confusion. "Of course not! Typhon is the most fearsome monster ever to inhabit the universe! If Zeus hadn't defeated it and imprisoned it in the Underworld at the beginning of time, it would have destroyed the entire Cosmos."

This topic was doing nothing to ease my nerves. "Why don't you write a poem about daffodils or fluffy kittens?" I asked. "Something a bit nicer for once?"

Homer's face flushed. He was not the sort of artist who responds well to constructive criticism. "Great artists are never appreciated in their lifetime," he sulked.

33

"That's all right, then," said a voice from behind us, still thick with sleep. "You may not have long to wait."

It was Sibyl and she was in her sleeping gown. Worry was etched on her ashen face.

"What's the mat—" began Homer, but I shushed him and asked, "What's the matter?"

"I had a dream," said Sibyl flatly.

I shrugged. "What's so special about THAT? *I* had a dream last night, once I finally nodded off. Dreamed I was sailing in a giant pie on a sea of gravy. I don't know what it could mean. . . . Something about not feeling loved enough as a child?"

No one volunteered to interpret my dream. "What did your dream show you?" Homer asked Sibyl.

The obol dropped. "Oh," I said. "One of *those* dreams." Sibyl used to work at the Delphic Oracle, handing out predictions of what was going to happen. She still got the occasional glimpse into the future. My heart sank like a Boeotian-made warship (a line that foolishly featured viewing portals at the bottom of the hull so that the crew could keep an eye out for sea monsters).

"It was dark and I was lost," began the ex-priestess. "I was wandering about in some sort of maze of tunnels."

"The Labyrinth* at Crete?" asked Homer.

---

* Translator's Note: The labyrinth was a winding network of tunnels at the royal palace at Knossos on the island of Crete. King Minos had it built to house the Minotaur, a fearsome monster with the head of a bull and the body of a man. (Some of his advisers had suggested the alternative of a nice field with a fence around it, but Minos felt this wasn't sufficiently dramatic.)

Sibyl nodded. "I knew that there was something I had to do—one very important prisoner trapped in the labyrinth whom I had to find and free."

"Zeus?" asked Homer.

"Possibly," said the priestess, "I'm not sure. I didn't find him, anyway. I tramped through the tunnels for ages until I came to a central chamber. It was empty, but there was blood-red writing all over the wall. It said: NOBODY CAN DEFEAT THE BEAST IN THE DARK.

"Hope that was just red paint," I said miserably. "Otherwise you'd need quite a lot of blood to write that."

"That's not all," said Sibyl. "The next line said: NO ONE CAN SAVE THE COSMOS. I was standing there reading this, when suddenly I heard footsteps approaching. An unspeakable terror gripped me. The footsteps got closer and closer, and then—"

"WHAT?"

"And then I woke up and it was all a dream," said Sibyl briskly.

None of us spoke for the next few up-and-down lurches of the ship.

"So, do you think the footsteps were made by the 'beast in the dark'?" asked Homer at last. "Perhaps it was there to stop anyone from freeing the prisoner in the labyrinth? Like some sort of guard?"

"Perhaps," said Sibyl. "But where does Evil King Sisyphus come into all this?"

I listened to all this in silent amazement. "What is *wrong* with you two?" I erupted at last. "Didn't you understand the message on the wall? *Nobody can defeat the Beast in the Dark,* whatever it is! *No one can save the Cosmos!* So we're all doomed! Am I the only one who finds this just a tiny bit depressing?"

"I do," Homer confessed.

I blinked back hot tears and held down bitter bile at the sheer unfairness of everything. "Well, that's it then, isn't it? Your premonitions are never wrong. We might as well just turn this ship around."

Sibyl shook her head slowly. "No," she said.

"What do you mean '*No*'? You just said yourself that no one can save the Cosmos. So what are we still heading to Crete for? If everything's truly done for, why don't we find a nice island so we can at least enjoy the days we have left?"

My logic was watertight, but Sibyl chose to paddle on in the currents of irrationality. "Because we have to try," she said simply. "Who else is there?"

She turned her attention deliberately to the waters ahead of us, and I could tell that, in her mind, this conversation was over. We were going to Crete on a hopeless mission and that was that.

In some ways, her obstinate refusal to listen to the piggy voice of reason made things easier for me. As I looked at the resolute set of her jaw and the steely look shining in her eyes, I said to myself, *I don't know this person . . . not really.* I mean, there's determination, and then there's stubbornness . . . and then there's out-and-out reckless nuttiness with no regard for the feelings of others.

When I finally spoke, my voice sounded small and rasping, no doubt as a result of all the sea air and definitely not because of the cocktail of terror, guilt, and despair I was choking back.

"Listen, there's something I have to tell you. I'm—"

Sibyl looked around and held up a hand to cut me off. "I know, I know. You're the pig who saved the world," she said. "That's why we need you now, Gryllus." She turned back to the horizon ahead, where a band of black cloud stretched across the sky.

"That's not what I was going to say," I replied forlornly. But before I could say any more, I was interrupted by a guttural grunt from behind me: "Oogh, agh, oogh."

It was the primate formerly known as Captain Simios. Something had clearly bothered him, enough to make him knuckle-walk the length of the deck. Thick hair stood up all along his back, and his close-set eyes flashed in an agitated fashion.

"Really? That *is* terrific!" I said distractedly. This must have been the wrong thing to say, because Simios replied by baring his impressively big canines. He let out a distraught screech.

I attempted a different tack: "Oh, dear, what an awful shame, Captain!"

This turned out to be a more appropriate response, in that the baboon nodded his muzzle frantically.

"What's the matter, Captain?" said Sibyl.

We followed the primate's long, leathery finger as it pointed to the east—or was that the west? In this area of the sky, the bank of clouds looked thicker and darker and altogether more threatening. They also appeared to be moving quite quickly toward where we were heading.

"Oh," said Sibyl. "Oh, that doesn't look good at all."

I drew on my long years of service in Odysseus's crew and

gave my expert nautical assessment of those storm clouds: "Can you turn this thing around?"

The sea was noticeably less calm now. Homer was already bent over the ship's side (and he wasn't looking for fish).

"I think Gryllus might be right," said Sibyl, "for once. We can't turn back, but we should avoid that storm front. Can we loop around it?"

Simios grunted. The rest of the monkeys in our crew had picked up on his unsettled mood and began howling and shrieking in alarm. There was a sharp smell in the air, and we could only hope it was the whiff of panic.

The ship rose and fell on an immense wave.

"Oh, that's just swell!" I said, trying to ignore the corresponding wave of panic that rose and fell in my belly.

But then I saw it: a tiny slice of land in the distance, out beyond the boat's prow. It was the first land we'd spied since leaving Aeaea, and the sight of it filled me with a desperate hope. If there truly was nothing to be done to save the Cosmos, shouldn't we be heading for just such a place—a nice little island in the sun where we might enjoy the last days of existence as best we could? Didn't that beat the certainty of failure on Crete—not to mention danger, pain, and any number of other things that are best avoided?

There was just one problem. If the storm front moved just a few stades, we'd have to pass right through it to reach the island.

I reminded myself that a true hero has to keep his head while all about him are hopping up and down hysterically.

Lifting my snout, I forced myself to sniff the air calmly. "Actually, no need to worry," I pronounced at last. "Judging from the wind speed and direction, combined with the size of those enormous clouds and the . . . er . . . air humidity, I can assure you that the bad weather front will pass by to the south of us. We can hold our course."

Sibyl narrowed her eyes. "Are you *sure?*"

"Yes, actually! Have you forgotten I was a crewman on one of the greatest ships of all time? That I saved the entire Cosmos?"

I turned to the baboon captain. "You can trust me on this one."

I'm not sure how much Simios understood, but the heroically confident tone of my voice seemed to calm the giant baboon.

Twenty minutes later, the storm hit us.

BOOK VII

An ill wind blows no good (and this wind is so ill that it's in critical condition).

With each surge of the ocean beneath us, the ship rocked a little more violently, until soon the prow was smashing down into the seething waters and saltwater spray was flying in our faces.

Normally, Sibyl would have contacted Poseidon, God of

the Sea, and Aeolus, Lord of the Winds, but we knew this would do no good now. No, it was just us and the uncontrolled elements. Looking at those towering storm clouds, I couldn't help thinking that it wasn't going to be a fair fight.

"We'd better batten down the hatches," said Sibyl grimly.

"Yes, what does that mean, 'batten'?" I asked. "I've always wondered."

But Sibyl had turned to help a proboscis monkey haul in the last of the oars and strap them down. I concentrated on keeping my balance—not easy on a wet deck when you're equipped with hooves.

Soon the wind was howling louder than a boatful of noisy monkeys—this is an actual fact that I can vouch for. The rain began to fall, not bothering with the preliminary spitting and drizzling phases but going straight to torrential downpour. (No sense of dramatic buildup, the rain.) Far-off lightning flashed and flickered in a random way that confirmed that Zeus wasn't at the controls.

"Nothing you can do out here," Sibyl shouted to me. "You'd better join Homer! He's up on the poop deck."

"But . . . I can't go in there till he's done, surely," I protested.

"Listen!" Sibyl yelled, and even the roaring of the wind couldn't mask her irritation. "*Poop deck** doesn't mean what you think it means. Now GO!"

As you can imagine, it pained me to have to leave the sodden

---

* Translator's Note: The poop deck is the name of the raised deck at the stern of a ship, as any junior trainee sailor would know—which makes you wonder how much attention Gryllus was paying during basic training.

monkeys to their valiant struggle, but what Sibyl had said was true. It would serve the common good better if I tucked myself away somewhere safe and dry.

I staggered up to the small hut on the poop deck. Inside, Homer had lashed down the furniture and now sat on the bench at one side of the hut. One look told me why the poet was not out helping on deck. He was a shade of bluish green most commonly associated with months-past-its-sell-by-date yogurt.

"Keeping track of all this, are you?" I shouted. "So you can put it in a poem?"

Homer tried to reply, but what came out of his mouth was not the sort of thing you would want to put in an epic poem, if you know what I mean. (More like modern art, actually, if you know what I mean again.) Good thing he had a bucket on his lap. He was keeping a tight grip on a wooden beam with the other hand.

Which was more than I could do, of course. The pig possesses many fine physical qualities—I mean, it's not bad having a sense of smell that can detect a pie from twenty stades away. But there are drawbacks, too, and the lack of fingers and handy-dandy opposable thumbs is high on the list, especially in situations like this. This design flaw left me with only my mouth to grab on to things.

I did this now, gripping hold of a knot of rope with my teeth. The ship rocked sickeningly. At times it felt as if we were being swept high into the air. This was followed by a dreadful moment of anticipation when we knew that the ship was poised at the top of a mountainous wave. There was just time for Homer to wail (unpoetically), "Oh, no-oooooo!" And then we'd plummet down, falling so fast that my stomach decided it no longer liked its usual spot and would rather set up shop in my throat, thank you very much.

After the downward plunge, we'd have scant moments to ready ourselves before the next go-round. It was during one of these brief lulls that the door flew open and Sibyl gripped its frame. Behind her the rain lashed the deck, the wind shrieked . . . or was that one of the simian crewmates? Either way, it didn't sound promising.

"How are you doing in here?" Sibyl shouted above the din of the storm.

"Terrible!" I answered.

In order to pass on this vital information, I had to loosen my toothy grip on the rope. Alas, at that precise moment the ship pitched violently and I began to slide across the floor.

"Watch out, Gryllus!" yelled Sibyl. "Grab something!"

A brilliant idea, but not wholly feasible. Once my bulk had begun to move, it would take choppers stronger than mine to stop my momentum by grabbing something. I hurtled across the floor, straight toward Homer, who looked like a hedgehog frozen in the path of an oncoming hydra. He snapped out of it just in time, leaping to one side quickly before he could be splattered.

That just left the wooden walls of the hut to bring me to a stop — and they would have done so, too, if only shipbuilders nowadays could actually construct decent, sturdy ships the way they used to in the good old days. But oh, no, they have to use the cheapest materials they can find, don't they? They cut corners and take no pride in their work, and what are you left with? Flimsy planks of wood that just smash and splinter the first moment a speeding, out-of-control pig crashes into them.

CRUNCH!

The next instant, rain and wind were slapping against my face. I was out on the deck! I had smashed my way through the walls of the poop-deck hut and was now sliding around on the deck, as it plunged and rose. I looked around desperately for something to sink my choppers into, but each new wave sent me skidding and sliding in a different direction. Monkeys were screaming angrily and leaping out of the way as I slid and crashed all over the place, until the ship plunged forward and suddenly I was belly-sledding the length of the main deck at top speed.

The cargo hold lay straight ahead of me. There was a bit of a gap on either side of it. I tried to adjust my weight expertly so that I would pass it on the left. Then at the last moment, it occurred to me that the space on the right was a tad wider, so I attempted to reshift my weight and go that way.

Alas, I paid a terrible price for my indecision. I struck the cargo hold head-on, before plunging into an unconsciousness as black as some very black stuff indeed.

I woke up to good news and bad.

On the plus side, the storm had died down, the ship was still afloat, and we didn't appear to have lost any of the crew, who were scurrying about and carrying out repairs and generally working like mad monkeys.

On the minus side, my head felt like it had been sat on by *whatsitsname*—Typhon, the most monstrous of all monsters.

I looked blearily at Sibyl, who was busy bailing water from the deck with a clay bowl. The sky above was an ugly smear of pale gray.

"Is there any grub?" I mumbled.

"Afraid not," she replied briskly. "We lost a lot of rations when something large and heavy struck the cargo hold at high speed. The crew rescued what they could, but most of it was swept away."

It was only then that I realized we weren't moving. The ship was lying at anchor.

"Where are we?" I groaned.

The former prophetess shrugged. "We got blown quite a long way off course. Won't know how far until we get a good look at the constellations. Still, it won't be long until nightfall, seeing as how you've been asleep for most of the day . . . while we've all been working the whole time." Sibyl gave me a withering look. "Anyway, it's a good thing we made it here."

"Made it *where?*"

"Oh, just look over the bulwarks, Gryllus!" she snapped.

"Never mind the bulwarks," I replied, looking instead over the wooden side of the ship. "Oh. It's an island." (I'm no geographer, but, hey, I know an island when I see one.)

Sibyl nodded without looking up. "At least we can patch the ship up here."

There was something about this island's landscape that niggled at me. Something about those sandy dunes and rolling hills that tickled the back of my mind. Something . . . *familiar.*

I was close to fishing out the memory from the murky depths of my brain when Homer squelched up to us. He still hadn't returned to his normal shade of pale after the day's storm. "The captain and crew need a few more hours to finish the repairs," he said breathlessly. "They want us to go and get more supplies . . . I think."

Sibyl sighed and reached for her trusty backpack. "Come on, Gryllus," she said. "Your nose will come in handy, sniffing out provisions."

I hesitated. Was now the time to refloat my plan to stay on dry land and try to ignore whatever problems the Cosmos might be facing? Judging from the all-too-familiar look of steely determination on Sibyl's face, probably not. She just wouldn't understand. The last thing I wanted to do was let the ex-priestess down. But then again, I didn't want *anything* to be the last thing I did, if you know what I mean. Maybe it would be best to spare the sentimental good-byes and just take my leave less openly? Could I do this?

"Well?" Sibyl demanded.

"Er, well, actually, I think I'll stay on the ship, if it's all the same to you. See if I can regain my strength."

Sibyl nodded sympathetically at the wounded-but-brave-little-soldier look in my eyes. Then she pointed to the hairy gang of crewmen, who (I now noticed) were all grunting and snarling as they eyeballed me from the rigging. "You're quite sure you're not up to it, Gryllus?" Sibyl pressed me sweetly. "Because I get the distinct impression that some of the crew rather blame you for all this damage to the ship. *And* for the loss of rations, which I gather they were particularly looking forward to."

I looked at the crew once more. They were humans who had been transformed into monkeys, but I knew it wasn't that simple. The form they'd taken had somehow seeped into their souls—they were a crew of veteran human sailors, but they were also a troop of wild primates who were not necessarily well disposed toward those of a porcine persuasion, which is to say, pigs. There was no telling which side of their dual nature would win out.

I jumped up to my four feet. "Just a jiffy!" I grunted. "Perhaps I *will* come . . . you know, to make sure you're OK."

Sibyl paused, one foot on the plank, ready to disembark. "Gosh, thanks a million, Gryllus," she said, rolling her eyes and elbowing Homer in the ribs so hard you might have mistaken her comment for sarcasm.

"Ow," whined the poet. "Don't *do* that, please."

BOOK VIII

Memory Lane is sometimes located on the wrong side of the donkey tracks.

As we trudged up the first long dune, my eyes warily took in the cliffs on either side of us.

"What's that weird sensation called when you're sure you've already experienced something?" I asked.

"Déjà vu," Homer offered. (His pronunciation of the foreign words—Egyptian, I believe—left a lot to be desired.)

"Oh. . . . And what's that weird sensation called when you're sure you've already experienced something?" I mumbled.

"Very amusing, Gryllus!" snapped Sibyl, not sounding all that amused. But I hadn't been trying to be funny. I was just distracted, unable to shake off the feeling that I really *had* been on this island before.

"Perhaps I was on vacation here when I was a kid?" I wondered aloud. I pointed my snout back to the cove at which we'd dropped anchor. "Yeah . . . I seem to remember building sand castles down there."

The island *did* look familiar, and yet . . . perhaps it *wasn't* the place I'd visited on vacation as a kid. I mean, there were no volleyball courts or signs for donkey rides along the beach.

You have to remember that memory is a funny old thing. Why is it that I find myself unable to remember simple things like the Greek alphabet, but I *can* remember tricky stuff like the name of the first girl who ever gave me a pie? (OK, *sold* me a pie.) I blame Mnemosyne. She *is* the patron goddess of Memory, after all. It's her job to help us remember things.

Sibyl had come to a halt. "Much as I'd love a chariot ride down Memory Lane with you, Gryllus, we *are* here to restock the ship's provisions!" She pointed down to a clump of something dark on the ground in front of us. "Look at this spoor."

I hopped back to avoid stepping in what she was talking about.

"Poop," I corrected her. "Sheep poop."

"And?" prompted Sibyl. "What does that mean?"

"Means I'm glad I didn't step in it. It looks quite fresh."

A weary sigh. *"And?"*

"And . . . er, the sheep on this island are well-fed, because I'm telling you, that is not a very small pile of—"

"It means there are *sheep* here!" Sibyl exploded. "Which means there'll be meat! Maybe cheese and milk!"

"Well, obviously it means *that*," I said, taking care to give the item under discussion a wide berth.

Homer, who had fallen behind on account of his thin-chested feebleness, caught up. Luckily for him, he spotted the offending article just in time; he too managed to hop to one side before his sandal made contact.

"I did that," I said, watching the lad's nimble footwork.

The poet wrinkled his nose. "Couldn't you have gone behind a tree or something?"

As she struck off for the hillside, Sibyl was muttering something that sounded a bit like a prayer to the gods. "This way," she called over her shoulder.

My eyes followed her purposeful stride, but my legs didn't. That instant, I realized a grim truth: Sibyl wouldn't give up, no matter what happened. She was made of tough stuff, forged in the intense heat of the all-girls preparatory temple of Apollo. But we couldn't all be made of such tough stuff, could we?

"I'll just check this hill over here," I suggested casually.

Sibyl's look pierced me. "OK," she said uncertainly.

I watched as she and Homer continued on their way. I turned the other way, feeling the cold, clammy hand of treachery squeezing my heart. All I had to do was walk over the hill and then keep on walking. But guilt gnawed at me like a rat in a cheese factory. How could I, the one-time savior of the entire Cosmos, even consider abandoning my companions? Without so much as a good-bye?

A silent debate raged within my brain.

You'll never be able to look at your own reflection again if you do this, said the nobler part around the frontal lobes.

So? replied the bit that seemed to dwell under a rock in my brain stem. *That's the beauty of being a pig. You don't have to look in the mirror to shave.*

But they're your FRIENDS. You won't be able to live with the guilt.

Yeah, but you can only feel guilty if you're ALIVE to feel guilty.

"What's that you're mumbling about, Gryllus?" said Sibyl suddenly, from behind me. When she saw my puzzled look, she just said, "Our way was a dead end. Thought we'd join you."

My opportunity to slink away had gone. Numbly, I followed the priestess to the top of the ridge. "That's more like it," she was saying as she pointed to something up ahead.

A thought as cold and uncomfortable and pointy as an icicle down the tunic hit me. Perhaps we mortals forget some things for a good reason; perhaps some things are just so horrible that Mnemosyne, in her Olympian kindness, *allows you NOT to remember them.*

I looked up, my pig's head suddenly heavy with unidentified dread. Sibyl was pointing to a gaping entrance in the rock face ahead of us, one ringed by overgrown laurels. I've got a bit of a phobia about caves, but it was more than that. As I gazed ahead now, my stomach clenched tight into a fist, which then proceeded to pummel my brain relentlessly.

"We haven't got all day, you know," said Sibyl—or something like that; to tell you the truth, I was hardly aware of what was going on. A red curtain of confusion had dropped over my senses, leaving me unable to resist when she gave me a push on the rump to move me toward the cave.

"B-But—" In a daze, I allowed Sibyl to shove me along, but my haze of confusion was turning into something altogether harder and sharper, and that would be *fear.* One buried part of my brain was frantically trying to bring a fragment of memory to the rest of the mind's attention. Meanwhile the other portion of my brain was desperately trying to pretend that there was really nothing wrong, *honest,* that I really *wasn't* back in the one place that had provided the setting for my worst nightmares.

Sibyl herded me into the cave, past the familiar outline of the arch-shaped boulder. It was dim inside, but not so dim that I didn't register the interior design—Stone Age chic, just as I *had known it would be.*

I tried to speak, but a whimper was all I could manage. Sibyl didn't notice, anyway.

"We've hit the jackpot!" she cried, looking around the cave. "This must be a pirates' den or something. No need to search for provisions now!"

I knew she was referring to the towering stacks of cheese and meat and the buckets of whey and the sacks of vegetables piled up on one side of the cave. I knew this; I knew it *without looking* because . . . because . . .

"It's not *that* cold in here," said Sibyl when she saw me trembling. "Anyway, it won't take long to load up, write a thank-you note, and then be on our way."

"Er, Sibyl?" Homer interrupted her from a smaller connecting chamber of the cave. "Have a look at this, will you?" He held up a bronze helmet that had a big hole on one side of it. Well, not just a hole; more of a . . . *tooth mark.*

Various other objects were scattered on the rocky floor — mismatched leather sandals, a few sword hilts, a crumpled shield. They had the look of items that had been chewed a bit and then spat out.

Sibyl picked up a bow and examined it gloomily. "Er, yes, well, we'll just take what's absolutely necessary."

My mind was churning like a butter churn, only you wouldn't want to spread *these* thoughts on your toast. I *had* been on this island before, oh, yes, but not as part of any vacation package.

Meanwhile Homer was reaching up to a cloak, thrown over the top of a nearby boulder. "By Hera's holy handbag!" he gasped when he saw what lay underneath.

We were looking into a face. I could describe at length the curly hair, the closed eyes, the noble nose, the full lips pressed shut, but these might detract from the most noticeable feature: the face was on a head that had at some point in its troubled history parted company from its body. It was just a head and no more. It sat there, as forlorn as a jigsaw piece lost down the back of the sofa of life.

I felt dizzy. Any minute now, the pressure in my head would become too much — my mind's cork would pop and the sparkling wine of my fear, chilled to icy terror, would burst out and make a mess all over the insides of my brain.

"Oh, deary me." Sibyl was one of those sensible girls who can take the grisliest things in her stride, but even she sounded rattled. "Yes, well, we really will just grab the essentials," she said hurriedly. "We can skip the thank-you note."

"What about . . . *him*?" Homer asked in a hushed voice. "We can't just leave him here, can we?"

"No . . . no, I don't suppose we can," replied Sibyl, whose temple training allowed her to maintain a strong sense of proper behavior, even in extremes. "We'll have to take it . . . *him,* and give the poor soul a proper send-off to the Underworld."

She reached a tentative hand toward the head, but squeamishness got the better of her.

"Homer, tie that cloak into a bag, will you? Hold it out and I'll just sort of . . . knock him off." She lined up the wooden bow and got ready to clock the side of the head and roll it into the waiting bag.

While all this was going on, I became aware of a faint noise in the distance.

BOOM.

Was it the pounding of the surf? Another storm approaching? No, it was followed too quickly by another:

BOOM.

Something fluttered in my heart, and it wasn't the Bluebird of Happiness—more like the Dirty Great Black Crow of Dread.

Another pair of rumbling booms, still in the distance but a touch louder now.

BOOM, BOOM.

The rhythm made them sound almost like . . . footsteps?

In the gloom of the cave, Sibyl was unaware of anything but the task at hand, namely getting the gray head in the bag without actually having to lay a finger on it. "One," she counted, holding the bow by one end like a bat and swinging it to make sure it would connect squarely with the head.

BOOM, BOOM came the noise from outside, a bit louder now (CLOSER!).

"Two," Sibyl counted.

BOOM, BOOM.

Homer was cocking an ear—he had heard it, too.

"Two and a half . . ." Sibyl winced.

BOOM, BOOM.

My brain was spinning (OH, GODS, ALL THIS HAS HAPPENED BEFORE).

"What *is* that?" murmured Homer, still holding out the cloth bag but looking around toward the cave's mouth. The rumbling sound was now being accompanied by a faint bleating.

"THREE!" exclaimed Sibyl, steeling herself to whack the head, but she never managed to deliver the blow because . . .

BOOM, BOOM.

. . . the eyes on the bodiless head snapped open.

"Waah!" Sibyl yelled.

"Waah!" Homer yelled.

"Waah!" I yelled, but not because of the pale eyeballs staring at us. No, the chained-up memory in my head had burst free like a sideshow escape artist—*ta-DAA*! Terror nailed me to the ground, incapable of movement.

OH, DEAR GODS, I WAS BACK!

BOOM, BOOM.

Make that WAAAAAAAAAAAAAAAAAAAAAAAAAAA-AAAAAAAAAAAAH!

. . . because what we could hear outside was the sound of two very large feet carrying someone — someTHING — home after a long day's shepherding. And I knew the owner of those feet would be in the mood for A SNACK!

"In fact, let's forget all about the provisions and just make a move!" Sibyl gabbled. She turned away from the eerily staring gray head, but she and Homer quickly realized that they would never make it to the cave's entrance in time, not given the rate at which those gigantic footsteps were getting nearer and nearer.

BOOM, BOOM.

Sibyl hissed something, and the two of them scurried off across the cave. I did nothing, was capable of nothing. Without making any comment, the prophetess trotted back and gave me an almighty shove. I was oblivious to everything; I was no more than a pig-shaped statue made of blubber and fear in equal parts, but I must have moved because the next thing I knew, we were around the back of some enormous clay jars of olive oil.

BOOM, BOOM.

The flock appeared first. These were no ordinary sheep — they were enormous. Any one of them could have provided woolly mittens for the Colossus at Rhodes and still have had enough wool left over to deck out all nine Muses with new pairs of leg warmers.

The overgrown animals knew the drill, making their way

into the cave in an orderly fashion. As they guided themselves into the fenced enclosure, the cave echoed with their bored bleats.

BOOM, BOOM.

And then an immense shadow filled the entrance to the cave. *This is exactly how it happened before!* screamed my brain. *First the sheep, then the shadow, then the you-know-what.*

WE WERE IN THE CAVE OF THE CYCLOPS!

BOOK IX

Mr. Bunny teaches an important philosophical lesson.

How to describe the one-eyed giant? No doubt Homer would rattle on, comparing him to the wooded peak of a mountain or something. For my money, descriptions like that just soften the blow. The truth of the matter—the unadorned truth—was this:

- The cyclops was big.
- The cyclops was ugly.
- The cyclops had the look of something that could eat something the size of an adult human (or, say, a pig) in one go without batting a single eyelid. (I wasn't just guessing this. I knew it from dreadful experience. I knew it because I had been trapped in this cave once before, back when I was human, along with Odysseus and several of my crewmates.)

What else? His hair was still matted and filthy; his face still covered in stubble as long as nails. His teeth still looked like brownish-yellow tombstones, and it seemed unlikely that he'd ever changed the animal-skin, patchwork loincloth I'd first seen him in. The only real difference since last I stared at the cyclops in utter terror was the huge single eye. The bloodshot eyeball was now squeezed into a permanent squint.

The giant hung his enormous head close to the sheep pen. "Settle dahn now, you fluffy baa-sheeps," he murmured.

I suppose I should have been surprised to see that the cyclops had much of an eye left at all. According to Odysseus, we had left the one-eyed monster completely blind. But then again, if truth were string, Odysseus would spend a lot of time hitching up his undies. Anyway, at this moment I had other things on my mind, notably the paralyzing thought that I would soon be making my way down the giant's gullet.

The cyclops had rolled the boulder across the cave entrance. It wasn't a perfect fit, but it was snug enough to prevent us from making an exit. Once again I was trapped in this nightmarish cave, only this time I had Sibyl and Homer for companions instead of one of the mightiest heroes of the Trojan War. A glance at the pale faces of the poet and the priestess didn't fill me with much hope of ever spying the sun again.

The giant had begun to make a fire, which was soon crackling and spitting. Most of the smoke went up through a hole at the top of the cave, but enough remained to make it difficult not to cough and splutter. I heard a contented sigh and massive knee joints cracking as the cyclops settled down, resting his gigantic back against the rock wall. Suddenly, a strangulated, high-pitched voice echoed around the cavern.

"Hippety, hoppety, hippety hop. Oh, I is just a lickle bunny rabbit wot is lookin' for carrots."

Frank astonishment appeared on Sibyl's and Homer's faces, alongside the fear and despair. They peered out through a gap in the clay pots. Even I sneaked a peek, to see the giant holding up one gigantic hand with two tree-trunk fingers raised. The fire cast this hand's shadow against the wall so that it looked like a huge silhouetted rabbit hopping along. The sheep let out a chorus of contented baahs.

"Oh, 'ello," squeaked the cyclops in his bunny voice. "Oo is you, ven?"

The giant had raised his other hand. The bulky shadow of its clenched fist faced off against the giant bunny on the rock face.

"Why, I is Mr. Fist," growled the giant in his normal voice, jerking the fist up and down to indicate speech.

Back to the bunny: "Oh . . . well, can you tell I, where is vem lickle carrots wot I is lookin' for?"

Mr. Fist: "Listen, I is not interested in carrots wot is salad muck and not even proppa grub. I is interested in meat wot is right delishus and tasty for I."

Bunny (uncertainly now): "But . . . I is meat."

Mr. Fist: "Heh, heh, I knows you is meat, you stoopid rabbit! Vat is why I is goin' ta squash you and snarf you for me supper."

With the speed of a striking cobra—but the bulk of a well-fed ox—the clenched fist smashed onto the other hand. As Mr. Fist pummelled Mr. Bunny flat on the cave wall, the cyclops timed his words to the rhythm of the pounding:

"GOOD . . . BYE . . . MIS . . . TER . . . BUN . . . NY. . . . IN . . . TO . . . ME . . . CHOPS . . . YOU . . . GOES!"

The final punch echoed in the sudden silence.

"Ve end," the cyclops declared affectionately to his flock, "so now youse fluffy baa-sheeps go ta sleep or else youse'll be goin' into me chops an' all."

In fact, the sheep were hardly bleating now, apparently calmed by their ultraviolent bedtime story. They leaned against one another in their enclosure, swaying gently like woolen waves in a moonlit sea of sheep.*

The bedtime story had not had the same calming effect on me, however.

To my terrified mind, the cyclops's shadow-puppet play was the world boiled down to its bitter essence, like soup left untended on the stove, and its burned and blasted message was this: *In this world of ours, the carrots are never found before poor old Mr. Bunny runs into Mr. Fist and Mr. Chops.*

And, a worse message still: *First Mr. Bunny . . .*

. . . then Mr. Pig.

The cyclops, possibly drained by his dramatic performance, opened his mouth in a vast yawn. "All right ven, Ed," the cyclops groaned as he stretched out farther. "Do yer stuff."

---

* Translator's Note: The manuscript appears to have been amended here from the original Greek, which reads "swaying gently like a load of old sleepy sheep. Oh, and it was dark."

"Who's Ed?" Sibyl mouthed silently, her brow furrowed. *Another cyclops?* asked her eyes. Homer, who had spent much of his solitary youth cataloging supernatural beings on index cards, shook his head in bewilderment.

It soon became clear who the cyclops was addressing—it was the bodiless head that Homer had unveiled earlier. The cyclops moved it closer, holding it between thumb and index finger, and carefully set it down. The head's eyes were open; they sparkled in the dying fire's glow.

"Ve usual, lickle head, and make it snappy," sighed the cyclops, his one eyelid drooping.

"So it's *head*, not Ed," Sibyl whispered. Her tone revealed her to be the sort of person who gets cross at the sound of a dropped *h*, even when the very thread of her life gives every sign of rapidly unspooling. You have to admire that level of dedication to good diction. (Then again, what teacher at the Titan Elementary School would have dared correct the cyclops's pronunciation? Answer: a soon-to-be-dead one.)

An expectant hush fell over the cave, and then, despite the total absence of lungs, the little gray head took a breath and began to sing.

And what a song! I don't know if your musical tastes run to jazzy riffs on the Pan pipes, or teenybopper bands like Ganymede and the Cup-bearers or Nymphs Aloud. Either way, you've never heard a song sung like this. In a voice so clear it was practically see-through, the little head delivered a song so lovely it *throbbed* with loveliness. It was a thing of beauty in this dark and hellish place. That head sang his heart out, if you know what I mean.

I closed my eyes and listened:

"The gods have fled, the moon is high.
Let golden slumber close your eye,
To dream of mortals come to call
So you can CRUSH AND CRUNCH THEM ALL!"

It was a classic lullaby right up to this final line, at which point the head's silky tenor switched up to a shrieking falsetto. The final word was the vocal equivalent of a pickax to the ear.

This abrupt ending didn't disturb the giant. His single eye was already closed, and a trail of dribble ran down his chin, winding around the stubble like a stream through bulrushes. The cyclops was asleep.

"That song was . . . incredible," breathed Homer, who made it his business to know about such things.

Sibyl paused before delivering her own verdict: "Good tune, nice voice . . . shame about the lyrics."

BOOK X

A former hero suffers a long, dark night of the piggy soul.

As the giant's wet snores filled the darkness, Homer and Sibyl whispered their desperate plans. The epic poet hoped we might just lie low until morning, when the cyclops would let the sheep out and head off to the fields, leaving us free to depart at our leisure.

Sibyl knew better. "Too risky. The sheep are the only thing that stopped him from sniffing us out." She glanced over at the sleeping giant. "When they've left in the morning, he'll be able to tell we're in the cave too."

No, she said, we had to look for a way out tonight. To this end, she set off to explore the back part of the cave, near the cyclops's feet, while Homer picked his way anxiously in the opposite direction, toward the remnants of the fire.

Me, I did nothing.

No, that's not true. What I did was, I sat in darkness and despair, listening to the giant's gurgling snores, and I faced up to some painful truths.

The pig who'd saved the world?

A hero, huh?

Huh!

Who was I kidding? I was nothing. I was Mr. Bunny in a world ruled by Mr. Chops and Mr. Fist; the only difference was that I *knew* that I would never be nibbling on one of life's carrots ever again.

Why did Sibyl and Homer still cling to hope? We would never find a way out. We were goners.

I still hadn't moved a frozen muscle when Sibyl returned. "No exit over on that side," she reported grimly. "A few cracks in the rock, but they don't lead anywhere."

Homer was back a few minutes later. His trip too had been as fruitless as the carnivorous cyclops's lunch box. The smoke hole, he reported, was high up in a bell-shaped section where the cave walls were impossible to climb.

Sibyl took in this news in dejected silence. "OK, Gryllus," she said at last. "Tell us again how Odysseus tricked his way out of here before."

My terror-stricken brain refused to engage in such frivolous activities as speech. All it could manage was:

"Meep."

"What?"

Homer leaned in. "I know what Odysseus did," he said. "Gryllus told me."

"Just give me the facts, then," Sibyl hissed. "No need for poetic flourishes, OK?"

"OK." The young poet nodded solemnly. "Well, they went out to explore the island, and Odysseus took a skin of wine from the temple at Ismarus, intending to give it as a gift to whoever offered them hospitality. When they ended up trapped here in the cave, he gave it to the cyclops instead, but—and here's the good part—he never mentioned that it was a drink for the gods and that non-Olympians needed to dilute it with water, twenty parts to one. The cyclops guzzled the wine down straight!" The poet glanced my way. "Right, Gryllus?"

"Meep."

"Of course," continued the poet, "the cyclops demanded more. Before long, he'd had a skinful—*literally*—and he fell into a drunken sleep as deep as, as . . ."

"No poetic stuff, remember!" said Sibyl. "It was a deep sleep—I get it!"

"Hold on," said Homer, a desperate glimmer of hope lighting up his peepers. "You haven't got any Ismarian wine in your backpack, have you?"

"Actually, I DID have some, but *someone* drank it on the voyage to Aeaea!" answered Sibyl, throwing me an angry glance. "Said it was for medicinal purposes."

"Meep," I apologized.

The poet went on, more despondently. "Before the giant woke up, Odysseus and some of his crewmates got a wooden stake. They sharpened one end, then they thrust it into the embers of the fire, and then they, they . . ."

"What?"

"Supposedly they plunged the stake into the sleeping giant's single eye! I always heard that they blinded him, but . . ."

Sibyl looked over at the sleeping giant, who was now sucking his immense thumb with dreadful slurping sounds. "Typical hero talk," she muttered. "They can't help exaggerating."

"Anyway," Homer continued, "the next morning, the cyclops couldn't see, but he still wouldn't leave his sheep cooped up. He rolled back the boulder, but he knew that Odysseus and the Greeks would try to escape in the middle of the flock. So he ran his hand across the back of each and every sheep as it left the cave. What he didn't know was that Odysseus had instructed his men to cling to the *undersides* of the sheep, which the cyclops wasn't checking because . . . well, you know, it was the *undersides* of the sheep." Homer made a face to show how full of germs such a place must be. "And that's how the crew got away. Right, Gryllus?"

"Meep," I confirmed.

"OK . . ." Sibyl was biting on her bottom lip. "Well, we have the advantage that the cyclops doesn't know we're here. I suppose it *could* work again?"

Homer gave a helpless shrug.

"There's just one little problem," said Sibyl, but the look in her eyes hinted that the problem wasn't all that small. The problem was, in fact, large and huskily built.

The problem was me.

"How's Gryllus going to hold on to the underside of a sheep?"

The only indication of the new dawn was a thin arc of daylight framing the cave's blocked-up exit. It had been a long, busy night, though I can't claim to have contributed much to the busy part.

Sibyl and Homer were putting the finishing touches on my disguise. As the former priestess stuck down the last bits with clay from the cave floor, Homer optimistically fluffed up the bits that were already on.

"How does that look?" he asked hopefully.

"Like a pig randomly covered in bits of wool," said Sibyl, who did not believe in sugar-coating the bitter truth.

But we were many stades past the point of no return. Sibyl and Homer tiptoed over to the sheep pen, steering me in the right direction. The cyclops's breathing no longer had the faraway sound of deep sleep. He would soon be awake.

As we crept under the bottom rung of the fence, the natural stupidity of the sheep served as our ally—the animals made no fuss as we mingled with them.

All I can remember of the next few minutes is: the press of wool on all sides; the growing bleats as more and more of the flock awoke; the tangy aroma of farm animals that lacked all awareness of basic hygiene and didn't care who knew it.

"What are you doing?" I heard Sibyl hiss to Homer.

The poet wrinkled his nose. "Looking for one whose belly isn't so dirty. Otherwise it'll set off my allergies."

"Terrific idea," replied Sibyl. "After all, we wouldn't want you to have a runny nose when the cyclops shoves you into his mouth and starts munching."

Speaking of the cyclops's mouth, just then a tremendous yawn resounded through the cave. The one-eyed giant was waking up. The bleating all around me grew louder, more urgent. The sheep knew their master was up and about.

"Breakfast time," the cyclops muttered aloud.

Uh-oh. My mind foolishly tossed up the memory of when the cyclops had simply picked up one of Odysseus's men and started chewing. I would never forget the terrible snap, crackle, and pop of that awful meal. Was the cyclops going to start the day with a little protein now by reaching in and plucking out a sheep for his breakfast?

Thankfully not—the one-eyed giant grabbed a barrel of whey and slurped it down in one go.

"Stinkin' whey for breakfast," he grumbled. "Again." He burped wetly and wiped his immense forearm across his lips.

"Right, me byooties," he addressed the flock, "out you go."

I couldn't see over the sheep around me, but the sound of scraping rock told me that the giant was opening the exit. Pale light filled the cave.

Excitement was running high among the sheep. This must have been one of the highlights of their day. They jostled for position as the cyclops stomped across to open the gate to their pen. I could no longer see Sibyl or Homer, who must by now have been gripping onto the bellies of two unlucky sheep.

And then the flock was surging forward. I was carried along, a fact that spared me from undertaking the highly tricky process of putting one foot in front of the other. I squeezed my eyes shut, squinting just enough to make sure I was heading toward the light but ensuring that I could not really see the giant we would have to pass by.

The sheep's hooves clattered on the cave floor. The light ahead was growing stronger and stronger — so strong that I even started to think the unthinkable. . . . *Could this plan actually work? Would I live to see another day? Feel the wind once more through my bristles? Frolic once more through fields of grass* — well, OK, not exactly *frolic*, but *amble* at least?

"'Old on," grunted the cyclops. "This un in't right."

A fleshy wall descended in front of me. It was the giant's foot, and I hit it, head-on. The sheep behind me bumped into me, the one behind that bumped into *it,* and so on, in an enormous livestock pileup.

Suddenly, there I was, face-to-face with the cyclops's big toe. It was half the size of me, as blunt and hard-looking as some relentless, snub-nosed digging creature, yet it seemed to fill my world with its yucky hard skin and untrimmed, yellowing nail. I was almost hypnotized by the toe's circular whorls, like some ancient labyrinth of skin.

The cyclops brought his huge head down and sniffed. "Don't

smell right, does you? Right stinky. Is you sickenin', me byooty?"

Under other circumstances, I might have taken offense. After all, the wave of bad breath that came from the cyclops's mouth told me that he was not overzealous about brushing and flossing after eating some unfortunate creature whole. As for his armpits . . . well, you don't want to go there.

But I said nothing, did nothing. I was immobilized by naked terror. Total, utter, in the altogether, flapping-in-the-breeze-without-even-a-fig-leaf-for-decency's-sake, naked TERROR.

The cyclops's eye was a huge cracked mirror in front of me, and in the enormous disc of the pupil I could see myself—a fat little pig with scraps of wool stuck here and there across its back.

I looked . . . *bite-size.*

" 'Ere, you isn't no baa-sheep o' mine," growled the cyclops. Puzzlement hadn't turned to rage yet, but I knew his brain was poised on the edge of that plunge.

"Can't hardly believe me eye!" The cyclops squinted the aforementioned eye. "Wot you is . . . is an oinky-PIG!" he roared. Then he grinned, displaying the sort of gruesome choppers you might see in a "before" poster at the office of the world's bravest dentist.

"An' oinky pigs is better'n stinkin' whey. I LIKES oinky pigs for me grub!"

The dread hand of Fate held me squirming under its ginormous thumb. So this was it—I had managed to get away from the cyclops's cave once before, but that had clearly been a Cosmic mistake of some sort. It had taken a while, but now the Fates were about to rectify this clerical error. My destiny was about to be fulfilled in one bite or two (depending on the cyclops's appetite and table manners—so make that *one* bite).

Good-bye, cruel worl—

"Run, Gryllus!"

BOOK XI

When things go wrong, Nobody is there to save the day.

It was Sibyl, of course.

What's more, she wasn't that far from the exit. The sheep she'd hitched a ride under had made it past the giant. That meant there was nothing stopping her from riding all the way to freedom. But no, she had given up her chance of escape in order to come back and help me.

"Wo—?" grunted the cyclops, thrown off balance by all these deviations from his morning routine. "Oo is you?" he roared.

Most people would have felt impelled to answer a question bellowed by a carnivorous giant, but not Sibyl. She ignored the cyclops and yelled out again to me: "Run!"

Ah, if only it were that simple. If only I weren't rooted to the spot like a terrified bunny in the path of a Persian battle chariot, one of those scary ones with the big spiky wheels.

The cyclops was scrambling to his feet. The hand that reached out for me could have squeezed the life out of me like juice from a lemon . . . only who'd want to drink lemonade like that? (Apart from the cyclops, that is. . . .)

Suddenly another noise emerged from the pileup of sheep behind me, a distinctly unsheeplike one. It was a cough, and it was enough to dislodge Homer's feeble grip. He had succumbed to his allergies, and now the poet dropped to the floor with an "Ow!"

The cyclops's single eye blinked in incredulity, and his giant calloused hand wavered in front of me.

"Oo is YOU?" he cried. "Ow many lickle humings is in 'ere?"

Before any answer was forthcoming, Sibyl started running, *back* into the cave. As she did so, she swung around the bow that had been slung over her shoulder. Once she had an arrow in her hands, she slowed down and took aim.

OK, dear listener: armed with a puny bow and arrow, what target would you choose on a foe as fearsome as the cyclops? The throat? The heart? The huge eye that was currently flitting between Homer, Sibyl, and me? Good guesses, one and all.

Sibyl's arrow zipped through the air and struck ME in the rump.

"Ye-ow!" I cried, but the prick of that arrow got me moving at last. There was no thought involved; it was just a physical reaction to a sharp object hitting a tender spot. I ran. Sibyl was running, too, and she was level with me now. "This way!" she cried as we overtook Homer, and her feet skittered across the rocky floor toward the back of the cave. Unable to make any decisions for myself, I followed.

Bad move. There was nothing in the rear section of the

cave—we were trapped. Using both hands, Sibyl shoved me into one of the vertical fissures that ran up the cave wall.

"As far back as you can go!" she yelled.

And then I was alone, pushing myself so hard into the rock that I was almost a pig-shaped smear. I was dimly aware that Sibyl and Homer had run into similar crevices on the same rock face. But there wasn't time to wonder how they were faring, because the cyclops was now approaching the back of the cave.

He squinted and craned his head, sniffing deeply now that the flock had gone.

"Lickle humings, lickle humings," he called, in an amiable singsong. "I smells you, you an' your lickle piggy."

The roof of the cave became lower and lower the farther back you went, and soon the cyclops was crouching, then shuffling along on his knees. At last he fell forward, taking his substantial weight on his arms. The mini-caves of his nostrils twitched again, their nose hairs stirring like reeds in the breeze. The giant moved his heavyweight head as close as he could to the back of the cave—right in front of my hiding spot.

"'Ello, 'ello," murmured the cyclops. "Oo's in 'ere ven, eh?"

Silence. The cyclops's voice grew angrier.

"I am not stoopid. I smells you. I smells your fear, din' I?" (Fear was one word for it.) "So oo . . . is *you?*"

Some more silence, then:

"OO IS YOU?"

"No one you need bother yourself with!" I wailed, and I was speaking from the heart. "I'm just nobody!"

The effect these words had on the giant couldn't have been worse if I'd said, "Get lost, you one-eyed pea-wit!"

"NOBODY!" the cyclops roared. "Oh, I's bin waitin' for Nobody to come back! I's sworned to kill Nobody, an' kill Nobody I will! I's gonna rip Nobody to lickle bits! I's gonna guzzle Nobody's blood, I is!"

These might all seem perfectly decent, pleasant things to say—and you might interpret them as a sign that the cyclops had turned over a new leaf and decided to become a tree-hugging, vegetarian pacifist and all-around Boy Scout. Maybe, but I wasn't about to emerge from my hiding spot and sit around the campfire singing "We Are the World"* with him just yet. No, the giant's enraged bellowing suggested that he was every bit as fearsome as ever, even if the content of that bellowing was all this lovey-dovey stuff about wanting to hurt nobody.

Suddenly the cyclops thrust his hand into the crevice to grab me. His enormous fingers came close, too, close enough for me to see the grime caked beneath his nails, each one as big as a Spartan battle shield. Then his giant raw knuckles scraped against the rock walls—the huge hand could go no farther.

"I'sll be back," he growled. "An' ven Nobody's in deep, deep trouble."

I squeezed my eyes shut, all two of them, and tried to ignore the sounds of the cyclops stamping about the cave.

---

* Translator's Note: According to Thucydides, the full title of this song was "We Are the World (well, at least the Greek-speaking part of it)."

It wasn't long before he returned, and now he was fiddling with what looked like a broken flagpole. The giant was attaching something to one end of it. The pink tip of his tongue poked out of his gargantuan mouth as he struggled to do such finicky work with enormous, thick fingers and one dodgy eye.

Finally the giant was done, and he proceeded to feed one end of the pole into the crevice in which I was cowering. As it neared me, I saw that something was dangling from the pole. It was the head, the one we had heard singing a lullaby just hours ago. It now hung from the end of the pole by a piece of fishing net that had been fashioned into a basket of sorts. The gray face did not move, betrayed no flicker of emotion, but its eyes were open.

"Right ven, 'ead," snarled the cyclops. "Oo can yer see? Is it Nobody?"

The head was so close to me I could have felt its breath— if it had been breathing, that is. And yet, as I looked into the pale, unblinking eyes set in that gray face, I *knew* they were looking back at me.

In desperation I frantically nodded, in hopes that the head would report back that indeed nobody was in here now.

But when the head spoke, its dull eyes on mine, it said: "No." The voice was flat and uninterested. You'd never have believed that it was responsible for the song we'd heard the night before. "*Somebody* is in here," said the head.

This seemed to discombobulate the cyclops a bit. "Somebody, eh? But I is lookin' for Nobody!" he exclaimed.

He pulled the head back out of my hiding spot. Then he

must have inserted it into one of the other crevices, because moments later the cyclops growled, "Wot about this un? Oo is it?"

I had no way of knowing whether the giant had picked the hiding place of Homer or Sibyl. I strained to hear what the head's bored-sounding voice reported back: "I do not know. It . . . could be anybody."

Once again, this did not appear to be the answer the cyclops was looking for. "Anybody! I is not carin' about Anybody!" he roared. "I is lookin' for Nobody!"

The cyclops shifted along to check another potential hiding place, and he moved back into my line of vision. I had a dismal view of his furry loincloth and even furrier back. The giant leaned forward onto his elbows and fed the pole into yet another crevice.

Suddenly, something else came into view. Sibyl! While the giant was focused on the next fissure in the cave wall, the priestess had emerged from her hiding place. The giant would only have to look back over his shoulder to spot her. He only had to shift his legs the wrong way to squash her as flat as a Peloponnesian Potato Pancake. (Try saying *that* when your life's in imminent peril.)

What was she up to, anyway? The former prophetess was clutching something in one pale hand — a small rock? Keeping her eyes on the cyclops's back, she drew back her skinny arm and hurled the rock across the cavern and into a larger chamber in the rock face opposite.

"Wot were VAT?" boomed the cyclops. He whirled around, but Sibyl had ducked behind a boulder.

The cyclops wasted no time. He scrabbled across the cave floor and thrust his head-on-a-stick into the empty chamber.

"Quick! Oo is it, 'ead?"

"Nobody," came the truthful, and emotionless, response. "Nobody is in this one."

The cyclops let out a screech that could curdle blood like year-old raspberry yogurt. "NOBODY! NOBODY!! LET ME AT 'IM! NOBODY'S TIME 'AS COME!"

Tossing the head and its pole to one side, the giant lunged forward, thrusting his head into the chamber to see for himself. Enraged beyond the flimsy confines of language, he let out a savage "Raaaaarrrrgghh!"

This was followed by a puzzled "Huh?"

This was followed by a sheepish "Erk."

Here's why: the cyclops, being a giant, had an appropriately large head. Throw in a huge pair of sticky-out ears that wouldn't have been out of place in a lineup of the Corinthian royal family, and it meant just one thing. Having approached the entrance at a lucky angle that allowed him to get his head *inside* the chamber, he now found himself unable to pull it *out* again.

He was stuck.

He began to thrash his legs up and down like a toddler throwing the world's most extreme temper tantrum. Sibyl skillfully dodged his flailing feet as she raced to the entrance of my hidey-hole, the miserable spot I had assumed would be my final resting place (only, I'll tell you, it wasn't all that restful).

"Hop to it, Gryllus. We haven't got all day."

BOOK XII

Every silver lining comes with a great big cloud.

I've always had a fair complexion, me. Her "little pink Milesian rose," that's what my mom used to call me (unfortunately within earshot of the other kids on the island, but that's another story). I have always burned very easily in sunshine, a tendency that got worse when I became a pig. I only had to spend an hour or two out of the shade before someone would start asking who was frying ham. Put it this way: unlike certain barbarian tribes, I am not a sun worshipper.

But right at this moment, as the three of us charged out of that cave, the sun on my back was one of the greatest sensations ever. I was ALIVE! Sibyl and Homer had to be feeling the same — they both wore the silly grins of people who'd expected not to be squinting in the sun ever again.

There was just one thing bothering me. "What exactly happened back in there?" I asked.

"Simple," Sibyl replied, a hint of self-satisfaction creeping into her smile as she trotted along. "The cyclops thinks Nobody is a person."

"But . . . everybody is a person, aren't they?"

"Oh, yes, I forgot that part!" said Homer. "Odysseus told the cyclops that his name was Nobody, didn't he?"

I vaguely remembered this happening, although at the time I had been a tad too distracted to concentrate. "Yeah, why did he do that?"

"So when the cyclops shouted for help, he kept saying 'Nobody is attacking me!'" answered Homer. "So he didn't receive any help."

"Get it?" asked Sibyl.

"No."

Her brow furrowed. "Well, words like *nobody* and *somebody* don't operate like normal names or nouns. Do you follow me?"

"No."

"The word *nobody* doesn't refer to an actual person. It's not a name. If I say, 'Nobody's at the ship,' it doesn't mean there's a person called Nobody who's at the ship. Do you see?"

"No."

"It's a word that draws its meaning from how it works in a sentence. Look, Gryllus, this is elementary Greek we studied at the temple in Year Two, Term One. Do you really not get it?"

"No."

Sibyl sighed. "Let me put it this way. The cyclops is a big dummy who wouldn't know his bum from a ditch in the ground. NOW do you get it?"

"Loud and clear," I replied knowledgeably. "Why didn't you say that in the first place and spare us the mumbo jumbo?"

All the while we had been legging it back toward the safety of the ship. For once, Homer was a fair bit ahead of us. He had left the rocky path and was plunging into a stretch of pine woods below, clutching a sack of food he had stolen from the cave. Meanwhile, Sibyl and I had reached the summit of a hill. The craggy cliffs were still right behind us but, in the other direction, the island looked lovely from here. Admittedly, some of the trees didn't look the healthiest, but the land rolled appealingly down to the sea.

Suddenly Sibyl froze.

"Hold on!" she said. "I've just had an amazing thought. . . ."

"Can it wait?" I gasped.

But a grin was spreading across Sibyl's face. "Maybe that's the answer we've been looking for." She beamed. "An alternative way to interpret the prediction!"

"I'm not following you," I said, adding impatiently, "*again*."

I'd never seen Sibyl looking so exhilarated. "It's one of the things I learned at the Oracle: predictions can be really tricky. You think they mean one thing, and it turns out they mean another. Do you see?"

"Yes." (This answer was not entirely accurate.)

"The cyclops called you *Nobody,* as if that were your name, right? What if *you're* the Nobody in the premonition?" I didn't like where this was going, but Sibyl didn't stop to let me off.

"Remember the dream I had about the labyrinth — 'Nobody can defeat the beast in the darkness.' Maybe that means it *could* be defeated, by someone called Nobody . . . which would be YOU. Isn't that brilliant?"

Sibyl was showing me altogether too many teeth. "Quick!" she said. "Let's go and tell Homer the good news!"

She veered off the path and began to race down to the trees.

"I'll be right there . . ." I gasped. "I just need to catch my breath." My legs did ache, but more important, my exhilaration at still being alive had fizzled out, despite this news that the end of the world might not be inevitable after all. The real problem was the vital role Sibyl seemed to think fell to me. *Brilliant* was not the word that sprang most readily to mind. A more appropriate word would have been . . . whatever was the opposite of *brilliant*.

Poopy.

I watched Sibyl continue down the hill with her backpack and the bow she'd picked up. Suddenly the taste of my continued existence wasn't so sweet. I might have earned another temporary respite from the jaws of the cyclops, but the crucial word here was *temporary*.

As if to underscore this thought, a cloud passed across the sun behind me and I heard a rumble of thunder. The land in front of me suddenly looked altogether shabbier. *Perfect!* I thought morosely. No doubt Homer would have called that cloud one of those *whatchamacallits* . . . literary symbols, and what it symbolized was this: nothing lasts—not sunshine, not safety, not happiness, not yogurt.

Not life itself.

"Come on!" Sibyl shouted from down the hill. She turned to look up at me and then screamed, "GRYLLUS!"

As things turned out, the sudden shadow was an even more apt symbol of life's transience than any mere innocent passerby of a cloud. That's because the shadow was, in fact, thrown by something standing behind me—something very, very big. (Here's a hint. We weren't on the Island of the Cyclops; we were on the Island of the Cyclopes. The clue is in the name—CyclopES, plural.)

Yep, it was only another cyclops, wasn't it, this one even

bigger than the one in the cave. There was no time to wonder how something so enormous had managed to sneak up on me, before a vast hand reached down and scooped me up into the sweaty darkness of its balled and grubby fist.

BOOK XIII

Table manners vary from place to place (and we're not talking about eating peas off your knife).

So, all in all, the day was not shaping up well. Consider:

1) I was now trapped within a makeshift pen created by two uprooted trees and a broken section of old fence.

2) Three hideous cyclopes — count them, THREE! — were squatting on nearby boulders.

3) Their topic of discussion was dinner and had direct bearing on my immediate future (or lack of it).

4) I had the beginning of a headache.

Added together, it all falls short of the perfect day. Hard to imagine that getting eaten would do much to turn the day around, either.

So much for Sibyl's brilliant interpretation of the premonition! Far from being destined to save the Cosmos a second time, I was destined to become a light supper.

"Wot's it gonna be ven, bruvvers?" demanded the largest of the three cyclopes. "Raw or cooked up?"

"You get all o' vem luvverly crispy bits wiv cooked up," commented one of the others.

"Yeah, but raw's better, for yer heart an' vat," added the third piously. "You know, on account of it 'avin' more *New Tree Ants,* innit?"

The other two gave him disdainful looks. "Wot is *New Tree Ants?*" growled the biggest, whose name I later learned was Brontes—the Thunderer.

"*New Tree Ants* is fings wot jump in yer food an' is good for ya, innit," said the health-conscious cyclops, whose name was Arges.

"Is you bonkers?" exclaimed Stereopes, the middle brother. "I ain't eatin' no insicks wot'll wriggle about inside me guts!"

"I says . . . *cooked!*" declared Brontes in a voice that brooked no argument (unless you fancied arguing with a fist the size of a well-fed ox).

While big brother assembled the fire and struck the flint, Stereopes could hardly contain his excitement. "Bags I the 'ead! I likes to roll 'em around me chops an' crunch 'em up!"

"You'll git wot you git an' like it." Brontes gave his brother a cuff across the back of the neck.

The three settled down and waited for the fire to get going. Part of me—the teeny, tiny bit not drowning in terror—noted with amazement that the sky was darkening. They do say time flies when you're having fun; shouldn't it, therefore, crawl when you're spending your time quivering and cowering? Not so today. The daylight hours had whizzed by and we had reached that time of the evening when, throughout the civilized world, wine and conversation flow, opinions are shared, and tales told. Unfortunately, the cyclopes were running a bit low on the old sparkling conversation.

"Where's Polyphemus, ven?" said Arges in an obvious attempt to fill the silence.

"In 'is cave wiv 'is sheeps, I expeck," said Stereopes.

I realized that they were talking about the cyclops we had left behind in the cave. It seemed that Polyphemus was their little brother. They didn't appear to hold him in high regard.

"Yeah, lickle twit loves vem sheeps, dunnee?" contributed Brontes.

They all let out forced chuckles.

"Yeah . . . he loves vem sheeps."

"Sure do."

"Yeah . . . sheeps."

The silence returned, as awkward as an ice-skating emu. All three giants turned a hopeful eye to the fire, but it was not yet roaring.

Suddenly Stereopes put down his gigantic club and leaned forward, lifting himself slightly from the boulder.

"Ere's sumfink wot's good," he promised. He readied himself like an Olympic wrestler, bent forward, gritted his teeth, and then:

POOOOOOOOOOOOOOOM!

The island shook as the giant broke wind massively.

It's a well-known fact that such occurrences are not funny, a position convincingly argued by Aristotle in his philosophical treatise, *On Humor*.* The cyclopes must have skipped this important academic work in their studies.

"Har, har, har, har, har," laughed Brontes and Arges in clear appreciation of the decibel level of their brother's performance. And, admittedly, it was nothing to be sniffed at.

Once the laughter had died down, an unspoken challenge hung in the air (not the only thing). Being the oldest brother, Brontes raised his enormous haunches.

"Vat weren't nuffink," he spat. With a quick check that the back flap of his loincloth wasn't tucked in, he rolled his head on his neck and readied himself like an Olympic boxer. He crouched low and grimaced, until:

PAAAAAAAAAAAAAARP!

A line of trees was bowed back under the sudden gale, and I realized why much of the island's flora had a stunted look. The younger cyclopes let out murmurs of honest admiration as they fanned their great hands in front of their faces.

The full-grown male cyclops is a competitive beast; there was no question that it was Arges' turn next. Arges readied himself like . . . well, like an Olympic synchronized swimmer,

---

* Translator's Note: The only surviving quotation states that "the simple act of expelling gas is a biological necessity shared by all mammals and is amusing only to the feeble-minded." Aristotle first outlined this theory in a lecture at the Athenian Academy. Unfortunately, after a heavy lunch, the great philosopher found himself providing a living example of the topic under discussion. The assembled students lacked Aristotle's intellectual insight into the workings of humor and fell down laughing.

actually. His single eye squeezed shut. His brutish face contorted with effort, until:

. . . . *squip?*

His older brothers pinned Arges with an unimpressed eye (one each).

"I've not bin meself lately," mumbled Arges.

"Har, har, har, har," sympathized Brontes and Stereopes.

The one-eyed giants were not deterred by the ungodly smell that had settled over the island like a low-pressure weather front. They were having a blast. So much so, in fact, that they failed to notice Sibyl, whose pale face peered out of the woods on one side of the clearing.

I saw her, but the sight didn't fill me with even the slenderest of hopes—what could a human-size ex-prophetess do in the face of such enormous brutes? Nevertheless, Sibyl clamped a hand over her nose and coolly assessed the situation.

Brontes was up on his gigantic feet again. The mood was suddenly more serious. Fun and games were over, and now the oldest brother was about to assert his natural authority.

"Awright, step back, youse wood nymphs," he growled, "cuz vis is sumfink wot's gonna blow yer eyebrow right orf."

He planted his feet wide and leaned forward, gulping in vast quantities of air. He began to strain, his face going from pink to purple, with barely a pause at red. Tendons thick as branches stood out on his neck. His single eye bulged alarmingly. A series of gurgles began to emit from his vast belly, getting louder by the second. Something was coming!

Suddenly, there was a cry from the hillside above us. "Bruvvas! 'Elp me, bruvvas! It's Nobody! Nobody comed back to me cave!"

The first cyclops—what had they called him? Polyphemus—was bounding down the hill. The top half of his vast head was ringed by a bloody scrape, no doubt from when he'd finally managed to yank it out of the chamber in the cave.

Arges rolled his eye. "Not again," he muttered.

"Nobody *ever* comes to yer cave, you stoopid lickle twit!" yelled Stereopes.

Brontes did not contribute to this discussion, being otherwise engaged. The gurgles in his stomach had taken on a raucous life of their own.

I glanced back in Sibyl's direction. The priestess was gone. She must have run off, considering the situation to be hopeless. Disappointment speared me.

No, wait! Sibyl *wasn't* gone! She was coming closer, crawling her way toward the fire, like a commando in the Spartan elite SAS (Swords, 'Ands, Shields squad). She clutched an arrow in one fist.

Polyphemus continued stomping down the hill. "No, lissen! *Somebody* was wiv 'im too. An' anuvver one—it were *Anybody*!"

Sibyl was crouching beside the fire now. She had ripped a strip off the bottom of her ceremonial robes and was bundling it around the head of the arrow.

"Oo's SHE?" Argus exploded, finally noticing the human intruder who had gate-crashed their barbecue.

Stereopes looked, but not Brontes. He had accrued a phenomenal buildup of gas, and now there was only one place for it to go—out into the big, wide world. . . .

Arges and Stereopes leaped to their feet and charged toward Sibyl, but she managed to control her trembling arms sufficiently to finish bandaging the arrow and dip its business end in the fire. . . .

Brontes shut his eye and let nature take its course. It was all a matter of that newfangled physics now — *What goes up must come down*, *Nature abhors a vacuum*, and *When you've gotta go, you've gotta go.* . . .

The opening note from the giant's nether regions was at the lower end of the scale, like a horn calling a barbarian horde to battle.

Even with his poor eyesight, Polyphemus was now close enough to the campsite to spot Sibyl.

"Vat's one of 'em!" he cried.

Sibyl skipped nimbly to one side and lifted her bow in the direction of the approaching giants.

Meanwhile Brontes' blast grew louder, and it was clear that this was no mere bodily function; this was a natural wonder, a cataclysm the likes of which the world had not seen since monstrous Typhon threatened to rip the Cosmos apart.

VOOOOOOO . . .

The world quaked. While she was still able, Sibyl let fly the flaming arrow; it zipped up past Arges and . . .

missed!

It wasn't going even remotely in the direction of any of the cyclopes' head or neck areas. It —

No, wait! The arrow crossed the path of the mighty wind unleashed by Brontes the Thunderer! This wind, being of a highly combustible nature, ignited immediately. The air exploded into a wide swath of flame, a sideways column of yellow-blue fire that streaked out as far as a line of (appropriately named) ash trees. In the other direction, the pillar of fire flashed backward until it reached its original point of departure.

Brontes' bum.

"Yoooooooooweeeeeeeeeeeeeeeeeeeeeee!" wailed Brontes in a manner that was really quite undignified (although fair enough, all things considered). Cheekwise, the cyclops's hands moved from the upper set to the lower.

Sibyl was already yanking back that section of fence that kept me prisoner.

"Here we go again," she said. "Come on."

As we ran across the scorched earth, I noticed that three of the cyclopes had been hurled backward by the blast.

The only one still upright was Brontes. He was running up the hill, still wailing piteously. I felt a pang of sympathy for him, even if he *had* been about to host a picnic with me as the sole item on the menu.

I mean to say—something like that was enough to bring tears to your eye.

BOOK XIV

A band of heroes gets ahead.

The monkeys were not very pleased that we'd returned with just one measly bag of provisions. They were even less pleased to discover that Homer's bag did not, in fact, contain any provisions at all, but rather the bodiless head we had found in the cyclops's cave.

Things got even worse when the primates realized that this head was still alive, despite being a solitary body part. Captain Simios was the first to notice. He promptly let out a startled shriek and dropped the head, which then rolled around the deck.

By the time an irate Polyphemus and two of his bigger brothers appeared at the cliffs overlooking us, the crew of monkeys was positively miffed. And when the one-eyed giants started hurling dirty great boulders to try and sink us . . . well, now the monkeys were very agitated indeed.

Of course, by this stage, the primates had pulled up anchor and were frantically rowing to safety. Luckily the cyclopes' aim was off today. In addition to the usual difficulty of gauging distances with just one eye, Polyphemus's poor vision let him down. Stereopes and Arges also threw poorly, and who could blame them? Like their brother, they had been knocked over and out by the recent firestorm, and they still had a dazed, singed look about them. (Meanwhile Brontes was nowhere to be seen on the cliffs. He was probably soaking his sore bits in a nice, cool pond somewhere.)

"I'll get ya!" Polyphemus roared, bending down for another boulder. "I'll rip Nobody's 'ead off!"

The boulder landed short with a mighty *KER-PLUNK!*

His brothers got into the spirit of things too, joining in with:

"He'll crunch up Somebody's boneses!"

And:

"He'll slurp up all o' vem *New Tree Ants* out of Nobody!"
(I'm pretty sure this one was Arges.)

And:

"He'll pluck off Anybody's armses and legses like he woz
a lickle fly!"

The rocks went on ker-plunking into the waters around
us, but our luck was holding out. Another few strokes and
we'd be in the clear.

"Faster!" I yelled at the rowing monkeys. Then I looked back
at the trio of giants on the cliff top. A hurricane of emotions
whipped up in my heart. Fear, disappointment, shame . . . and
anger, anger at these overgrown, one-eyed bully boys. How
dare they live here, of all places? Who did they think they were,
with their ravening appetites and their giant boulders and their
oversize single eyeballs? How *dare* they?

As another rock sploshed into the water, I rushed to the
rail and shouted, "What a useless shot! You couldn't hit Typhon
from twenty paces, you couldn't! You're useless!"

The three cyclopes didn't seem to like this, and their
frustrated rage fanned my own anger.

"And don't bother trying to follow us!" I went on trium-
phantly, especially now that we were well and truly out of range.

"Shhh!" Sibyl hissed, but I wasn't listening. The blood was
pounding in my piggy ears as I shouted, "It's a long way to
Crete, you big goons!"

"Gryllus!" Sibyl barked, and the look on her face informed
me that perhaps I shouldn't have specified our precise
destination.

Luckily, even after the rotten day I'd had, I was able to think on my hooves. "Hah! Fooled you!" I yelled. "We're not even going to Crete! You'll find nobody on Crete, so there!"

Confident that I'd set right my little slip, I was surprised to see Sibyl slump back in apparent despair. There's no pleasing some people.

"What?" I asked. "What now?"

The priestess gave no answer. Meanwhile, on the cliffs behind us, Polyphemus the cyclops paused, another boulder above his head, ready to hurl it. A horrible grin spread across his horrible face, but who could say why? They're not easy to read, cyclopes.

We settled back into our seafaring routines soon enough, and yet everything was different now. Sibyl spent most of the days up by the front of the ship, apparently willing it to go faster toward our appointment with destiny on the island of Crete. If truth be told, the former priestess had lately been giving me the willies. OK, she had saved my life back on the island, and for that I was duly grateful. But WHY had she saved me?

It was only because she had come up with this nutty idea that I was the "Nobody" who could defeat the mysterious Beast in the Dark of the Cretan labyrinth and set free the imprisoned gods.

What Sibyl *didn't* know was that I had been considering slinking away on the island of the cyclopes. Every time she spotted me on the ship now, she gave me a giant thumbs-up and a frighteningly intense grin. It was too much to take. I began avoiding her company.

That left Homer. He seemed like an altogether new budding poet since our stop, and it wasn't hard to work out why. It was the head that he had grabbed on the way out of Polyphemus's cave. Almost as soon as we were clear of the cyclopes' island, Homer had found a comfortable resting place for it in the hole at the top of a coil of rope.

Desperate for any distractions, I wandered over to find out more. Homer was fussing about, making sure that the head, whose eyes were once again shut tight, could not roll out.

"Is he our new mascot, then?" I asked.

Homer gave me the sort of look—all offended and pained and irritated and monumentally misunderstood—that teenage epic poets specialize in.

"Do you know who this is?" he asked.

"Well, *either* he's a bit careless with his body parts *or* he's pioneering the world's most radical weight-loss program."

"This is *Orpheus*," Homer whispered reverentially. "Well, part of him anyway."

"Gotcha, gotcha." I scrutinized the head. "And, remind me . . . who was Orpheus?"

The young poet blinked in astonishment at the abyss-like depths of my ignorance. "He was the greatest singer, the greatest lyre player the world has ever known. Obviously."

"Oh. . . . Probably not much good on the lyre now though, is he?" I gave Homer a friendly wink. "I suppose he could play it by ear. D'you get it? Play by ear? Eh? Eh? 'Cause he's still got—"

"Shhhh!" Homer hissed like something nasty from under

Medusa's hairnet. "You'll wake him! Anyway, what do *you* know, Gryllus? You can't even play the lyre, can you?"

"I don't know," I replied. "I've never tried."

"Orpheus's song was so beautiful, it could make the trees themselves weep."

"Ah well, there's money to be made in the music business, if you've got your head screwed on. Do you get it? HEAD screwed on? It's a joke, 'cause buddy boy here's just a head. Do you see?"

Homer ignored my dazzling wordplay. (It went over *his head*—do you get it? Eh? Eh?)

"The rocks rang out in sorrow at the loveliness of his voice," continued the starstruck young poet. "The wild beasts of the woods stopped and listened as he—"

"Hold on, I've got one!" I barged in. "When he was at school, right, I'll bet he was—wait for it . . . at the head of the class! Get it? HEAD of the class?"

Not a peep from Homer, but I persevered. "I know, I know. I should quit while *he's* ahead. You know . . . he's A HEAD? It's a sophisticated play on words, you see, because he actually IS a . . ."

I became aware that Orpheus was looking dolefully up at me.

"Oh. Er . . . hello there, little fella," I attempted cheerfully. "Bet you didn't think you'd find yourself on a big ship like this, did you? Not to worry, you'll soon get your sea leg— er, you'll soon get the hang of it."

The head's uncanny gaze did not waver. The overall effect

was a bit creepy, so I began to blather: "Anyway, must be nice to be out in the sun! Get some color in your cheeks. That'll cheer you up, eh? Give you a bit of a, er . . . head start in your new life. . . . And we can move you around a bit, every half hour, just to make sure you get tanned evenly. . . ."

The unwavering gaze remained just that.

"What d'you say, little fella?"

"I am lacking a body," replied Orpheus. "Not a brain." His voice was as eerily flat and lifeless as . . . well, as lifeless as the head itself looked (despite the fact that it could look around and hold conversations—though not, apparently, friendly ones).

"Cheer up, sunshine," I said. "Look on the bright side. In your condition, I bet you could ride on any ferry in Greece for half-price. At least! You might get on for free as luggage, if you played your cards right."

Orpheus's expression was sarcophagus-grim. Homer rolled his eyes.

"What?" I cried. "Those ferry tickets can be pricey."

OK, we hadn't got off to the smoothest of starts, but I was confident in my interpersonal skills. And rule number one of getting to know someone was to find common ground. Therefore:

"Actually, I'm a bit of a singer myself," I told the greatest singer who had ever lived. "I never went professional, but I had plenty of offers. The thing is, I'm a bit of a purist, artistically speaking. I won't sing any old rubbish just 'cause that's what the unwashed rabble want."

No response.

"Would you like to hear a song or two?" I offered, one artiste to another.

Orpheus's sigh rattled eerily in his unconnected neck. "Do you know, you're getting on my nerves?" he said.

I scanned the contents of my brain. "'You're Gettin' on My Nerves'? No, don't think I know that one. . . . But you hum it and I'll do my best to join in."

"Pay no attention to our pig, Mr. Orpheus." Homer jumped in before the head could even choose a key for me to sing in. "He's just a pig. Myself, I'm an epic poet—well, one day I *hope* to be an epic poet, that is—and I'm a huge fan of yours and . . . well, do you mind if I ask you something?"

Again no response emerged from the head, but Homer plowed optimistically on: "It's just . . . how did you end up, you know, like THIS?"

The head was silent for so long I thought he'd nodded off again. But then Orpheus sighed and said, "I was wandering in the east, alone with my lyre. I was far out in the wilderness, singing my songs of woe, when a crocodile crept up and attacked me." Even recounting these dramatic events, Orpheus sounded completely uninterested.

"Here, hold on," I said. "*He* just said all the wild animals would stop and listen to your song!"

Orpheus sniffed. "They *did*. My song could calm the most savage of breasts. However, when a creature is afflicted by a lack of auditory ability . . ."

It took a moment for all these fifty-drachma words to sink

in. "You mean to say, you got attacked and eaten by . . . a *deaf crocodile?*"

Orpheus's tone was noticeably more clipped. "Yes."*

"Unlucky," I commiserated. "But what was it with all the sad songs anyway? With a voice like yours, you should have been singing to packed auditoriums, not wandering off on your lonesome—"

Homer was shaking his head violently and drawing his hand across his neck in a repeated, fluttery motion. What? Was he trying to tell me that Orpheus had lost his head? Well, DUH! By the time I realized Homer was actually trying to tell me to stop, it was too late. Orpheus had closed his eyes. The meaning was clear: he did not wish to speak further.

"What did you have to go and say that for?" Homer whispered hotly as we tiptoed away. "Stop embarrassing me! Just think before you open your big snout next time."

And he stamped off to his cabin, making sure he slammed the door behind him and leaving me to think: *Teenage epic poets, eh? What can you do with them?*

---

* Translator's Note: According to most accounts of his demise, Orpheus was killed by the Maenads, the wild followers of the god Dionysus. This revised version probably originated because the Greek tragedian Euripides considered the true story about the crocodile to be "as believable as Heracles doing long division without an abacus or a mathematician on hand."

BOOK XV

Heads and tales

All in all then, my onboard social options were turning out to be quite limited.

Each day I found myself attempting to navigate safe passage between Homer and his chuckle-free head on one hand, and Sibyl and her depressing talk of labyrinths and endangered gods on the other.

With the monkeys no more favorably disposed toward me, that gave me lots of free time, which I chose to spend feeling sorry for myself. It was on one of my numerous solitary circuits of the deck that Sibyl managed to catch up with me.

"Gryllus!" she said with suspicious enthusiasm. "I thought you were going to join me for dinner."

"I . . . skipped dinner," I said, in what may have been the most outrageously unbelievable lie of my life.

Sibyl had to know this, but she just said, "And how's our new shipmate?"

"Orpheus?" I grunted. "He's . . . not the friendliest talking head I've ever met."

"Has he said anything about the situation on Crete?" she wondered.

"Can't you ask him for yourself?"

"There's no point," Sibyl murmured. "He just closes his eyes as if I'm not there. One time he mumbled something about me reminding him of someone and the memory being too painful. . . ."

"Maybe he used to know another bossy boots at some other temple?" I offered.

"He was talking about Eurydice," said Sibyl.

"Right, right, of course. And . . . just give my memory a quick refresher. . . .Who was Eurydice again?"

Sibyl shook her head sadly. "Eurydice was his true love. They thought they would be together forever, but one day she got bitten by a snake."

"Nasty bite, was it?"

"She died instantly."

"So really quite nasty, then."

"Orpheus's love was so great that he followed her to the Underworld itself." Sibyl had always struck me as a young Hellenistic woman of the modern era, but her eyes came over all misty for a moment.

I bristled. "Yes, well, it's not as if I haven't been to the Underworld myself, *twice.*"

"This was different. Orpheus sang to win Eurydice back. His love song so moved Pluto,"* continued the ex-priestess, "that the Lord of the Underworld agreed to let her shade return to the land of the living with her husband. But there was a catch."

"Isn't there always?" I grunted.

"Orpheus was permitted to lead Eurydice back out of the

* Translator's Note: Pluto, the Lord of the Underworld and Zeus's brother, was also known as Hades. Apparently he was sometimes called Old Misery Chops, too, but not often to his face.

Underworld, but he was not allowed to look back and check that she was with him."

I knew what was coming next. "He looked back, didn't he?"

Sibyl nodded. "He looked back. Instantly, Eurydice faded back into the shade-world and Orpheus had to return topside without her. He never got over it. That's when he set out alone, traveling beyond the civilized world with just his lyre for company."

It was dark now, but Sibyl didn't even glance at the stars above. The sky was a total mess. Without the gods to keep order, the constellations had fallen out of their tidy patterns and connect-the-dots pictures into a shambles.

"So after he went and lost his head," I said, "how did he end up in the cyclops's cave?"

Sibyl shrugged. "Apparently, the head went floating off down the river, still singing its song of love for Eurydice." (I almost said "Awww!" before realizing that this was more creepy than cute.) "According to legend, the strength of his love for Eurydice kept him alive. He must have floated out to sea, and the cyclops caught him in a net full of fish."

Sibyl gazed out into the darkening night as if, with the application of just a little willpower, she could discern what future it held for us.

"From what I've seen," she said at last, "I think Orpheus has got something missing."

"Oh, you do, do you? Hmmm, now what could that be? A certain faraway twinkle in the eyes? A winning smile? He hasn't got a mustache. No, hang on, I've got it—what the amazing talking head is missing is HIS ENTIRE BODY FROM THE NECK DOWN!"

Sibyl held my gaze. "According to Aristotle, sarcasm is the second lowest form of wit,"* she informed me coolly.

"What I mean is," Sibyl went on, "he seems kind of . . . disconnected."

"That's right." I spoke as if to a bewildered toddler. "Disconnected from his shoulders. I will remind you of something—Orpheus is the original Billy No Body."

"Look, I'm not talking about anything *physical*," Sibyl snapped, no longer able to suppress her temper. "It's something about *him,* his personality. He doesn't seem to care about anything, he's . . ." She broke off in midsentence. "Wait! What did you just call him?"

"The amazing talking head?"

"No, after that."

"Billy No Body," I answered. "You know, 'cause he's just a head. . . ."

Sibyl's eyes shone. "Gryllus, you might not know it, but you're a genius!" she pronounced. She almost gave me a pat on the head but thought better of it and then hurried off up the deck, leaving me alone and slightly confused.

"I *do* know that, actually," I said. But the only things that

* Translator's Note: According to ancient sources, Aristotle's full list of the lowest forms of humor was:

    1. all reference to bodily functions (see footnote on page 82)

    2. sarcasm

    3. practical jokes involving poisonous deadly hemlock

    4. domestic animals wearing little tunics and doing tricks

    5. any joke that begins, "An Athenian, a Corinthian, and a Boeotian go into a bar. . . ."

heard me were the stars and a lone monkey on night watch, and, quite frankly, what do they know about genius?

I took the long way back to my sleeping area. I told myself that it was to give me a chance to think, but that wasn't the whole story. The route took me near the bodiless head of Orpheus. Homer was nowhere to be seen, and the head was alone, just sitting there (not surprisingly).

If truth be known, I *did* know what Sibyl had been going on about. Orpheus *was* disconnected, and this came down to his lack of concern for all things bodily. There was a kind of otherworldly calm about him, which made him the total opposite of the cyclopes. Think about it: the one-eyed giants were nothing *but* bodies—all guts and appetites, burps and farts and bones and sinew, and chubby hairs sprouting out of nostrils and knuckles. They were bad breath and worse body odor and hideous big toes (*gigantic* toes), and sweat and snot and blood. They were just so utterly . . . *physical.*

Orpheus, on the other hand, being in ownership of only a small portion of his physical body, gave the impression of being simply beyond much of this. And from this unique perspective he had developed a worldview in which nothing really mattered very much. In a strange way, I couldn't help envying him.

But then, as I made my way back to the poop deck, I heard a low sound coming from the head. Orpheus was singing softly to himself in the dark.

It was the first ditty I'd heard from him since the cyclops's lullaby, but this was something altogether different. Even without catching the lyrics, I knew it was the saddest, most beautiful song I'd ever heard—so beautiful it somehow transcended the sorrows of the world. No, more than that—it took the sorrows of the world and transformed them into something wondrous. No, that's not quite right either. It sort of . . .

Oh, look, it was a nice song, but a bit sad.

I moved slowly forward, sliding my hooves so they wouldn't clack on the wooden deck. I was close enough now to see that his eyes were shut. Was he singing in his sleep? Dreaming? If so, it couldn't have been a happy one because in the glow of the moonlight a single tear made its unhurried way down one gray and sunken cheek.

BOOK XVI

Songs of innocence, songs of pies

I was unable to sleep that night, and for once I could not lay the blame on my habit of eating too much cheese before bedtime.

No, it was that song, the one Orpheus had been singing on deck. There was something about it that felt . . . well, the only word is *true*. The song felt *true*, if that makes any sense. And what's more, its truth seemed contagious: with the mournful refrain still echoing in my mind, I looked up into the dark of my cabin and faced a few truths that related specifically to me, the main one being:

I cannot do this.

My experience on the island of the cyclopes had brought this realization home; actually it had brought it home, tucked it in, and then nailed up the doors and windows.

I. Cannot. Do. This.

If Sisyphus really was powerful enough to capture the gods and imprison them, what would I be able to do? I KNOW I had saved the world once — I just didn't have it in me to do it again.

This wasn't cowardice on my part — I had philosophical reason on my side. I mean, consider the body — every single part of it has its own purpose, its own job to do, right? The eyes are for seeing. The legs are for walking. The liver is for . . . well, now wasn't the time to get all bogged down in medical details; obviously the liver does something or other.

The big question was this — what was the point of the *sum* of all these parts? What was the point of ME? What purpose did this little piggy serve? Well, look at the clues — there was my ample girth; the frivolous design of my curly little tail; my natural inclination to overeat and oversleep, often at the same time; my deep-seated, biological aversion to danger. Added together, these features didn't suggest that my purpose on this Earth was to save the Cosmos AGAIN, did they?

Did they?

I could only answer with a resounding *No!* Forget being a hero! Forget saving the world! Good gods, I couldn't even save dessert for later!

There was nothing else to do. I had to come clean, had to

tell Sibyl. I scrambled up, rushed out onto the deck, and made my way hastily toward Sibyl's quarters. All was quiet now. Orpheus had fallen silent, and the only crewman awake was the macaque at the ship's tiller.

I was almost at Sibyl's cabin when the door flew open.

"I was just coming to see you, Gryllus," gasped the ex-priestess. "I've got something important to tell you. Remember that premonition I had?"

How could I forget? (And trust me—I'd really tried.) "That's what I wanted to talk about." Guilt gave me a fresh squeeze. "Perhaps I should go first?"

"No, listen!" said Sibyl urgently. "I don't think my interpretation was right." She paused. "Gryllus, you *are* listening to me, aren't you?"

Pies, pies, pies, pies.

"Er, sorry . . . what?"

"I said I don't think . . . Gryllus, pay attention! This is important!"

Pies, pies, pies, pies.

"Can you hear that?" I asked.

"Hear what?" Sibyl tilted her head. "I can only hear waves and wind. Oh, and a couple of seagulls."

Pies, pies, pies, pies.

"You can't hear that? It's . . . singing, but it's not Orpheus doing it."

The monkeys had heard it as well. One or two began to whoop on deck, and then more of them joined in, their hoots quickly turning into full-out howls and screeches of excitement.

"What on earth is going on?" asked Sibyl, looking around. What was going on was that the monkeys had gone nuts, jumping about in high excitement. What's more, they were all gazing in the same direction, over to starboard—or, indeed, port . . . one of those two.

The monkey manning the tiller was swinging us around, but not fast enough for the jabbering pack of primates that wrestled for control of the rudder. Captain Simios won this little scuffle, blessed as he was with the longest reach and most fearsome canine teeth on board.

Pies, pies, pies.

The delightful song continued from up ahead, where the crash of waves and bursts of foam suggested there was an island. Hardly able to contain themselves, the monkeys were leaping and hopping and doing backflips and zipping up and down the mast and rigging. Their close-set eyes blazed. A pack of sodden gibbons crowded onto the foresail, rocking their narrow shoulders back and forth like a pack of little hairy jockeys, as if this would speed up the ship's progress.

Just then a second, equally glorious element of the song from the island broke in, going:

Fresh out of the oven, fresh out of the oven!

Sibyl marched up to the tiller. "Just *what* is going on, Captain?" she demanded sternly. "If you hold this course, you'll crash us straight into those rocks!"

But the only sea-captainy part of Captain Simios just now was the part steering the tiller. The rest of him was pure baboon. As such, he let out a warning grunt and waved a hairy fist at Sibyl.

"Gryllus, a little help might be nice," Sibyl shouted back to me, but I wasn't really listening. Well, I *was*—I just didn't care. No, like the monkeys, like Homer, who was now up by the foresail, I too was gazing at the island ahead. Even at this distance and in the moon's poor light, I could see the welcoming glow of an inn. What's more, I could make out the sign over the door. It said:

DELICIOUS PIES, ALL YOU CAN EAT!

And, even better than this, below it:

DOMESTIC ANIMALS DINE FOR FREE

I didn't pause to wonder *why* I was able to read this despite the fact that I had never in fact learned how to read (I was absent on the day they taught reading at school).

No, my attention was focused on the three women who stood outside the inn. It was a toss-up which one was holding the biggest tray of pies in her hefty arms, but every last one of those pies looked grand. None of the women looked like a total stranger to pies themselves either, which is, of course, the sign of a tip-top baked-goods establishment. (You can't trust restaurants owned by skinny whippets. How can the grub be up to much if they won't even take the opportunity to overindulge in it themselves?) The outside tables heaved with pies—I had never seen anything actually *heave* with pies before, but let me tell you, it was a wondrous vision.

While the two alluring pie ladies on either side kept up

the background chant of *Pies, pies, pies,* the statuesque beauty in the middle unleashed her glorious soprano:

"Come and get 'em.
Fresh an' hot.
Cost too much?
Oh, I think not!"

Oh, yeah, this kind of song was right up my alley, that particular locale being Greedy Pig Avenue. The singer winked—at *me!*—and this little piggy's heart melted. Was this love I felt or simply greed, and did it matter, anyway?

"Pies aplenty,
Pies galore,
So be a pig an'
Have some——"

The crescendo of the song was lost, wrenched away from me, and I felt a quick stab of anger in the same heart that had only just melted into lovestruck goo. I felt cold, too, suddenly aware again of the wind and the salt spray whipping against me.

The reason I could no longer hear the pie song was because of the little noggin himself: Orpheus. Sibyl was crouching next to him (so *she* was responsible!), and the head had begun to sing. His song wasn't half so enticing, by which I mean it offered not one single promise of tasty, filling, hot snacks (that cost nothing!). No, Orpheus's song was altogether sadder, but I have to admit, it *was* more beautiful. Its melody and words are lost to me now, no more than snippets from an old dream. It was something about returning to the place of one's birth, about wandering the pine forests in the predawn light and watching as the village's lights came on one by one. Bit of a downer really, and yet the song's honest simplicity suddenly made the other song, the pie anthem, sound shrill and false.

Actually, come to think of it, the sound from the island really was shrill—more like the raucous cry of a gang of gulls than a bevy of pie-wielding ladies.

I looked that way and let out one of those gasps, the sort you make when you realize that you have been eyeing up what turns out to be a gaggle of birdlike monsters, all equipped with fearsome talons designed for the tearing of flesh. What those talons held in their grip were not pies at all, but rather pale bones that had been picked clean. The creatures' blazing yellow eyes followed us hungrily as we neared the stark cluster of black rocks on which they roosted.

"Their song is enchanting!" Sibyl yelled to me.

"D'you think so? I've gone off it," I called back.

"No, their song is *magical*! They're sirens. They lure sailors to their doom!"

The monkeys at our end of the ship had changed their tune too. Their shrieks went from excitement to alarm, as they clapped eyes on the reality of the vulturous bunch up ahead.

Unfortunately, the wind was so strong that Orpheus's voice could be heard by only the handful of monkeys nearby. The rest of the crew, including the hirsute captain at the helm, were still intent on getting us to that island. Who knows what they imagined they could see there. I shuddered at the thought.

It wouldn't be long before we were dashed onto the rocks, but once again Sibyl was ready. Orpheus's head was still singing away as the ex-priestess lifted it and placed it in a wicker basket. (She took the time to pull her sleeves down over her hands to do this.)

"Gryllus, take him up to the middle of the ship," she ordered, holding the basket out to me.

"Er, maybe you'd be able to do a better job with that," I began. "I've got this nasty crick in my neck and—"

"Just do it!" yelled Sibyl. "I've got to take the tiller!"

OK, so she wanted to try and wrestle a feral alpha-male baboon for control of the ship. Given this, I couldn't really argue with my assignment. (I did try, in fact, but Sibyl had already taken off up the deck.)

Gingerly I put my teeth around the handle of Orpheus's basket. The head was heavier than I'd expected, but nevertheless I began to carry it to a more central spot so the singing head could de-entrance the crew. As we came within earshot, monkeys shook themselves as if coming out of a nap and they blinked in confusion at what was going on around them.

Sibyl had her hands on the tiller now, but Simios had not yet relinquished his grip. (I wouldn't like to say who I'd have put my money on here. Simios's primate physique surely gave him the edge in sheer physical strength, but Sibyl's education at the all-girls preparatory temple of the Delphic Oracle had left her with a will of iron.)

Up ahead of the ship, the piercing cries of the sirens were getting louder and louder.

Unfortunately, I was paying so much attention to what was happening on the island that I failed to pay quite enough attention to what lay immediately beneath my hooves. I slipped on an apple core, which some complete twit of a crewman must have simply dropped onto the deck. (Come to think of it, it might have been me.)

My front legs skidded out from under me. Naturally, I regained my footing with swiftness and agility, but not before Orpheus's head had tumbled out of the basket.

As the head rolled, I became faintly aware that the sirens' screeches were sounding more and more pleasant, but then Orpheus took up his song again. Sadly, now that he had rolled under one of the rowing benches, he was unable to make himself heard to anyone but me.

I knelt down and tried to reach him, but there wasn't enough room for my own head, which in all fairness could not be described as petite. Meanwhile, I could hear the whoops of the monkeys around me becoming all enthusiastic again.

Thinking quickly and acting decisively, I positioned the basket sideways and then trotted around to the other side of the bench. From there I was just about able to reach the top of Orpheus's head with one hoof. Now all I needed to do was take aim and pop the head back into the basket.

My extensive taverna training paid off—it was a perfect shot! Orpheus could feel no pain anyway, and he didn't skip a beat in his song as he rolled neatly back into the basket.

There was just one thing—yes, Orpheus was back in the basket, but now he was facing the wrong way, that is, facedown

INTO the basket, which meant that I was *still* the only one who heard his achingly lovely song—which was quite muffled now, though no less achingly lovely.

The other noises around me *weren't* quite so achingly lovely—the monkeys hooting and hollering excitedly, the sirens screeching, Sibyl shouting, "Gryllus, what are you doing!" The ex-priestess had bested Simios for control of the ship's tiller, but the captain had been replaced by a knot of other monkeys, all determined to steer us toward that island.

I had dashed back around to the basket and was now wondering exactly how I might turn the singing head around in such a confined space with just a pig's snout to do the job.

I was still thinking this over when another, even louder noise joined the general cacophony. It was the front of our ship smashing right into one of the jagged rocks that encircled the sirens' lair. Every living creature on the ship pitched forward. All that stopped me was another rowing bench, which I now found myself wedged under, fixed as tightly as a cork in a jar of olive oil.

To my amazement, I saw that the jolt had turned Orpheus's head the right way around in his basket! However, it wasn't time to crack out the sparkling honey wine and celebrate just yet—not when the ship was breaking apart and a roiling wave of water was sluicing toward us.

I sank my teeth into the basket's handle and clung on for all I was worth (not much, I had started to think). Right about now would have been a good moment to send up a few well-phrased prayers to the gods.

If only there were any gods around to hear them. . . .

BOOK XVII

A hero finds himself drifting in life.

Turns out I *didn't* plunge into the raging sea and get pulled down to a watery grave. Nor was my fragile mortal body dashed and smashed against the jagged rocks that ringed the island. Nor, I'm pleased to report, did the gruesome sirens gather to feast on strips of my flesh, or suck the marrow from my bones, or cook me up with caramelized onions, or whatever it is they do for supper.

So, all in all, things could have been worse . . . but that's not to say everything was hunky-dory. When a ship starts to come apart, it's every man/woman/child/pig/poet/head/monkey for themselves.

My misfortune in getting stuck under the bench proved to have something of a silver lining: I didn't have to watch all the panicked running around and hysterical attempts to bail the ship out, and so on. It was bad enough *hearing* it.

Suddenly icy seawater slapped against me and then . . . *CRUNCH!*

My section of the ship slammed into a rock. My head came free and I looked up to see that the ship had come completely apart. I was on one chunk that had become detached from the rest, spinning wildly out of control.

As we whipped around and around, I caught a fleeting glimpse of another, larger section of our ship. All the monkeys were huddled on it. I spotted Sibyl and, I think, Homer, too.

They were too busy to see us, struggling as they were to right the collapsing mast and bail out water.

Then the raging waves swept Orpheus and me off in the other direction. We almost ran aground, but a cross-wave swept us away from the black rock.

The seething currents continued to push us away from the sirens . . . and from the other part of the ship, which was being carried in the opposite direction. "You can pack it in now," I muttered to Orpheus, who was still singing.

As soon as the head fell silent, the sirens' screeches became more melodious to my ears again.

"Come back, come back, these pies won't wait;
They'll soon be past their eat-by date."

As the distant, mournful voice crooned on, I was tempted—more than tempted—but we were at the mercy of the waves, and the waves were merciless. Soon we had been swept too far away to see or hear anything of the sirens' island. And that left just the three of us in the darkness: me, Orpheus, and a raging black sea teeming with stuff I'd rather not think about, especially its teeth.

It took a long time for the waves to die down sufficiently to let me sleep, so you can hardly blame me for sleeping in a bit the next day. By the time I woke, the sea was calm and glassy. I took grim stock of the situation in a typically heroic fashion. I was alive, but I was adrift on a raft. There was no land in sight, and I had no idea where I was. Even if I did know, I had no way of navigating or steering the raft. I was dry enough at the moment, but who could say how long this raft would stay afloat. There was no food and no drink. And, to make matters worse, the only company I had was Orpheus. The head was lying on his side looking at an oarlock from a distance of less than two finger-widths.

I set him upright, and then asked gloomily, "What now?"

In the absence of shoulders to shrug, Orpheus went to the effort of raising one eyebrow instead.

"Don't you care?" I exclaimed.

The head gave this due consideration. "Not really. . . . Not now."

I couldn't believe this. "You mean, you don't care if we get rescued or . . . the *alternative?*"

"It doesn't really matter." Orpheus wasn't even bothered enough to lift an eyebrow to indicate that he wasn't bothered. "Nothing matters."

"OK, Mr. Head," I said. "If you really don't care what happens, why did you sing to distract the crew from the sirens' song? Answer me that."

But Orpheus had gone back to being the strong, silent type, only probably not all that strong.

I looked around. Our world had shrunk to the cramped confines of this little raft. Beyond that, the Cosmos consisted of nothing but sea and sky, two endless realms, one of dark and one of light blue, separated only by the pale line of the horizon.

I couldn't help thinking that, in a sense, our entire existence is just like this — you know, philosophically speaking. I mean, sooner or later on the journey of life, we all find ourselves adrift on Fate's raft in a comfortless world, with nothing but . . . um . . . a moody, severed head for company. (I'm not sure yet how that severed head part fits in — you can work out the fine details for yourself, can't you? If you're going to swim in the waters of philosophical wisdom, this pig for one is not going to provide you with a surfboard and a pair of inflatable swimmies.)

The day crawled by. I suppose we could have kept track of the time by following the course of the sun across the sky, but really, what was the point? Also, I didn't know how.

I couldn't help envying Orpheus his apparent ability to remain untroubled by everything, to cut himself off from it all on the grounds that in the long run our problems didn't amount to much. I tried to do this, but I kept on thinking about how my delicate skin was getting fried by the sun. Also, my stomach had become quite vocal about the breakdown of regular food supplies. But this was nothing compared to the complaints of my throat. The worst part of our predicament was that I was dying of thirst, and here I was, surrounded by water for as far as my piggy eyes could see.

"Water, water everywhere, nor any drop to actually get down your neck 'cause it's all so bloomin' salty," I croaked.*

In an attempt to take my mind off the pain, I valiantly tried to keep up morale with a game or two. To my surprise, Orpheus actually agreed to join in, although his enthusiasm did leave something to be desired.

* Translator's Note: A scribbled note alongside the text here says something about liking the poetic effect of the second part of this line but wanting to rework the first part.

This unhelpful attitude became clear to me a few hours later when I said, "I spy, with my little eye . . . something beginning with *W-D-S*."

"The wine-dark sea," Orpheus sighed instantly. "AGAIN."

"Well, excuse me, I'm just trying to keep our brains occupied. You try and think of one we haven't done, then, Mr. Heady-Head-Head."

Orpheus didn't respond. Was he thinking of a new I Spy or just sulking? The silence went on so long it would have been quite awkward if this were a dinner party and not a never-ending nightmare on the open seas. It went on for hours, in fact, during which time the sun did not slack off in its job of beating down on us mercilessly.

I was suffering now. As the zoologists and swineherds among you will know, we pigs are not able to sweat. That's why we wallow in the mud: to cool off. (If you ever hear someone say, "I'm sweating like a pig," you should say, "No, as a matter of fact, you're sweating like an idiot, because pigs do not actually sweat," and then get ready to run like crazy.)

So, as there was no nice cool mud in the vicinity, I took to trailing my back legs in the water behind us.

It was a while before Orpheus's monotone broke the silence: "Something beginning with *S*."

"Easy peasy," I grunted listlessly, not even looking up. "It's the sea."

"No," said the head without emotion.

"The sun."

"No."

"The sky?"

"No."

"Give me a clue, then," I said, perking up a little. "Is it on the raft?"

"No."

"So it's something in the water."

"Yes."

"Is it bigger than an oil jar or—WAAH!"

It was pure dumb luck that I turned my head at that exact moment, just in time to see the huge, dark fin slicing through the water toward me, and then a terrible head broke the surface and a good-size mouth was there, and it was open wide to reveal a lot of pointy-looking teeth. The creature's glassy eye seemed to roll back in anticipation of digging into the unexpected treat of a pork dinner.

"SHARK!" I screamed.

I yanked my leg up out of the water a split second before the shark's choppers could snap it up. The terrible beast splashed back down into the water, and its fin thudded into the raft.

"Correct," said Orpheus without animation. "It was a shark."

It was around this time that I decided that I'd had enough of I Spy . . . and, to be perfectly honest, enough of my bodiless companion, too. I rolled onto my side with my back toward Orpheus so I wouldn't have to look into those pale, unblinking eyes of his.

It took some time for the hammering of my heart to slow down, but when it did, an irresistible fatigue was lying in wait for me. The gentle swell of the sea was lulling me. I gave in and let it drag me off to sleep, a sleep that pulled me far down, far from the terrible pain of my parched throat and the awful ache of my empty stomach and the weariness that caused my entire sunburned body to throb with pain.

I slept like a baby (well, you know, like a baby who's a good sleeper and not like the crybaby next door to me when I was growing up, the one who never slept for more than fifteen minutes at a time before he'd be up and wailing for his mom, and did I mention he was fourteen years old?).

Z
  Z
    Z
      Z
        Z
          Z
            Z
              Z
                Z

I awoke to the most wondrous sight in my entire life. No, it wasn't a luxury ship sailing up to rescue us. It wasn't even a beach with a handy little snack bar.

It was a pie!

There it was, just sitting on the raft in all its glorious *pieness*. The crust looked done to golden perfection. And if my goggling eyes weren't deceiving me, it was *flaky* pastry, the uncontested King of Crusts. Steam rose seductively from the little slits cut into the domed top of the pie. Oh, gods, it even had those fancy little pastry leaves on the top!

Who knew how it got there? Did it matter? Here it was, patiently waiting to be consumed like a good little pie should. I gave my lips a frenzied lick. This had to be the supernatural doing of an Olympian, but now was not the time to wonder which mysterious deity had provided such salvation from on high. Now was pie-eating time!

Suddenly the pie spoke. "What are you looking at?" it asked (in the sort of voice you might not expect a pie to have).

"Heh, heh, heh," I answered, silently complimenting the pie's provider on the nice magical touch of making the pie appear to talk. It's these little details that separate the true Olympian gods from the minor deities. Ravenous hunger gave me renewed strength, enough to get to my hooves. My parched mouth conjured up enough saliva to indulge in a spot of drooling.

"Er, what are you doing?" asked the pie teasingly as I staggered across the raft.

My voice was as cracked as a village idiot's flower vase, but I still managed to croak, "Oh, you know what I'm doing all right, little pie. . . ." The mad grin on my face made my snout ache.

"Little *what?*"

My stomach was demanding that I simply gobble the whole thing down in one go, but Johnny Brainbox was still in control enough to insist on restraint. I would enjoy the pie much more, the old gray matter urged, if I took my time. (*Delayed gratification,* that's what they call it up in Athens; *eating your pie slowly* is what we call it out on the islands.)

And so I slowly reached out my snout to take the tiniest

possible nibble of crust, just to see if it was as totally and utterly delicious as it looked.

I hadn't even bitten into it when the pie's vile taste hit me. "YUCK!"

It tasted like, like dirty socks or . . . I don't know, like earwax or some other profoundly un-pielike substance. Whoever had come up with this pie should have spent less time on the fancy magical talking effects and more time on the basics, like making sure the pastry was edible.

"Get off me!" said the pie irritably. I recoiled in alarm, and as I did so, exhaustion got the better of me. The world seemed to shudder and stretch unpleasantly. When reality snapped back into focus, the pie was no longer there in front of me. Instead, I was looking down at the all-too-familiar head of Orpheus. My snout still hovered over the singer's right ear. I could make out faint pink toothmarks on the otherwise gray-white flesh.

"I do not find that amusing," Orpheus intoned.

I knew now why the world had shuddered, and it was my turn to shudder at what I had nearly done. So it had come to this, then. Cast adrift on the cruel seas, I was reduced to nearly eating the ear of a severed head I didn't even particularly get along with.

I hopped backward, spitting again and again to get rid of the awful taste of Orpheus's earhole. "Oh, gods! Yuck! *P-too! P-ter! P-too!*"

I did such a good job of getting the taste out of my mouth that I forgot about a possibly even more important job: that of staying on the raft. I hopped straight back into the dark waters of the Aegean Sea. *SPLOOSH!*

I was submerged for only a few seconds, but it was long enough to confirm my gut feeling that salt water is not a good habitat for a pig. My head burst out of the water, brine stinging my eyes and nostrils.

The raft had drifted quite some distance from me. I began to kick my way toward it, while the head of Orpheus watched my efforts gloomily.

My natural buoyancy kept me afloat. However, as hard as I kicked, the raft did not seem to be getting any closer. I did my best to control my breathing and pace myself, but suddenly my finely tuned animal intuition was screaming at me to get a move on because SOMETHING WAS WRONG!

Then I glimpsed it—a shape out of the corner of my eye, something triangular and fast-moving, just above the surface of the water. Something that appeared to be *circling* me.

"What was that?" I gasped. "That dark shape behind me?"

"It was a fin," said Orpheus matter-of-factly.

Oh, gods. "And was it the fin of a friendly, intelligent dolphin, here to help by pushing us with its snout to a nearby island?" I panted in desperation. My legs were beginning to throb with pain, but under the circumstances I wasn't about to grant them a breather.

It took Orpheus a moment or two to phrase his answer, perhaps because he didn't want to panic me.

"No."

Water slapped against my snout as my four legs scissored

ever faster. Why, oh why had the Grand Designer of the Universe not equipped pigs with webbed hooves? Such lack of attention to technical detail was exactly the sort of thing to make a philosophical pig lose faith in the essential rightness of this world of ours.

I glanced over my shoulder, just in time to see the dorsal fin zooming toward me. It was a little waterborne announcement saying, "No hard feelings, bud. This is just the way the world works. Some of us are meat eaters, and some of us are made of meat." It was nothing less than an aquatic retelling of Mr. Bunny and Mr. Fist, and I give you three guesses who was stuck going hippety-hoppety as he tried in vain to swim to safety.

I am no stranger to death—I'd died twice before, after all. And yet my wealth of experience as a dead bloke did nothing to ease my fears now.

But then the shark just swam right past me. With a flick of water from its tail, it was gone.

My relief came with a large side order of puzzlement. Presumably I hadn't just encountered the world's first vegetarian tiger shark. It was unlikely to be sticking to a seafood-only diet (even though this was probably the healthiest option for any cholesterol-conscious mindless killer of the deep). Why, then, had it passed up on what was, after all, an unusually tasty square meal floating right in front of it? (OK, more of a *circular* meal.)

And that's when I saw the even larger shape, some distance behind the shark. What broke the surface there looked less like a fin and more like the glistening coils of some very, very big ocean-dwelling serpent.

So that shark had been making its high-speed exit to avoid an even more fearsome predator. Whoever said sharks were just mindless killers of the deep was way off the mark — they were *downright sensible* killers of the deep.

I glanced back in time to see a toothy mouth as big as an archway rise from the water. It was the entrance to a path that led to certain death.

There was just time for one last thought to flash through my brain like summer lightning: *Well, isn't this just fan-bloomin'-tastic!*

Intermission

The Pig Who Saved the World will return momentarily. Village storytellers are urged to give listeners a break and to strongly recommend the following products, all personally endorsed by Gryllus the Pig.*

Come on down to Big Stavros & Gorgina's refurbished Kebab and Grill for one of our

Super-Size Monster Kebabs

They're so big, even Typhon, monster of monsters, couldn't finish one!

Serving suggestion

Big Stavros says, "Have two and we'll pay for your burial rites!"

New Improved Formula

You'll love Medusa's
Snake Oil Shampoo and Dandruff Treatment

from Narcissus Beauty Products

BOOK XVIII

Our hero encounters a bit of a tummy bug.

On the bright side, I wasn't dead just yet.

Then again, I was inside the sea monster's belly, which was pitch-black and cramped and, all in all, not very homey. Warm liquid sloshed against my legs and I could only hope it was seawater.

"Why aren't I dead?" I said aloud. I wasn't really expecting an answer — it was more a matter of preferring my own voice to the various gurgling and popping noises all around me. But a matey voice from somewhere off to my left replied with:

"Ah well, that's the crucial question, I suppose."

"WHO'S THAT?" I cried in alarm.

"Don't say you don't remember me!" the small voice tutted. "I'll give you a clue . . . handsome face, compact physique, lovely set of mandibles, prominent back legs?"

"Hoppy?"

"Bingo!" chirped little Hoppy the grasshopper, a.k.a. Tithonus, former boyfriend of the goddess Eos. "Glad you could join me!"

The pleasure's all yours, I thought sourly, but what I said was: "What are you doing here? What happened to that pelican?"

"Judging from where your voice is coming from, I'd say what's left of its bones would be . . . just to the left of you." (I inched quickly to the right.) "No, wait — that's *my* left, your *right*." (Something sharp was poking into my ribs. I scooted back to the left, even faster this time.) "Yes, I'm afraid the pelican decided to stop for a bit of a rest in open water," the ancient insect explained. "There it was, just bobbing up and down and riding the waves, when it got chomped. Which means I got chomped too."

"You don't seem all that bothered," I commented.

Hoppy the grasshopper didn't pick up on the sarcasm. "One mustn't grumble," he replied. "When you've been around as long as I have, very little can surprise you. It's not as if I've never been in the belly of a sea monster before! Not all that bad, once you get used to it, actually. Anyway, how're you getting on, Gryllus, my old chum?"

Well now, let's see, I thought hotly. Since my last meeting with the relentlessly chirpy insect, I had nearly drowned, *twice.* I had faced not one but *four* cyclopes, not to mention a gaggle of sirens, and I'd come up short on all occasions. I had been forced to look deep into the dark pit of my soul and I hadn't found much there. Plus, I hadn't had so much as a nibble of pie in days — in fact, I had nearly starved to death while adrift on the high seas. I had almost been snapped up by a shark, surviving only because something with an even *bigger* mouth had come along to swallow me whole. *How was I getting on!*

"I think it's fair to say I'm feeling *a bit droopy,*" I said through gritted teeth.

"Oh well, look on the bright side," advised Hoppy. "I assume you were on your way to Crete to find Circe?"

"Sort of," I said cagily. Now was not the time to go into my precise feelings about reaching Crete, I felt.

"Well, not to worry, then! You're *still* headed in the right direction! This sea serpent likes to bask in the shallow waters off the Cretan coast," the insect announced.

"What exactly is going on at Crete?" I asked tersely. "You never told us before. What's Sisyphus up to? What's he done to the gods?"

"It might help you to know his full title—*Evil* King Sisyphus," Hoppy replied. "You do know that he was condemned by the gods to eternal punishment in the Underworld, right? And that he broke out and returned to the Overworld?"

"Yes, yes!" I snapped. A sudden realization struck me: Sisyphus must have made his escape from the Underworld around the time that I had been there to thwart the plans of Thanatos and Chaos. (What? You're not telling me you've gotten this far and *still* not asked your village storyteller to recount the first batch of scrolls to you? Well, you're on your own now, kiddo.)

"Well," Hoppy went on, "Sisyphus set himself up on Crete in the abandoned palace at Knossos and started planning his revenge against the gods. And, being an evil genius, he came up with a doozy of a plan."

"He hasn't . . ." I searched for a nice way to put it. "He hasn't *bumped the gods off*?"

"No need," replied the grasshopper. "He found a way to send them all to sleep. *Indefinitely* to sleep."

"How's that?"

"Easy. Ever heard of the lotus fruit?"

A long-buried memory popped back into my mind. Oh, I knew about the lotus fruit all right. I'd last heard mention of that fruit when I was still a human member of Odysseus's crew. We had only just begun our long journey home from Troy when we stopped off at a small island:

While the scouting party was inland, I had a quick look around and found some fruit trees not far from the beach. I zipped back on board and whipped up a quick pie. I planned to give half to Odysseus, thereby putting him in a good mood for when I asked if I could be excused from rowing duties.

During dinner, I overheard Odysseus tell the first mate how odd the locals had been. They had offered the scouting party something called the lotus fruit. One of the crew had sampled it and immediately fallen into a sort of drowsy trance. Odysseus concluded that the fruit must contain a powerful drug of some kind. It had been lucky that more of the crew hadn't sampled the lethal fruit, he said, as he reached for dessert.

"Mmm, pie," he said with a grin. "My favorite."

I found my voice. "Stop! You can't eat that!"

"Why not?" Odysseus snarled.

"Because . . . we haven't got any ice cream! You can't have pie without ice cream, can you? That would be positively barbaric!"

The captain was already forking a wedge into his mouth. "Then let us be barbarians for once!"

I'll spare you the details about how every crewman seated around the table slumped forward into his bowl. Or how the next day they all roared and raged, demanding to return to the island this instant for more of the addictive fruit, and how the rest of the crew was forced to lock them in the hold.

Or how, when the coast was clear, one particular crewman had tiptoed to the back of the ship and chucked the other half of the pie overboard.

Now, in the belly of the beast, I said, "I have a *vague* memory of the lotus fruit. But what's that got to do with Sisyphus?"

"He devised a way of concentrating the effects of the lotus fruit. Got it so powerful that it would affect even the Olympians. It puts them into a kind of sleepy trance or some such. All Sisyphus had to do was get it into the gods' supply of nectar and ambrosia. From what I've heard, all the Olympians have been given the stuff, and plenty of the minor deities, too."

"But WHY?" I exclaimed.

"Isn't it obvious?" answered the grasshopper. "Sisyphus wants to rule the world, of course! The only way to stop him is to go to the Labyrinth at Knossos and set one particular prisoner free."

I remembered Sibyl's premonition: she had mentioned a feeling that she had to free one especially important prisoner in the labyrinth. "That must be Zeus," I said. "Right?"

It was too dark to see if Hoppy nodded. He went on: "But anyone who wants to get to the prisoner must first get past the Beast in the Dark."

I shuddered at these words. "What is that, the Beast in the Dark?" I asked.

"I don't know for sure," answered the insect, "but it doesn't sound good, does it?"

"You don't know the half of it." I told him about the part of Sibyl's dreadful premonition that said, "Nobody can defeat the Beast in the Dark."

In response, the grasshopper just hissed, "Shhh! What's that noise?"

Once I stopped talking, I could hear it, too. In addition to the usual background level of internal stomach noise, there was something else, a bubbling noise—sort of like someone speaking underwater.

There was an easy explanation for that—it *was* someone speaking underwater, and I had a good idea who.

"There's someone else in here," said Hoppy.

Alas, the grasshopper lacked the necessary bulk and muscle for the job that had to be done. I took a deep breath and counted to three, then I plunged down into the water.

On some islands there's a children's game known as "Bobbing for Apples." Now try imagining the world's creepiest session of bobbing for apples ever. OK, how close does it come to this? A talking pig bobbing for a disembodied head in the jet-black liquid sloshing about inside a sea monster's belly, while a wizened grasshopper cheers him on. (If your answer to this question was "Quite close," your bodily humors are clearly out of whack. I advise you to run along to your local physician or village barber for some medical treatment, possibly involving the placement of leeches on your forehead.)

I burst out of the water with Orpheus in tow. After altogether too much uncomfortable fumbling in the dark, I found a scrap of driftwood to balance him on.

"How long have you been down there?" I asked him, wishing that a pig's hooves were dextrous enough to remove a strand of hair from between its teeth.

I heard Orpheus spit out a jet of water before he answered, "Twenty-three minutes."

Hoppy chirruped appreciatively (possibly in place of an appreciative whistle, for which he lacked the necessary mouth parts). "That's pretty good."

"But a Billy No Body like you doesn't actually need to breathe, right?" I said to Orpheus. "Not having lungs or most of the other apparatus typically associated with living organisms?"

"I *don't* have to breathe," sniffed the head, "but that does not mean I enjoy being underwater. It gets up my nose and gives me a headache."

I had to sympathize—after all, a headache has got to be rough when you're nothing *but* head.

BOOK XIX

It's hard to keep a good pig down.

"Well, this is cozy," Hoppy declared with inappropriate cheerfulness. "I never expected company on the way to Crete."

"Why are you going to the island?" I asked. "Didn't you say that Sisyphus did you wrong one time?"

"I can't let him go taking over the world, can I?" he replied. "Who knows how things will end up? No, I intend to make my way to the labyrinth and sort out this Beast in the Dark." The tiny insect didn't seem to share my concerns about his chances of succeeding.

"What about Sibyl's premonition?" said Orpheus gravely.

Hoppy did not seem unduly put off. "Ah well," he chirped,

"when you get to be my age, you learn that you have to approach premonitions with an open mind. Right, Gryllus?"

I froze in the clammy dark. Did Hoppy know about Sibyl's interpretation of the premonition—her mad idea that I was the "nobody" it referred to, just because this was what the cyclops had mistakenly called me? But how could Hoppy know that?

I began to stammer that I couldn't possibly be the one to save the Cosmos.

"You?" the insect interrupted me. "Of course not! No offense, old chum," he added. "No, I think the solution must lie with your bodiless friend here."

"What, Orpheus?"

"Indeed! It was you who gave me the idea, Gryllus, when you referred to him as 'Billy No Body.' I bet he's the one who can defeat the Beast in the labyrinth because he's got NO BODY. It isn't *nobody;* it's *no body*. We need to get Orpheus to the labyrinth."

"That's silly," I exclaimed. "Isn't it?" But even as I spoke, I remembered the moment on the ship when Sibyl's eyes had lit up and she had called me a genius. Hadn't I just used the same affectionate term for Orpheus back then, too? Maybe Sibyl had reached the same conclusion as Hoppy; she just didn't have time to tell me before we encountered the sirens.

From the pandemonium of thoughts and feelings in my skull, one particular notion sprinted to the front. If this was true, then maybe there was still a chance that everything would turn out OK. Also, it let me off the hook, didn't it? If the premonition referred to Orpheus rather than me, then I wouldn't have to face the Beast in the Dark—or even explain to anyone why I was unable to do so.

"What do you think, Orpheus?" I asked.

I heard the head sigh in the dark.

"I think—" it began, but then he rolled off his bit of driftwood and hit the water with a splash. The stomach walls around us had begun to expand and contract with sudden violence. There was a distant roaring noise.

"What now?" I cried, struggling to keep my balance.

"Nothing to worry about," the grasshopper shouted. "The monster must be moving into shallow water. It'll be close enough to the island any minute. Get ready to disembark!"

I heard a series of little splashes. When he spoke again, Hoppy's voice was coming from a different direction. "Shake a leg! The exit's this way!"

The obol finally dropped for me. "You mean . . . we've got to walk back along the esophagus toward the mouth? That's our only way out?"

"No, no, you're quite right—there *is* one other exit." Hoppy spoke with the bitterness of experience. "I just assumed you'd prefer this way, but of course if you'd *rather* go in the opposite direction . . ."

It took a moment to work out what he was getting at. "Ah."

So, back toward the mouth it was, then.

If only I'd had some strands of seaweed, plus the time to fashion them into a basket, not to mention the ability to do so . . . I could have used it to carry Orpheus's head. As it was, I had to grab a clump of his hair with my teeth. (Still, it could have been worse — what if Orpheus were bald?)

The esophagus trail was easy for an insect like Hoppy. Not so for us bulkier types. As the tunnel became more and more constricted, I began to doubt that I would make it.

"Are we supposed to wait until it yawns or something?" I asked.

"You don't want to try and go out through the teeth again," said Hoppy. "You were lucky enough to be swallowed whole the first time around. No, it's the gills we're after."

He started to rattle on about how the gill system of monstrous aquatic serpents differed from those of fish and amphibians. It was fascinating stuff — probably — but we weren't exactly in the ideal learning environment just then, and I let all the biological terminology wash over me.

It boiled down to this: we had to wait for the right moment, then shove our way through the archway of cartilage in front of us.

"How will we know when's the right momen —?" I began, but then a load of fish (some whole, some gruesomely not) shot through the archway at me.

I heard Hoppy yell, "Now!" I rushed forward, through the archway and toward the light, to a separate fleshy place where water rushed against my face. The monster's mouth opened up ahead and I spotted a glimpse of gray light, framed by teeth.

It was hard not to get pushed back the way I had come — this, in fact, was where the solid matter was *supposed* to go. Instead, I battled forward and made a sharp left, following the water current through a series of platelike thingies and toward a row of vertical narrow slits ahead, which expelled the unneeded water back into the sea. Not surprisingly, these weren't designed for something the size of a pig to make its way through.

"Push!" I made out Hoppy's voice. "It'll give!"

Using the head of Orpheus to lead the way, I shoved and shoved until at last the gill opened a little. The swift current of the water outside came as a shock to me, so much so that it swept Orpheus's head out of my grip. But there was no time to worry about that now. I pushed again, and the last words I heard from behind me were, "Suck your gut in!"

My head was through now, and my shoulders, but not the rest of me. There was nothing I could do but hold my breath and look out into the inky water. Suddenly the sea monster began to thrash its head, possibly motivated by the discomfort of having a pig wedged in one of its gills. It whipped its head back and forth a couple of times, finally doing so with such force that the rest of my body was blasted out in an explosion of bubbles. I shot through the water at high speed.

Luckily a slab of submerged rock was there to slow me down.

I was a child again.

It was the middle of a never-ending summer, and I was on the beach. The air was filled with the joyous cries of the local children, and it seemed the most natural thing in the world to add my own voice to the chorus, and so I shouted, "Mom! The island kids have buried me up to my neck in sand again!" Then I noticed that the tide was coming in and waves were beginning to lap against my chin.

My eyes fluttered open, and the dream of my idyllic childhood faded. It wasn't the cries of frolicking children I could hear, but gulls. Water *was* lapping at my chin, but not in a pleasantly nostalgic way.

I scrambled to my feet, feeling quite bashed up and achey, but not actually dead.

The waves had deposited me on a desolate stretch of beach. There wasn't much around here. In one direction the sand curved gently into the distance; in the other, a finger of rock jutted out into the sea. The only building hereabouts was a run-down wooden beach hut.

Where were the others? I looked back into the crashing waves, thinking I had spotted the briefest flick of a scaly tail as the sea monster submerged itself. But there was no sign of either Hoppy or Orpheus.

I was alone.

So. This was it — the end of the road. Mere minutes after spying a glimmer of hope, I had gone and lost my head, and along with it all chances of becoming human again — not to mention rescuing the gods from the latest pickle they were in, saving the Universe, and anything else you'd care to mention.

What could I do now? There was nothing *to* do, nothing but live out the rest of my time — however much time there was left, that is — as a pig. I suppose there are worse things to be — I don't know, like a jellyfish. (Just imagine the sort of petty-minded discrimination you'd encounter. Let's face it, they're not invited to many parties. And if they were, they'd probably be mistaken for dessert and set upon by a pack of sticky four-year-olds armed with spoons.)

This thought did little to lift my spirits. There was no denying it: I had failed. The notion filled me with a stifling sense of regret. A phalanx of *what-ifs* laid siege to my mind, all chanting, "Wasted your life, wasted your life!" Who could say what I might have been if I hadn't joined the Greek Army all those years ago? Or what I would have gone on to do if I'd been transformed back to my true shape and stayed with Odysseus? All these alternative lives—*better* lives—seemed as closed to me now as the money bag of my old crewmate, Stingy Petros.

Now I would never attain my dream job (pie tester to the crowned heads of Greece). I would never be given a hero's welcome as I entered the gates of Athens. I would never—

Hold on, what was that? Something little and round, bobbing up and down in the water. Every time a wave nearly brought it up the shore, the undertow would drag it back out again. Finally, an eddy spun it around, allowing me a glimpse of Orpheus's long-suffering expression.

It took a few goes, but finally a wave deposited him farther up the shore. I trotted over and set him upright, even going so far as to remove a clump of seaweed from his forehead.

"You took your time," Orpheus said.

Leaving the head in the sand, I spent some time searching for Hoppy. The little insect was nowhere to be seen. Perhaps he had been carried off by the waves, or maybe he was inside the belly of some lucky fish. Whatever the reason, the insect had not made it onto the shores of Crete.

At last I returned to the little head. Orpheus's flat gaze filled me with doubt. Could Hoppy's interpretation of the premonition have been right? Was Orpheus really the one who could overcome the Beast in the Dark of the Labyrinth? It seemed like quite a long shot, but what did we have to lose?

There was only one problem, and it was a big one—if Orpheus was needed to save the world, he still had to be taken to Knossos, and, sad to say, there seemed to be only one candidate for that job (i.e., yours truly).

I slid my front legs down so that I could look right into his blue-gray eyes. "Tell me something," I asked. "Why did you help out on the ship, back at the sirens' island? I thought you didn't care what happens."

Orpheus took a long time answering. "Sibyl told me that if I helped, there was a chance I might be reunited with . . . someone I knew a long time ago. Someone very dear to me."

"Eurydice?"

I took Orpheus's lack of response as a yes. "So what changed after we were shipwrecked? Why did you go back to not caring?"

Orpheus tried to look away, but the absence of a turnable neck did not work in his favor. "After the ship broke up, I was left with just you, and I didn't think . . ." He was polite enough to let the sentence dangle.

I felt the wind on my pigskin, the sand beneath my hooves, and I remembered the time I had looked down on the Earth when I was on the Chariot of the Sun. How delicate it had looked. How *worth saving,* in spite of all its flaws.

"Yeah? Well, listen," I told the head. "If Hoppy was right, then perhaps there *is* a chance that you'll see Eurydice again. But we have to get you to the Labyrinth at Knossos." I sighed. "I don't like it much—I'd rather be sitting by a pool somewhere, sipping cocktails while you all just get on with it—but there's no one else, so I guess I'm going to try to get you to Knossos. I'll take you to the outskirts of the city, and then that's it. I can't do any more than that. . . . What do you say?"

I held my breath, waiting for a yes or no. But one of my ears was waterlogged, and what I heard the head say sounded more like, "Soldiers."

"What's that?" I leaned in. "You'll have to speak up."

"Soldiers," Orpheus repeated, louder. "Coming up the beach."

BOOK XX

The importance of not losing your head in a crisis

It was a military patrol on horseback. Were they Sisyphus's troops? I wasn't sure how far from the palace of Knossos we were here. Whomever they served, the soldiers were still a long way off, but they were definitely heading this way.

Fleeing was not an option—they'd run us down in minutes. That left only hiding. Alas, this beach was totally useless when it came to hiding places—no forests to disappear into, no sand dunes to pop behind. Our only chance was the dilapidated little beach hut.

This hope was dashed when we ran around to the other side and looked inside. It contained nothing except a single wooden bed with a stack of woolen blankets neatly folded at the foot—nothing to hide in, behind, or under.

The wooden porch was little better, featuring one chair and a large sack of grain or something propped against the wall.

With enormous effort I hauled the sack up onto the chair. Then I ran inside the hut, returning moments later with the bedding in my mouth. I began to arrange this over the sack on the chair.

"Pointless activity may keep your mind off a problem, but it will not make it go away," commented Orpheus.

I stepped back and scrutinized the cloak-covered sack. It did resemble a human torso, sort of. Grimacing, I picked Orpheus up by the hair again and swung him up onto the top of the sack. It was a perfect fit—the head nestled in the indentation I'd made with one hoof.

I spat the vile taste out of my mouth, then pulled the top blanket up to cloak the singer's severed neck. Then I hastily arranged a second blanket into a rumpled *himation.**

"This cannot possibly work," critiqued Orpheus, who was turning out to have a real defeatist streak.

But he'd voiced his doubts too late. Horses' hooves played an ever-louder drumbeat outside. I quickly took up position, pretending to nibble some of the reeds at the side of the hut. Moments later, the patrol appeared.

"Good morning, sir," called the lieutenant in charge as the

---

* Translator's Note: The *himation* was a woolen garment worn over the *chiton* (tunic) and fastened at one shoulder. Colors varied, but in fashion-conscious Athens, the "in crowd" favored stylishly black *himatia*. (To appreciate the universal nature of this phenomenon, go to any fashionable New York or London hangout and see how many plaid sweaters or Day-Glo orange trousers you can spot in the sea of black.)

patrol halted. He had dismounted from his horse and was holding his plumed helmet under one arm.

As I continued pretending to munch away, I held my breath. Was Orpheus going to play along?

My fears were unfounded, because the next instant the singer was responding: "Morning." (He remained non-committal as to its goodness.)

"We're investigating a report of unusual activity," continued the lieutenant. "Possible sighting of a sea monster. Have you seen anything out of the ordinary coming along the beach?"

"No," answered Orpheus.

"Come to think of it, we haven't seen you before. This *is* your hut, yes?" asked the lieutenant.

"Yes." Presumably Orpheus was trying not to get tangled in a web of overly elaborate lies.

Nice strategy, I thought, keeping my head down. We might even get away with this, as long as Orpheus could keep his h—. . . as long as he could stay calm.

The lieutenant was gazing at Orpheus's unmoving body.

"Are you feeling OK, sir?" he asked.

"Yes."

Then, in an uncharacteristic torrent of words, Orpheus added, "Never better."

The puzzled lieutenant mounted his horse again. He was about to give the command to move along, but at that precise moment a fat fly buzzed through the air. It executed a few lazy banks and loops, before settling on a good landing spot . . . the tip of Orpheus's nose.

The lieutenant hesitated.

"Er . . . looks like you've got a fly on your nose there," he said, scratching his own nose in sympathy.

"Yes," Orpheus answered calmly.

The fly began rubbing its front legs together in that disgusting way flies do when it looks like they're cleaning themselves. (Who do they think they're kidding?)

The lieutenant tried to stifle his revulsion. "So . . . um, aren't you going to shoo it away?"

"No," Orpheus improvised. "I like it. It's . . . a pet."

"A *pet* fly?"

"Yes."

"*Your* pet fly?"

". . . Yes."

"OK. What's its name?"

". . . . ."

The silence stretched, until:

". . . . . Gryllus," said Orpheus, his voice uncertain.

I looked up sharply. *Mouthy little head! Of all the names he could have come up with, he had to go and nab mine!*

Meanwhile, Orpheus had begun wrinkling his nose rapidly in an attempt to dislodge the six-legged visitor. The fly—clearly of an easygoing disposition and currently enjoying its afternoon break—seemed untroubled.

The lieutenant and the rest of the soldiers just stared in horrified fascination. As far as they were concerned, this peculiar bloke in the beach house had not bothered to move a muscle since they arrived. And now he was contorting his face wildly while his pet fly continued to perch contentedly on the tip of his nose.

Finally Orpheus gave a violent double-barreled sniff. This was followed by an ominous sound.

"Ah . . . ah . . . ah . . ."

I stopped my fake rooting in the yard. Oh, gods, Orpheus was about to sneeze!

I looked up just as the fly, now well rested, saw fit to take off and resume its epic quest for a nice bit of cow poop to call home. Meanwhile, in a positively Heraclean effort, Orpheus held his breath, bit his lip, and somehow, incredibly, managed to stifle the sneeze. His head rocked back and forth alarmingly, but it remained in place.

The lieutenant and his soldiers just gazed, openmouthed.

"You're quite *sure* you're OK?" asked the lieutenant, antsy now to get away from this wack-job on the beach.

Orpheus was getting touchy. "I *told* you, I'm perfectly fi—ACHOO!"

The second sneeze came out of nowhere. Well, actually it came out of Orpheus's nostrils, and it did so at maximum speed and volume.

"Gods bless y—" began the lieutenant, but good manners deserted him as soon as Orpheus's head tumbled forward. It hit the wooden floor of the porch with a sound like two halves of a coconut being struck together—*CLOP!*—and began rolling toward the mounted soldiers.

"Waah!" cried the young lieutenant, drawing his sword. This situation had presumably not been covered in his officer training manual. The troops followed his flustered lead. The horses began to neigh hysterically. With a muffled thundering of hooves on sand, they reared back in a fearful attempt to avoid the disembodied head, which was bumping down the steps and heading their way.

"Don't let those horses step on him!" I blurted out.

The soldiers threw alarmed looks at the talking pig.

"Waah!" they said as they took this new factor under consideration. What must have started out as a routine patrol along the beach had now taken a sharp left into the nightmare territory of detachable heads and eloquent animals. *Welcome to my world,* I thought bitterly.

Orpheus tried to rectify the situation the only way he knew how—by singing. He broke into an inappropriately jaunty tune . . . or at least he started to. He'd only sung a couple of lines before he rolled into a mound of sand. The music died as he was forced to spit sand off his tongue.

Unsurprisingly, the soldiers were all for getting out of there at top speed. It was only the lieutenant who, faced with the sight of both me and Orpheus, kept *his* head (as it were).

"Come back!" he commanded his scampering men. "The Princess Aurelia will want to see these two. Apprehend them immediately."

One of the soldiers looked down uneasily at the head on the ground but made no move to pick it up. Perhaps he was worried about catching a cold so bad that one sneeze could blow your head off?

"Can I use my shield to pick it up?" he asked at last.

BOOK XXI

A royal princess displays her heart of gold.

Orpheus and I were shoved into the patrol's single wagon. There followed an hour's ride along the coast road — over exceedingly bumpy terrain, incidentally. I took no pleasure in the magnificent sea views, but once we had passed the first sentry's outpost and entered the military camp, I peered out in amazement.

The patrol was part of a decent-size army. We passed a number of tents, outside which troops were engaging in such military pursuits as spear throwing and hand-to-hand combat practice.

We passed siege towers and battering rams, and then more soldiers, all readying themselves for war — sharpening blades, filling quivers full of arrows, hammering dents out of shields.

Of course I was no stranger to sights like this. It was just like being back at Troy. What I was looking at could be nothing but a siege army. I felt strangely at home — it wouldn't have surprised me to spot a handsome, sandy-haired bloke engaged in the vital military task of peeling potatoes.

There was another similarity with the forces at Troy. The wide array of styles of armor and weaponry indicated that this army had been patched together from all corners of the civilized world. There were Scythian archers shooting at practice targets, while Spartan swordsmen trained with wooden blades and Boeotian spear-throwers jabbed at hanging dummies to hone their disemboweling skills.

"Is this the army of Sisyphus?" I asked the leader of our patrol.

"Not likely," muttered the soldier nearest to us.

"We follow King Midas of Phrygia," the lieutenant answered.

"Until his money coffers run out, that is," added one of the troops.

One of the other mercenaries said something about this probably coming sooner rather than later. There was no time for me to press the issue, because the patrol had pulled up outside the largest, swankiest tent in the encampment.

We were unloaded and led inside — Orpheus still balancing on the inside of a shield and me with a dagger at my neck.

The tent was full of soldiers. An air of nervous expectation lingered in the air, and the sort of noise that only a large number of military types shuffling from foot to foot could make. Each unit of soldiers stood around its own stack of objects, and the various groups were all jealously eyeing up what the others had brought. The lieutenant of my patrol was anxiously trying to spruce up the plume in his helmet and shine up his breastplate with a little spit and polish.

"What now?" I asked.

"Hush, pig!" hissed the hoplite with the dagger. "You don't want Princess Aurelia to hear you, do you? She's got a heart of gold, you know."

Heart of gold? I immediately imagined one of those simpering princesses you hear about: the sort who spend their gilded lives spreading royal loveliness and putting flowers in their shimmering blond hair. The sort who tend to injured woodland animals (which then fall in love with her and pathetically attempt to make her a dress out of leaves and twigs and their own droppings, and she's such a delightful soul that she won't say what junk it is and how they ought to enroll in the Woodland College of Fashion and Design if they want to pursue a career making royal ball gowns).

Suddenly a horn fanfare silenced the nervous chatter. Four slaves entered the tent, carrying a litter on which reclined a portly older gentleman decked out in fine purple robes. This had to be King Midas, judging from the way everyone in the tent dropped to one knee and bellowed, "Hail, King Midas!" He responded with a distracted little smile. (Midas was one of those kings whose physical presence makes you wonder if the royal families really do have Olympian blood in their veins. He looked more like a fruit-and-veggie merchant in fancy dress.)

The king's litter was followed by a second one, but this required *six* slaves to carry it, all quite a bit beefier than the first group. It wasn't that the person on this litter was so much heavier. But whereas Midas's was made of polished wood, the second litter appeared to be solid gold. It was so heavy that the porters all grunted with the effort and made little shuffling steps that suggested they might be in the process of doing their innards serious injury.

I couldn't see very much of the teenage girl on the litter. That's because she was largely hidden by the sheer amount of gold ornamentation all over her — golden rings, golden bracelets up both arms, a golden crown, and golden anklets up to her kneecaps. She glittered with golden earrings, necklaces, pendants, and brooches. She was clearly someone who had never taken to heart the ancient wisdom that "Less is more," at least when it came to gold.

A lanky figure in long, flowing robes stepped out of the shadows behind the golden litter: a priest of some sort. "The Princess Aurelia wishes to review the spoils of your day's work," he declared primly.

"And they'd better be good," snarled the princess in a voice like a piece of gold being scraped down a blackboard.

The patrol next to ours stepped forward. Three of its soldiers hauled forward a golden statue for the princess's inspection.

The unit's leader gestured flamboyantly to the statue. "We got it at the temple of Athena, Your Golden Majesty," he boasted. The statue did indeed depict the great goddess Athena holding an olive branch in one hand and her battle helmet in the other.

"Ooh, that looks nice, doesn't it, my buttercup?" said Midas to his daughter with the desperate air of a hen chitchatting with a fox.

I couldn't help agreeing. I have actually seen Athena face-to-face, and I can tell you, this was a pretty good likeness (even if the nose wasn't quite beaklike enough). Aurelia, however, did not care for such artistic considerations. She was only concerned with two things: the *amount* of gold and the *quality* of gold. She tapped the statue with one gold-painted fingernail. Then she cried, "Are you making a joke, Father? Because if you are, you will have noticed that I am not gracing

the room with the melodious tinkle of my golden laughter!"
(The king did not look as if he had noticed anything, staring
down as he was at his sandals.) "This piece of junk is cheap
copper ALLOY! It's rubbish! It might as well be gold-*plated*!
It might as well be BRASS!"

The king looked down some more at his (ornate but highly
impractical) sandals. Meanwhile, the first unit's leader had the
look of someone who has just wandered into a snake pit,
having believed it to be a cake shop.

"But . . . but it's top-quality merchandise," he spluttered.
"That's what we were told when we plundered it. . . ."

Aurelia hopped to her gold-clad feet. "Are you implying
that I don't know gold?" she snarled.

Now the officer had the look of someone who has just
wandered into a snake pit, having believed it to be a cake
shop, and has promptly been bitten in the head by an irate
cobra.

"No, Your Highness, but . . ."

Aurelia's eyes blazed yellow. "Am I not the princess with
the heart of gold?"

"Yes, but . . ."

"Then get this junk out of my sight and go and . . . GET
ME SOME DECENT **GOLD!**"

The unit's soldiers effected a tactical retreat at top speed.
For a few awkward seconds, the only sound in the royal tent
was the scraping of gold—but not, apparently, high-quality
gold—being hauled away.

Midas was the only one with the nerve to break that silence, but only just. "Aurelia, my dear . . ." he began, sounding as nervous as a substitute lion tamer fresh from the temp agency. "I've been wondering and . . . well, the thing is . . . do you think maybe you've got *enough* gold now? We've spent months going from island to island."

The contempt in Aurelia's eyes was pure and brilliant. "Do you hate me *so* much, Father?" she demanded. She said the word *Father* as if it were a euphemism for *imbecile*.

"Of course not, my golden nugget . . . but we already have an army of gold miners working back home and . . ."

Aurelia pasted a wounded look on top of her affronted one. "Am I asking for so very much, Father, after all I've been through? *Am* I?"

Midas blinked uncertainly. "Well, some people would say that all the gold in the entire world *is* an awful lot of gold for one person, I suppose, but . . ."

"Is it that I'm not worth it? That I don't deserve anything nice and shiny? Is that what you're saying, Father?"

"No, my precious metal, of course not! It's just . . . well, I was hoping that you'd draw a more . . . positive conclusion from all that unpleasant business of a few years back."

Aurelia switched tactics, facially speaking, her features drawing now into a pinched expression that put me in mind of the sirens' true faces. "Perhaps you would care to explain how *positive* I should feel about my own father completely and utterly ruining my entire life?"

"Come now, Aurelia, that's not——"

But the princess was in no mood to listen. "You were

granted, were you not, the greatest gift in history? A power such as no one else has ever wielded—the ability to *create gold itself*! And what did you do with it? You GAVE IT UP!"*

Aurelia's fury was as hot and deadly as molten metal, with no prizes for guessing which kind.

"But, Aurelia," pleaded the king, "it wasn't possible to live like that. I couldn't even eat when the very food in my hands turned into you-know-what."

Aurelia was as unbending as a metal rod. "Father, I have just one word for you . . . GLOVES! But oh no, you had to give up at the first little hiccup!"

"But, sweetie . . . you yourself were just a statue. . . ."

Aurelia's eyes narrowed until her pupils were just yellow pinpricks of hate. "JUST a statue?" she hissed. "I was made of GOLD—pure, shiny, beautiful, solid gold. My hair wasn't *like* spun gold—it *was* spun gold! I was *perfect*! And you had to go and muck it all up and turn me back into *this*!" She raised her arms, clearly displeased with the dull pinky-brown of the skin that peeked from under her many golden bracelets. "Thank the gods I didn't have to revert *completely* to flesh and blood," she added with a pout.

"No, my dear," Midas agreed with a sigh as heavy as the heaviest of precious metals. "You still kept your heart of gold. . . ."

Yeah, I thought, the obol finally dropping—*all hard and cold.*

---

*Translator's Note: King Midas was granted a wish by the god Dionysus and requested that everything he touched should turn to gold. He realized the foolishness of his wish when he broke a tooth on his supper of chicken nuggets, which were now real gold nuggets. Finally, Dionysus agreed to reverse the effects of the wish.

The priest alongside Aurelia's litter cleared his throat in a way that suggested he wanted the room's attention rather than a cough drop.

"Beta Patrol, bring forward your spoils," he commanded with a brisk clap of the hands.

The lieutenant of our patrol stepped forward.

"Your Shiny Highness," he began loftily, "I regret to inform you that we didn't find any gold, as such."

Displeasure rose like steam from the princess, but the lieutenant pressed boldly on into hostile territory. "However, we did find two items that we thought might amuse you."

At a nod from the lieutenant, one of the soldiers stepped forward, carrying Orpheus on a shield.

"It's a head," Aurelia pronounced spikily.

"It's not just any old head," the lieutenant continued hurriedly. He turned to Orpheus. "Go on, then. Say something."

Orpheus rolled his eyes once, before closing them.

"He's . . . he's just feeling shy," said the lieutenant. "He was talking up a storm earlier. Singing, too. He's got a golden voice, he has."

"A *golden* voice, you say?" The princess perked up. "Do you mean his vocal cords are actual gold? Because our court physician could easily remove them. . . ."

The lanky priest leaned forward and murmured, "Your Majesty, I suspect that the phrase 'a golden voice' is merely a metaphor."

"A metaphor!" Princess Aurelia spat in disgust. "Correct me if I am mistaken, but I was under the impression that one cannot wear a metaphor around the neck so that it sparkles and shimmers stylishly in the light! Therefore, metaphors are worthless!"

"But, darling, look at its eyes," Midas tried gamely. "You have to admit, it is rather good. It would be frightfully amusing at royal functions. You could hide it under a platter at high table as a practical joke. . . ."

"I am NOT looking for something amusing," replied Aurelia haughtily. "I am looking for something metallic and malleable and highly ductile and yellow and shiny and——"

"Yes, dear," sighed Midas. "I understand."

The soldier bearing Orpheus began to shuffle awkwardly backward. I noticed the priest move toward him, but then my attention was drawn to matters closer to home. That's because the soldier with the dagger had prodded me forward. With less confidence now, the lieutenant said, "There's more, Your Highness. We also found . . . *this.*"

There was no point in playing dumb at this stage, not when so many witnesses had heard me speak. My best bet was to ensure that the princess simply had no interest in me.

"I'd just like to say, I am completely made out of pig," I announced. "One hundred percent, twenty-four-carat oinker, I am."

Midas was beaming and clapping his hands together with forced jollity, but Princess Aurelia just gazed in disgust at my all-around lack of goldness. In her eyes, not only was I not gold, I was *the opposite of gold*.

She was about to speak, and I fervently hoped it would be something along the lines of, "Get that vile hog out of my sight!" But before she did, the priest leaned forward and cleared his throat again (more politely this time, as befitted his royal audience).

"What is it, Hieros?" snapped the princess.

The priest gave a twisted smile. "Your Majesty, tomorrow our armies march on the palace of Knossos itself. By nightfall you will be in possession of the greatest hoard of gold in the civilized world."

Aurelia's eyes glittered at the prospect.

"But our scouts report that the battle will not be easy," continued the priest. "The palace is well fortified, and Sisyphus has the reputation of being a wily opponent. What we need"—and here Hieros threw me a meaningful look— "is a truly special sacrifice. One that will guarantee success in the battle. One whose entrails will surely guide us on the path to victory."

Suddenly Aurelia was looking at me differently, her brain struggling to work while trapped under the weight of her obsession with the shiny stuff. Slowly a new concept was solidifying in her mind, like molten gold cooling into solid:

I might not be gold, but I was a MEANS to gold—lots and lots of gold.

King Midas was having a hard time keeping up. "So, you *like* the piggie, then, my golden nugget?" he asked his only daughter.

A tight grin flashed across Aurelia's face. Her eyes didn't stray from me as she said, "I love it, Daddy."

Midas smiled in obvious relief. "Well then," he said, "that's all that matters."

BOOK XXII

Sometimes you have to make sacrifices in life.

OK, guess where I was, bright and early the next morning?

Award yourself one point if you said in a wooden cage.

Two points if you mentioned that the cage was in a wagon.

And you can have a bonus point if you said the wagon was being pulled by a team of mules alongside phalanx after phalanx of soldiers, all on their way to lay siege to the palace at Knossos.

Once again, all this reminded me of my time at Troy—not a pleasant memory. I shut my eyes, but I couldn't escape the noises of imminent war: the thunderous sound of feet and hooves pounding the dusty earth, the clank and clang of people in heavy armor, the creak of battering rams and siege towers being towed along, the hearty greetings and friendly insults called from one phalanx to the next, the air thick with the unmistakable whiff of violence on the way.

Also—alas!—the same level of what passed for humor among warrior types. One soldier passing by said to his comrade, "They say there are so many archers at Knossos, the sky will be dark with arrows."

I opened an appalled eye. The speaker was clad in Spartan battle dress and carrying a spear, with a row of notches up it to indicate battle kills (unless he'd been using the spear to record his height over the years). He had a tattoo of Ares, God of War, on one arm.

His battle-hardened companion gave his beard a thoughtful scratch. "Then the gods are smiling on us," came his growled reply. "For verily it means we shall have some shade to fight in."

It was the straw that broke this pig's back. "By the hairy knees of Ares, have you never heard of UMBRELLAS?" I cried. "They keep you shaded *and* have the added advantage of not puncturing you in the neck and killing you." I paused. "Well, not unless you're *really* clumsy."

The two soldiers were unfazed. "The offering to the gods is chatty this morn," commented the tattooed one.

"Then the gods are smiling on us," growled his companion, after the usual beard-scratching routine. "For verily it means the sacrifice will go well."

I sank back into the straw, as the two mercenaries strode ahead in warlike fashion. *What was the point?* I thought glumly.

I didn't pipe up again after that, however idiotic the comments around me were. I threw all my energies into feeling sorry for myself.

I was making decent headway in this endeavor when twisty old Fate twisted again—Hieros rode up alongside my wagon. Because of his ceremonial robes of office, the court priest was forced to ride sidesaddle.

"Hey, Hieros!" I called. "You're making a big mistake, you are. I've got friends in high places—Zeus happens to be a personal friend of mine. When he finds out what you're up to, you'd better start shopping for a lightning-proof hat."

The priest did not respond. I tried a different approach. "Anyway, don't you know? Sacrificing animals and reading entrails is so out of date in this day and age, it's positively preclassical. Now I could put you in touch with a close friend of mine who used to work at the Delphic Oracle. . . ."

Again no response. Hieros didn't even glance my way.

"Besides," I persisted, "pigs are definitely *not* the species of choice for the busy entrails-examiner on the go. Too big! Too messy! Just think of all those entrails all over the place. That's a workplace accident waiting to happen, that is. You want something more compact, something you can carry in your robe pocket—a hamster maybe?"

Still not a flicker of emotion from the taciturn priest.

I was getting a bit desperate now. "Plus—just between you, me, and the temple pillar—I'm not sure *my* entrails are up to the job. Very unreliable, my innards are. I get plugged up very easily, you see. . . ."

Once more, no response whatsoever from the priest.

However, someone else *did* answer me. "Give it a rest, old chum. He's got earplugs in, so he can't hear a thing." The voice was very close—so close, in fact, that it seemed to be inside my head.

"Hoppy?" I asked, baffled.

The grasshopper's voice was louder than I'd ever heard it. "The one and only!"

"Where *are* you?" I whispered.

"I'm in your left ear, as it happens." To illustrate the point, the insect shifted a little and I felt an uncomfortable tickling sensation. No wonder my hearing had been a bit off the last day or so.

"I thought you were a buildup of earwax," I said. "How long have you been in there?"

"I hitched a ride when you made your exit out of that sea monster," Hoppy replied in a deafening whisper. "You've been doing awfully well, so I didn't want to put you off."

I gave the priest a sideways glance to see if he'd noticed that I had stopped pestering him and started muttering to myself. He hadn't.

"Oh, yeah, really? Well, thanks!" I replied huffily to Hoppy. "The only fly in the ointment being that I'm supposed to be slaughtered when the battle begins so that Chuckles over there can scrutinize my innards. In fact, in light of this information, I'd say you should feel free to jump in with suggestions anytime, Hoppy."

I hoped that he was about to reveal some brilliant secret plan that would lead me to safety. Before he could, the wagon halted and the grasshopper's butterfly interests moved on.

"What can you see? Tell me!" the insect's whisper blared in my ear.

I glanced up. "Just loads of soldiers on the march, same as before," I replied.

"No, what can you see the *other* way?"

With difficulty in such a confined space, I worked my way around. The wagon had stopped high up on a ridge. From this vantage point I had a decent view of the yellow stone towers and broad city walls of Knossos below. It was the sort of scene you might have written an enthusiastic postcard home about, if:

a) you weren't stuck in a cramped wooden cage with a bug in your earhole;

b) you weren't about to be ritually slaughtered;

c) you knew how to write.

The front ranks of King Midas's hired army were taking up position on the wide plain in front of the city's main gate. Not surprisingly, Knossos had the distinct look of being Closed for Lunch for the foreseeable future.

"Well?" insisted Hoppy. I was about to describe the scene to him in a few deft strokes, but then I became aware of events a little closer to our wagon. Beneath a makeshift awning, Hieros was kneeling and washing his hands in a ceremonial bowl. While this was going on, the priest's hooded assistant opened the side door of my cage and yanked me out by the rope around my neck.

"WELL?" Hoppy the grasshopper was sounding impatient.

I would have replied, only I was a little too busy being tied to the altar that had been placed at one end of the tent.

"*What* is going on?" persisted the insect.

"They're getting the sacrificial rituals started!" I hissed.

"Do keep your shirt on," said Hoppy. "You'll be right as rain; just you wait and see."

Next, Hieros sprinkled some water from the bowl on me.

"If you've got some sort of brilliant plan, better tell me now," I moaned to Hoppy when the priest turned away.

"No need to worry," the grasshopper's reassuring voice echoed in my ear. "There's loads of time for secret plans."

Hieros had taken out a handful of unground barleycorn from a leather purse around his neck. He proceeded to sprinkle this on me.

"I bet that was the barleycorn. Yes?" Hoppy commented. "He'll be sharpening the knife next, I expect."

Once my eyes had stopped watering from being pelted with

barleycorn, I could confirm that, sure enough, the priest was at the altar, drawing a smaller knife down the curved edge of a large, ornate blade.

"Is that what he uses to kill the sacrifices?" I whispered in alarm.

"Don't be silly!" scoffed Hoppy. "No, he uses the *ax* to kill you. Chop, chop! A swift blow to the noggin, just like that. He uses the *blade* to butcher you."

Even in the depths of my terror, a clanking noise from the plain below distracted me. There was enough play in the rope to allow me to turn my head. I was just in time to see the city gate of Knossos open up. Another army began to pour out.

Military strategy was never one of my strong suits — I was out sick the day they covered that at school. But even I knew that the rules of combat in the civilized world dictated that Midas's army must wait until their enemy had assembled. (Only dirty cheating barbarians would be so sneaky as to attack before that — which, come to think of it, might explain why barbarians win so many battles.)

Hieros the priest paused in his preparations to watch, too. As troops poured out through the gate, it became clear that the defending army was smaller than Midas's, but not by much. When these armies clashed, it was going to be big — if not the Mother of All Battles, then certainly the Great-Aunt.

Hieros resumed his priestly duties, holding up the curved sacrificial knife so that it glinted dramatically in the sun.

"Any progress on that secret plan?" I whispered to Hoppy.

"Goodness, I never knew you were such a worrywart," the grasshopper answered breezily.

Meanwhile the priest, satisfied that the knife was ready, now inspected the ax in the same way. Then he turned to face me.

"You don't think we're cutting this a bit close, do you?" I said to the increasingly irritating inhabitant of my left ear.

Hieros looked up the hill to where I'd seen the royal tent of Midas and Aurelia. The priest nodded—presumably a signal that he was ready, because seconds later a horn sounded the attack.

"See?" Hoppy said. "Told you there was nothing to worry about. He won't sacrifice you until after the first blood is spilled in battle."

"But that'll be in about two seconds, won't it?" I wailed.

I'm pretty certain Hoppy answered yes, but I couldn't say for sure because that's when the first lines of each army stepped forward to do battle.

BOOK XXIII

Cry havoc and let slip the pigs of war!

As armed hostilities began, the din was immense. Soldiers on either side roared as the first waves sprang forward and metal struck metal: sword on sword; shield on shield; in a few uncoordinated cases, helmet on helmet.

War is very different when you're close up. I'd never been so near the action during the Trojan War. I watched now in horror as one of Sisyphus's mercenaries thrust his sword right into one of Midas's soldiers. I was unable to watch as the victim fell, another senseless casualty on the altar of war. That's because he *didn't* fall. Instead, he looked down at his mortally punctured chest and whined, "Owwwww! That *really* hurt."

One of the primary goals of military training is to encourage the grunt to view the enemy as something less than human. Soldiers must be trained to think of the enemy as nothing but an obstacle to be cleared; a beast to be destroyed; a slab of kebab meat to be skewered. But the unexpected ordinariness of the wounded soldier's comment jolted his opponent out of his bloodlust.

"Er . . . sorry, mate," said the battle-hardened, scar-faced warrior, letting go of the embedded hilt.

Suddenly the scene no longer matched my memories of the fierce fighting outside the gates of Troy.

The injured soldier was looking down at the sword sticking out of his chest with some puzzlement. "That's OK, I s'ppose," he mumbled. "I was thinking of getting a new battle tunic anyway. This one's seen better days."

I could hear this unusual exchange because, almost immediately after the first clash of arms, the sounds of battle had pretty much died down. All along the front line, similar exchanges were going on. On either side, mortally wounded soldiers were wondering why they were still around.

I'm no acolyte of Asclepius, God of Medicine—I wouldn't know one end of a leech from the other (so never ask me to feed your pet leech)—but even I could tell something wasn't right.

"Shouldn't they be dead when they're run through with swords?" I mused aloud.

"That's what I've been trying to tell you," chirped Hoppy, even now still maintaining his jolly, seen-it-all air. "It's Sisyphus up to his old tricks, isn't it?"

"Is it?"

The grasshopper sighed. "Listen, Gryllus, how do you think you survived getting eaten by a sea monster? Stroke of luck, was it? How do you think you managed not to drown when you exited through the gills?"

"Well . . . I held my breath and swam expertly to safety."

Hoppy chuckled, an unpleasant sound when it's bouncing right off your eardrum. "I hate to be the one to burst your bubble, old chum, but you were stuck, hanging out of that gill, for ten minutes. Ten minutes underwater! Even a pig in tip-top physical condition couldn't have managed that, let alone yo—. . . Well, the point is, Sisyphus has gone and done it again."

"Gone and done *what?*" I snapped.

The answer came not from the grasshopper but from a helmeted soldier who appeared at the entrance to the tent.

"Gone and imprisoned Thanatos, that's what," said the soldier. "Or, if you prefer to refer to him informally . . . Death."

The soldier took off the bronze helmet and ran her fingers through her short, tousled hair.

"Fancy meeting you here, Gryllus." Sibyl smiled fiercely as she bent to cut my rope. "Rescuing you is becoming a bit of a habit."

"Who's this, then?" boomed the insect in my ear.

"It's Sibyl," I said.

"Duh!" said the former priestess, unable to hear Hoppy and thinking I was addressing her. "Of course it's me!"

I was struggling to keep up with everything. "So . . . the prisoner in the center of the labyrinth isn't Zeus — it's THANATOS?"

I became aware of movement behind me. Sibyl looked up quickly. "And where do you think *you're* going?"

"Nowhere," answered Hieros the priest haughtily. (And before you go and ask how come he could hear when he'd been wearing earplugs earlier, I can only say, "Hmm, maybe he TOOK THEM OUT!" Stop trying to be so clever and just listen to these scrolls.)

Sibyl moved to block the priest's exit. "Where's the head?" she demanded.

I was free now to look back and see the priest, who still held the ax in one hand and a saddlebag in the other.

"I don't know what you're talking about," replied Hieros. He was trying to maintain his imperious tone, but cracks were appearing.

"I know your sort," said Sibyl scornfully. "You don't care about the gods. If you did, you'd know there's no point making a sacrifice now. The priesthood is just a racket to you, isn't it? All you care about is making money from the gods. Someone like you wouldn't miss the chance to take the actual head of Orpheus."

"You are quite mistaken, young lady," Hieros huffed, clearly trying to pull rank on a less-experienced temple worker.

Sibyl pointed to a roundish bulge in the saddlebag the priest was attempting to hide behind the folds of his robes. "What's that, then?"

"It's . . . a soccer ball," answered the priest, who did not at first glance look like the sporty sort.

Sibyl gave the kind of grin you might see on an Amazonian warrior-queen just before she smacks your head in. "Oh yeah? Come on, then. It looks like the battle's off. Let's have a pick-up game, shall we?"

"Ah, it's . . . got a slow leak!" the priest squeaked.

"I don't mind. Bet we can get some of the soldiers to join in." Sibyl was rolling her shoulders as a warm-up. "You can be goalie, if that's what you're worried about."

The priest's voice went up a notch. "Ah, I'd love to, but this bad knee of mine . . ."

"I am *not* a soccer ball," a glum, muffled voice called from within the burlap sack. "Also, it smells funny in here."

Hieros had the decency to look aghast. "Oh, no, wait, you were talking about THIS bag," he babbled. "Sorry, I *quite* misunderstood you. Thought you were talking about . . . er, some other bag, the one I keep my ball in. Yes, yes, the head of Orpheus is in this bag. Quite so. And he's probably finished napping now, so, if you'll excuse us, I'll just take him back to the king so he can—" Sibyl's hand shot out and clamped onto the sack. The former priestess locked eyes with the priest. He was much taller than she and, though he didn't have too much meat on his bones, he *was* still carrying the very sharp ax with which he'd intended to do me in.

No matter. Hieros looked down into Sibyl's grimly determined, top-tier-temple-educated face and knew he didn't stand a chance. He yanked his hand away from the saddlebag as if it were a hot potato and he were a snowman.

"I've just remembered!" he warbled. "I've got to go and . . . see a man about a three-headed dog!" He began to move away into the crowd at high speed.

Sibyl looked around anxiously. Hundreds of soldiers on either side were crowding forward to see what was going on at the front line. Only a few actually knew that the score of battle casualties currently stood at 0–0, but it was clear to all that something was not right.

"We'd best get you two inside," Sibyl said to the head and me.

"You *three,* more like," I corrected her; then I directed my next comment to Hoppy. "Out you get then."

I tilted my head and shook it about until the grasshopper popped out onto the Cretan soil.

"I don't wish to be ungrateful," was all the little free-riding ingrate of an invertebrate said, looking up at me, "but have you ever thought about having your ears cleaned out?"

I don't know what they taught Sibyl at the Delphi preparatory temple for young priestesses, but it allowed her to take Hoppy's sudden appearance out of my earhole in her stride.

"You'll be Tithonus, then, I expect," she said primly.

"I usually answer to Hoppy these days, miss," said the little six-legger.

That's about all there was by way of introductory chitchat. Sibyl quickly folded Orpheus's bag back so that it was more like a hood. She tucked this under one arm and set off. I followed, with Hoppy clinging onto the bit of rope still around my neck.

As soon as we left the sacrificial-tent area, we entered a throng of soldiers, and we had to push and shove our way through. Confusion reigned and it was making a right old mess of things. The whole scene was in such disarray that no one saw fit to challenge us. I just fixed my eyes on Sibyl's back and followed in her wake as she got to work with the old pointed elbows and barged her way through.

After several minutes of slow progress, we reached less-crowded territory. We had made our way to the side of the palace walls. A wooden siege tower had been left here, but no one was manning it.

Sibyl pointed up the palace wall to a narrow ledge, some forty feet above our heads.

"And how exactly do you think I'm going to get up there?" I demanded.

Sibyl stuck two fingers in her mouth and blew, creating an ear-splitting whistle that almost made me wish I still had Hoppy tucked inside one ear, not to mention a friend of his nestling in the other one.

"I wish you'd say when you're going to do something like that," I complained.

A row of little hairy faces had appeared and were gazing down at us from the ledge—the assorted primate mugs of Captain Simios and the rest of the crew of our ex-ship. A human face joined them, one that looked less at ease in this high-stress situation. It was Homer, as pale and alarmed as you'd expect a sensitive artiste to be in a place like this.

Simios let out a grunt that must have meant something along the lines of "Watch out below!" because then he hurled a length of rope down to us. The coil landed in a cloud of dust, close enough to raise suspicions that I was its intended target.

Up on the ledge, the monkeys proved that they had retained enough nautical knowledge in their little primate skulls to tie the other end of the rope to a column.

"I hate to disappoint you," I told Sibyl, "but I'm not much good at rope climbing these days, what with being a pig and all." (No point mentioning that I had never been able to climb a rope, even when I was a human. Hard to say why, unless it had something to do with upper-body strength, agility, and technique.)

But Sibyl had begun to loop our end of the rope around my midsection.

"Breathe out," she instructed me, and she pulled in a couple of extra feet of rope to loop around me. "I see you've managed to find enough to eat since I last saw you," she commented snippily.

"Not true, actually. Been wasting away to skin and bones, I have."

I had no time to protest. Once the rope was secured and anchored to me, Sibyl began to climb up it, with Orpheus tucked into her trusty backpack. She was a proficient climber—of course!—and didn't take long to get up there. Then it was my turn. The gang of primates started to pull on the rope, hauling me and Hoppy into the air. They soon fell into a rhythm, coordinating their primate grunts, and before I knew it, we were halfway up.

"Wheee! This is the way to travel, isn't it?" enthused Hoppy from the back of my neck.

"You speak for yourself, mate," I replied, heroically ignoring the pain. "You haven't got a great big rope chafing you around your tummy."

From this height I was able to look out over the masses of soldiers in front of the palace gates. They had completely given up on the idea of fighting as a bad job, seeing as how it was impossible to kill the enemy; militarily speaking, this seemed to defeat the whole purpose of the exercise. Instead, there was lots of confused milling about.

As for me, I still hadn't fully digested the news Sibyl had imparted on the ground. So the prisoner trapped in the labyrinth was Thanatos, then? The supernatural embodiment of Death was an old—but not fondly remembered— acquaintance of mine. . . . Without this natural force to gather and dispatch souls to the Underworld, it meant that no one would die, didn't it? That explained why not a single one of the wounds in the battle below had been terminal. It also explained why I had made it to this island still breathing.

Well . . . so what? Was this state of affairs so terrible? If you couldn't die, that meant you'd live . . . *forever*! Think of it—a bright new world, free from the shadow of mortality! A world in which you could do whatever you liked—take a drunken walk along a clifftop, order dinner in whatever barbarian restaurant you liked, *anything*—without any fear that you might wind up in the Underworld for your trouble! Was that really such a bad thing? Maybe Sisyphus had done the world a huge favor. . . .

We were nearing the top of the ledge now. The monkeys pulled me onto it, and a rhesus macaque nimbly untied the rope. At one end of the narrow ledge, Sibyl stood at a small stone entrance into the palace. Homer already lurked in the darkness beyond, a lit oil lamp in one pale hand.

"Step lively, Gryllus!" ordered Sibyl.

But I didn't. I couldn't shake the idea that had taken hold of me. The imprisonment of Thanatos meant that every mortal could enjoy the privileges of the gods themselves!

I became aware that the baboon next to me was grunting something and jabbing me in the ribs.

"How splendid, Captain," I replied absentmindedly.

But the oversize baboon did not stop. He began hopping up and down and pointing at the ground below.

I peeked over the edge and saw a familiar face. It was the court priest, Hieros, and now he was flanked by two archers. He pointed up to us, and one of the soldiers began to draw his bow.

"Get a move on, Gryllus!" cried Sibyl, and for once she was unable to conceal the desperation in her voice.

At last I started to move toward the entrance, but it was too late; my hesitation cost us dearly. An arrow zipped up toward us.

I didn't even have time to select one of my wide range of panicked cries before the arrow struck. The thing is, it didn't hit me — it hit Sibyl, as she turned sideways to let me pass. The arrow went right through the priestess's back and then halfway out the front.

"OWW!" she cried. Her back arched and she unclenched her hands, dropping Orpheus. The head began to roll toward the lip of the ledge, but hairy primate hands scooped it safely up.

Sibyl whirled around and looked down over the ledge at the priest, who was furiously instructing the second soldier to load another arrow and fire.

"Well, really!" exclaimed the former priestess as the bloodstains on her robes spread, front and back. "Now that has gone and put me in a very bad mood indeed." Her eyes flashed. "Now MOVE IT, GRYLLUS!" she barked.

I have faced a good few monsters in my time, but not many of them compared to Sibyl when she was really, really grouchy. I scurried through the entrance and into the waiting darkness.

BOOK XXIV

The Labyrinth of Knossos has more twists and turns than a Carpathian soap opera.

Once the monkeys had closed the stone door behind us, our only light came from a couple of oil lamps. The little patch they illuminated was enough to give me an idea of where we were — slap-bang in the middle of downtown Trouble.

More specifically, we were in a corridor of some sort, one

that snaked off into darkness on either side. The outer wall seemed to be unbroken, apart from the low door we had just come through.

"What's the point of putting a door there that just leads out onto a little ledge?" I asked.

Homer pointed to the writing carved in big letters on the beam above the door. "EXIT AND GIFT SHOP," he read aloud.

"It's a not very nice trick to make people think they've found a way out," said Sibyl, her face struggling to mask her pain.

A way out of *what* was pretty obvious — at regular intervals, the corridor's inner wall opened into further passageways that twisted off into the darkness. This must be the world-famous Labyrinth of Knossos.

I looked dejectedly at the rest of my companions. The old gang was back together, and yet this wasn't the jolliest of reunions. The monkeys, in particular, seemed less than overjoyed to set eyes on me again.

"They hold you responsible for the ship going down," Homer explained. (I later learned that they had managed to construct a raft. After being picked up by a pirate ship, Sibyl had engineered a brisk takeover, and they had made their way to Crete. Here the ex-priestess had infiltrated King Sisyphus's hired army in her usual efficient manner. Meanwhile Homer, having been turned down on account of flat feet, had been forced to enter Knossos in the guise of a street entertainer, The Marvelous Mario and His Merry Monkeys.)

The arrow in Sibyl's chest was clearly causing a lot of

discomfort, but she was the sort of girl who considered showing this to be the height of bad form. "We all know what needs to be done," she grimaced. "Thanatos is imprisoned in the center of the labyrinth. Sisyphus has set someone — or *something* — to guard him, but I think I know how we can get past."

"Yes, about that. . . ." I began hastily. "The thing is, I don't think that premonition of yours refers to me at all, so—"

Sibyl cut me off. "I don't either. I didn't have time to tell you on the ship, but I think the premonition probably refers to Orpheus."

She bent down — painfully — and addressed the head.

"Are you in?"

"I am," he declared simply.

Sibyl turned back to me. "I've asked Homer to stay here with the crew," she said solemnly. "I'd like you to do the same, Gryllus. You've played your part — you got Orpheus here when we thought all was lost — and for that I thank you. But now it's up to me and him."

Everything was moving too fast. "Wait!" I cried. "Look at the state of your chest! You're bleeding all over the place. You're in no fit condition to go running around labyrinths."

Sibyl grinned the strangest grin. "I'll live," she said mysteriously.

"I just don't think we've thought this through!" I wailed. "Knowing that Thanatos is the prisoner changes everything, doesn't it? Well, doesn't it?"

"Listen, living forever is not a barrel of laughs," Hoppy piped up. "I speak from personal experience. You still get illness and pain and suffering and old age, and all that sort of business." The little grasshopper was bouncing up and down frantically at the nearest entrance in his eagerness to get going.

"It's just not natural," said Sibyl quietly. "Everything must have its time."

"Apart from the gods!" I blurted out.

Sibyl had a funny look on her face, and I don't think it was just the arrow poking through her chest that put it there. She looked sadder than I'd ever seen. "That's true," she said. "And we can only be thankful that we aren't them."

"But—"

She leaned in toward me. For a second I thought she was going to give me a hug, but I suppose the arrow sticking out of her chest would have gotten in the way. She patted me on the head instead.

"Good-bye, Gryllus."

"This is all very touching, but we really must GO!" Hoppy urged her.

Sibyl was already making for the labyrinth entrance with Orpheus's head in one hand and a lamp in the other. "Good-bye, Homer," she said. She jerked a thumb toward me. "Keep him out of trouble."

"Stop! Shouldn't we at least *vote* on it?" I exclaimed. "This new democracy thing they've got in Athens is supposed to be brilliant!"

But without another word or a backward glance, Sibyl, Hoppy, and the head plunged into the darkness of the labyrinth.

"Go, then!" I shouted bitterly after them. "See if I care!"

The rest of us were down to one lamp now, and our world

shrank accordingly. The monkeys' grunts had subsided to a low chorus of guttural murmurs, but it was Homer's reaction that surprised me the most. Tears were trickling down the epic poet's face.

"And you can pull yourself together," I told him. I have always felt uncomfortable in the company of snivelers and crybabies.

"We'll never see the likes of her again," Homer blubbered, wiping his nose on a sleeve. "She was a real hero."

"What do you mean, *was?*"

Homer's shining eyes met my piggy ones. "That arrow . . . it went right through her heart."

"So?"

"You do know what the heart does?"

"It's the seat of the emotions," I answered.

"According to some, the heart also pumps blood around the body," said Homer.

"So?"

"So . . . so, if Sibyl—no, WHEN Sibyl releases Thanatos . . ."

Homer trailed off and I was left to complete this grim thought for him: "She'll *die? Sibyl* will die?"

Homer's reply was a somber nod.

What? Sibyl was going to die! I *knew* she had rushed off without thinking this whole thing through. There *had* to be another way to sort this mess out. While there was still time to catch her, I dashed forward into the entrance to the labyrinth.

"Wait, Gryllus!" called Homer, but I was already charging along the twisting passageways in the direction they had gone.

Sibyl couldn't have gone too far yet. "Come back!" I shouted. "I *said* you were being too hasty!" I reached a junction and turned in the direction of a faint glow of light up ahead. "Wait for me, will you?"

As I neared the pale light, I realized it *didn't* come from the oil lamp in Sibyl's hand—it was a grille set in the ceiling above me. I looked up at a patch of wide-open, sky-blue freedom neatly divided into sixteen little squares, each and every one of them impossible to fit through. A nasty little thought wriggled into my consciousness: perhaps I'd never see the sky again, other than through a vent like this.

"Sibyl!" I shouted. "Can you hear me?"

No reply, but all was not lost. I closed my eyes and sniffed deeply. In addition to the musty smell of a labyrinth that obviously hadn't had a spring-cleaning in several dozen springs, I could detect the faint aroma of my companions in the maze. I would simply follow my nose! (This is no comment on Sibyl's bathing habits, more a reflection of the wondrous qualities of the pig's snout and its ability to pick out the slightest of scents. It also helped that Orpheus's disembodied head was getting a bit ripe these days.)

Barreling around yet another twist in the maze, I stumbled across a carelessly discarded pile of sticks. They snapped and crackled under my hooves; they had to be as dry as a . . .

Oops.

They weren't, in fact, sticks. Beneath the pale light of

another overhead vent, I saw that I had encountered a fellow wanderer in the labyrinth. More specifically, his rib cage.

The skeleton's vacant eye sockets seemed to stare at me accusingly, as if demanding to know why I had come too late to assist him — several decades too late, by the look of things. Without the cosmetic support of cheeks and gums, his jaws were fixed in a permanent grin at some secret joke. Well, let me tell you — I've heard the punch line of that particular joke, and it didn't have me rolling in the aisles. (Then again, skulls *always* look as if they're grinning. Zeus only knows what they have to be so happy about. OK, maybe they've succeeded in shedding those difficult last twenty pounds on their diet, but at what cost?)

The grin's skeletal owner must have been here since the labyrinth was first used, decades and decades ago, to house the bull-headed Minotaur. Now an even deadlier prisoner was being detained in the labyrinth . . . and here I was, heading straight toward him!

"Sibyl! Hoppy! Where ARE you?"

My words echoed back at me mockingly. No doubt the labyrinth was designed for just this purpose, acoustically speaking — lousy for staging an impromptu lyre recital, brilliant for leaving those inside its winding passageways feeling disorientated and dazed. I sniffed quickly, but any trace of my companions' scent was lost now, obliterated by the smell of bones and decay and despair.

There was nothing to do — I began to retrace my steps back to Homer and the primates. It was no great hardship for an intellect like mine to remember the turns I'd taken and simply reverse them. Right, right, left, double-back on myself, left again—before long, I was trotting back through the entrance and around the corner . . .

. . . straight into the solid stone wall of a dead end.

"Oof!"

For some inexplicable reason, I had taken a wrong turn. Had I miscounted? Run past an opening?

I set off again, more slowly now. If I'd been in a more philosophical mood, I might have reflected on how life was like this, really: a dizzying maze in which you can't see what lies ahead, where you're presented with one decision after another, and it's almost impossible to choose which option is the right one. Plus, it makes your feet hurt like nobody's business.

"Homer!" I shouted; then—because I was no longer sure which direction I was headed in——"Sibyl?"

I thought I heard a response amid the echoes, but it didn't sound like either an ex-prophetess or a would-be poet.

"Captain Simios?" (I was getting a bit desperate now.)

Still no answer, but I could hear something. I stopped. There it was again: the unmistakable shuffle of footsteps.

With the height of the ceiling changing all the time, and the walls twisting and turning this way and that, this labyrinth could really play tricks on your eyes. At first the figure approaching didn't seem especially tall, but then I realized that it was VERY tall—huge, in fact.

It was also familiar, and not in a good way.

Actually, it was Polyphemus.

The cyclops!

BOOK XXV

A brisk chitchat with the most evil person ever to set foot on this planet

"WHAT? Who dares to set foot—I mean to say, *hoof*—in this place?" bellowed the giant when his single eye spotted me.

I didn't stop to wonder how the cyclops came to be here or how the dim light of the labyrinth made the giant look smaller in some way.

Hey, he was still a cyclops, and he still looked hungry!

The giant took a step toward me, lifting one hand. In the gloom, the massive palm and fingers seemed oddly indistinct, blurred around the edges, but this didn't stop me from reacting as any warrior with a healthy sense of self-preservation would:

"Waaaaaaaaaaaaaaaaaaaaaaaaaaaaaaaaaaaaaaaaaaaaah!"

What more could I say? It wasn't the most informative response, but it captured the essence of my feelings perfectly. However, just in case there was any doubt as to what my heartfelt cry meant, I accompanied it with some high-speed hoofwork.

The cyclops's shout followed me: "Go, vile hog! Flee and never return to this place!" The monstrous voice didn't sound quite the same here in the narrow confines of the labyrinth, at once reedier and plummier—another acoustic quirk of the labyrinth perhaps?—but it was still a considerable motivational tool. Certainly, I was feeling extremely motivated—specifically, motivated to get the Hades out of there, chop chop!

Which is what I did.

I turned and ran blindly through the winding pathways of the labyrinth, charging to junction after junction and never once pausing to consider which way to go. The only direction I had in mind was AWAY.

My piggy ears were filled with the frantic scrabble of my hooves on stone and the ragged panting of my breath. It's moments like this that really bring home to you how you ought to have spent more time doing regular aerobic exercise, only, of course, out-and-out terror tends to dilute the impact of this important lesson.

But even terror has its limits—sooner or later, you still run out of steam. I had already slowed down a fair bit when I skidded around yet another corner and found myself eye to eye with a couple of soldiers. One of them held a sword and a shield decorated with the Cretan double-ax; the other was carrying a tray of food and a map of the labyrinth.

"Out . . . of . . . the way!" I gasped. "It's right . . . behind me!"

"What's right behind you?" asked the guard with the tray.

"Yeah, what?"

"The cyclops, you fools!"

I tried to barge past them, but barging was beyond me now.

"I don't see any cyclops," said the guard with the tray.

"Yeah," agreed his comrade. "Me neither."

Now that I had stopped running, I realized that there were no cyclopean noises echoing along the passageway behind me: no stomping feet or disgusting grunts.

I looked back. "Oh. . . . Well, it *was* behind me. It was . . ."

But the guards could not have appeared less interested if I'd been explaining Pythagorean numerology.

"Save it for the boss," said the one with the tray.

"Yeah," added the other, brandishing a short sword in my general direction. "Save it for Sisyphus."

The two guards led me away at swordpoint, using the map to navigate our way out of the darkened maze. Once we were out, it soon become clear to me that the rest of the palace at Knossos fell somewhat short of *palatial*. It had all the bells and whistles you'd expect—marble colonnades, wide balconies, elaborate mosaics on the floor, and imposing friezes painted on the walls—but none of them seemed up to snuff. The friezes of giant bulls were faded and smudged, the colonnades and balconies chipped and crumbling. Most of the mosaics had pieces missing, and I hadn't yet passed a statue that wasn't lacking the tip of its nose or some other vital dangly bit.

Finally, I was steered through a small anteroom toward a set of double doors. The soldiers prodded me through these and into the throne room.

"Ahem. Your Majesty, we found . . . *this,* coming out of the labyrinth."

The room was no doubt impressively grand . . . decades ago, that is, when Minos had been master of this palace and the very name of Knossos sent a ripple of fear across the Greek-speaking world. Now it looked more like a commuter-wagon waiting room in rural Boeotia. The decor was *so* last eon—all Minoan bull-jumpers and double-axes. Wide steps still led up to a throne, but it was in dire need of upholstering and a lick of paint.

There was plenty of space for the usual mob of royal hangers-on, elite guards, etc. However, now there were just two guards on the doors and one lookout at the window. Their mismatched uniforms gave away their status as more soldiers-for-hire—this, too, was an army that had been hastily cobbled together.

The only other person in the room was a tall figure in purple robes.* He stood at the balcony, looking down on the battlefield below.

As Sisyphus turned, I realized that his robes might well be royal purple, but they also had the ratty look of serial hand-me-downs. The king himself was a gaunt, bearded figure. His gaze was of the sort that is variously called *piercing*, *hawklike*, or *a bit on the rude side*. It didn't quite go with the enormous grin that occupied the lower part of his face. In the present situation, that smirk seemed about as appropriate as a knock-knock joke at a state funeral.

"A pig!" declared the king in apparent delight.

I fired back a look of both hatred and fear, fully aware that I was in the presence of one of the most notorious evildoers the mortal realm had ever seen.

"Yes," I snarled defiantly.

"And a *talking* pig, at that—splendid!" Sisyphus's grin grew even more wolfishly large.

* Translator's Note: Since ancient times, the color purple has been associated with royalty and wealth. Even today, if you wish to impress your friends and generally appear more dignified and regal, go to school dressed from head to toe in purple. (For best results, you can't go wrong with velvet.) This may be against the school dress code, but your teachers won't dare say a word because of the subliminal message of royal authority your bright purple gear will be giving off.

It was the perfect opportunity for a cutting comment to wipe that evil grin off his face. The only thing I could come up with was, "Oh? Splendid, is it?"

This blistering response didn't have the desired effect. "Yes . . . I just said that, didn't I?" he answered.

Evil King Sisyphus rubbed his chin in contemplation. "The question is, what to do with you. . . . Normally we'd simply execute all intruders, but executions aren't really what they used to be, at the moment."

One of the guards cleared his throat. "We could chuck 'im out the window, Your Majesty," he suggested helpfully.

Sisyphus nodded, giving the proposal due consideration.

"You can't do that!" I exclaimed. "I'd burst like a water balloon!" Even though I wouldn't die, what sort of existence would I have as a giant splotch of pig bits?

"You're right—it would make a terrible mess," conceded Sisyphus. He grinned and pulled a large gold coin from his pocket. "Tell you what," he said breezily, "we'll leave it to chance! Heads you can stay; serpent tails and it's out the window you go. Fair 'nuff?"

Before I could answer, Sisyphus had flipped the coin with his thumb. It arced into the air, twinkled at its zenith, and then fell to the ground . . . where it promptly rolled under the throne.

"Well?" demanded Sisyphus. "What is it, then?"

One of the guards got wearily to his knees. "I can't see. It's rolled right to the back, Your Majesty."

"Well then, go and get it!"

While the guard inched on his belly toward the coin that would decide my fate, Sisyphus beckoned me to the window.

"Come, look at the armies," he said, beaming. "They know there's no point fighting, but they're not sure what to do instead. Look at that platoon over there—they're using their shields as flying discs to play catch!" Sisyphus's eyes danced over the chaotic scene. "You have to laugh, don't you?"

"Not really," I replied, glancing at the disarray outside. "I don't see how all this helps you to rule the world!"

"What?" Sisyphus looked genuinely surprised. "Who said anything about ruling the world? Why would I want to do *that*?"

There was no polite way of putting this. "Well, because you're so . . . you know, *evil*. . . . I mean, why else were you condemned to everlasting punishment in the Underworld?"

Back at the throne, the first guard had gotten stuck. His two comrades were attempting to free him by tilting the throne up so that he could slide back out from under it.

"I'll tell you the reason for my punishment." Sisyphus chuckled. "Many years ago, I was on top of the world—an earthly king with untold riches. I had it all. And yet . . . the allotted thread of my life wasn't unspooling any slower. As the end approached, one question kept on coming back to me. Why must we mortals put up with such fleeting lives, while the gods enjoy the benefits of immortality? And so I devised a plan to trap and enchain Thanatos. The scheme succeeded wonderfully, but—surprise, surprise—the gods weren't pleased at the thought of lowly mortals enjoying the benefits of immortality. They took it upon themselves to free Thanatos and banish me to my eternal toil."

I was confused. Sisyphus—the legendary evil genius, once

Olympus's Most Wanted, the upper realm's public enemy number one—had been punished because he'd tried to escape death? That was *it*?

"But I'll say one thing for my punishment in the Underworld," continued the king. "It gave me plenty of time to think. As soon as I escaped, I knew what to do the second time around. I would first ensure that the gods were dealt with. This proved alarmingly easy—simply a matter of effecting entry to Olympus and spiking their nectar with a sleeping potion. And presto! The Olympians are slumbering like the infants they so surely are in spirit."

He turned back to the window. "The embodiment of Death, not being a god as such, was impervious to my potion. But I was now free to lure Thanatos into the labyrinth and enchain him once again. As for the workings of the Cosmos . . ." He waved a slender hand dismissively. "It turns out we really *don't* need any deities to assist the wind in blowing or the sun in tracking across the sky."

Behind us, all three guards were now lifting the throne and moving it to one side.

My head was beginning to throb. "So . . . you've done all of this because you were afraid of dying?"

"No!" cried Sisyphus, clearly offended that I might think him subject to such trivial considerations.

"Then *why*?" I whispered. "What's the point?"

"The *point*?" Sisyphus let out an unkingly giggle. "Oh come on! Next thing, you'll be asking for the meaning of life!"

I was silent. All my hours of philosophizing were a blur to

me now, wasted time I could have put to better use, such as stamp collecting or pie consumption.

"Er, Your Majesty, we got the coin," said the gruff voice of the guard. His knees were mucky from crawling to retrieve the coin.

"And what was it?" Sisyphus asked brightly.

"Tails, sire," answered the guard as he handed the wretched coin over.

Sisyphus smiled. "And I can't recall, did that mean in or out?"

A nasty grin spread over the guard's face, but before he could answer, a herald appeared at the main door. Lacking a trumpet or anything to make a fanfare, he just shuffled his feet a bit before announcing, "Your Majesty . . . King Midas and the Princess Aurelia are here!"

BOOK XXVI

The Cosmic Joke doesn't raise a laugh.

Midas entered, accompanied by a small entourage of armed guards. The Phrygian king was clad in Tyrian purple, too, but the cut and quality were clearly far superior. Midas's hair and beard were carefully set in little kingly ringlets, and yet somehow all these individual touches still failed to add up to much of a regal whole.

The same couldn't be said of Aurelia, who was loaded down with even more golden jewelry. She clanked in, her beady eyes instantly scanning the room for any signs of the yellow shiny stuff.

"Welcome!" Sisyphus bowed low to his royal guests, but the grin remained stubbornly on his face.

Midas blinked. "We are here to discuss terms, as your messenger requested," he said uncertainly.

Aurelia raised one arm—with difficulty, given the number of bracelets on it—and pointed at me. "That's MY pig!"

"Then the fates have blessed you," declared Sisyphus, "for he is a fine specimen of a pig, if a little perplexed." He studied the sheer volume of gold weighing the princess down. "And yet I'd hazard a guess that pigs are not your primary field of interest, Princess. I sense you have no doubts about what is *really* important in life—yes?"

"Nothing matters except gold," answered Aurelia, lifting her chin in defiance of both Sisyphus and the weight of the several crowns on her head.

"Well said!" declared Sisyphus. "Let's hear it for gold, a somewhat impractical soft metal that just so happens to be rather shiny!" Sisyphus turned to Midas. "And what of you, my fellow king? What is the most important thing in your life—the thing that gives it *meaning*? Wealth? Power? Fame, perhaps? A guaranteed spot in the annals of history?"

Midas was looking down at his pedicured toes again. "I wish only to keep Aurelia happy," he answered quietly.

"Bravo!" pronounced Sisyphus, with a smirk that belied his sincerity. He folded himself onto the shoddy throne. "I was once like you, Aurelia." He smiled. "Like all selfish children, I cared only about me and what I could get for myself: riches, power, whatever. But as I grew, I came to realize that my family, my loved ones, were just as important to me." He nodded in acknowledgment of Midas. "But *I* didn't stop there. I realized that all the people I knew were just as valuable to *their* own loved ones. There was only one logical conclusion: the lives of *all* my countrymen were equally valid. But why stop at the borders of my own small city-state? Surely the lives of every living Greek carried the same value. And then what of the barbarian non-Greeks? I came to realize that *all* lives count as much as our own. It was merely a matter of stepping outside of one's own selfish preoccupations, of seeing them as being no more significant than the preoccupations of anyone else. When I finally understood this, I knew I had to do something that would benefit *all* of humanity. This is why I first decided to imprison Thanatos—to liberate all my fellow humans from the shadow of death."

Midas and Aurelia shook their heads—one in embarrassed confusion, one in anger (at the unfavorable description of gold).

"But here's the funny thing," continued Sisyphus, the smile freezing on his face. "Once you've taken that first step outside yourself, it's hard to stop. Take a few more steps and every life looks not just equally important, but equally UNIMPORTANT. Our births are mere accident, our deaths insignificant, and there isn't much to brag about in between. From a distance— let's say from the viewpoint of the gods—the daily struggles of our lives are no more than the comings and goings of ants. Our ambitions are trivial, our achievements transitory."

I was about to hit back with a stunningly brilliant riposte, a philosophical boot that would slam into his intellectual house of cards and send it flying. The only thing was . . . I couldn't. I just stood there in numbed silence.

"That's absurd," I said at last.

"Exactly so—our lives are absurd!" crowed Sisyphus. "It can't be avoided. Each of us is the center of his or her own world, all wrapped up in the details of our own lives. But humanity's curse is our ability also to step outside and see just how insignificant we really are. In the big picture, our lives are meaningless, our dreams too trivial to contemplate. But even when we *know* this, we still can't shake the conviction that our lives *are* important, that they *do* mean something. And so we muddle on, trying to keep both beliefs in our heads. . . . It truly is absurd!"

Sisyphus caught my eye and gave me the coldest wink I've ever seen. "So much, then, for the meaning of life! Unless it's a joke . . . one huge Cosmic Joke. When I returned from the Underworld with the intention of capturing Thanatos a second time, I did so for very different reasons."

"So . . . you're doing all of this as some kind of joke?" I asked.

"You might say so," replied Sisyphus with a defiant grin. "Or, at least, I am removing the killjoys who don't wish to share the grand joke."

The gold coin was back in Sisyphus's hand. I looked nervously at the guard who had been so keen to remind Sisyphus of the outcome of the last toss.

"So then," said Sisyphus, "if Aurelia wishes for gold and you wish to keep Aurelia happy, gold is what we should toss for.

The spoils of war go to the winner!" He glanced at the guard. "And this time I won't stand so close to the throne."

Midas blinked uncertainly. "I . . . I don't think . . ."

"There is an awful lot of gold around in this palace," Sisyphus purred, waving the coin back and forth.

Aurelia's glittering eyes followed the coin. "We'll do it!" she snapped.

Sisyphus placed the coin back on his thumb. "Just one word of caution: if you win, your troops must steer clear of the labyrinth."

Aurelia pounced on this like a ferret on an arthritic chicken. "Why? Is that where all the gold is, in the labyrinth?"

"Alas not," replied Sisyphus, his smirk failing to match his sympathetic tone.

Midas still looked confused. "Whatever's in the laby-rinth . . . does it have anything to do with what just happened on the battlefield outside?"

Sisyphus nodded approvingly. "I can see why you're a king," he said, ". . . beyond the mere accident of birth that brought you into this world the son of a monarch rather than a dung shoveler."

"Thank you," said Midas, ". . . I think."

"I can tell you what's in the labyrinth!" I shouted. "It's where he's got Thanatos locked up! And there's a cyclops in there guarding him."

"Incorrect!" said Sisyphus.

"But . . . I *saw* it! Polyphemus the cyclops was in the labyrinth."

This was the cue for another bout of grinning on Sisyphus's

part. "No . . . you saw something that *looked* like a cyclops," the king corrected me. "To ensure that my guest of honor remains in the labyrinth, I have enlisted the services of a very special guard by the name of Proteus. He is a deity, but a somewhat *minor* one—one who feels that he doesn't perhaps get the respect he's due from the Olympians. His particular gift is the ability to assume any number of different forms." He turned to me. "Presumably this cyclops is something that strikes a special fear in your heart?"

"You might say that," I mumbled.

Sisyphus beamed, like a proud parent whose toddler has successfully reached a landmark moment—using the potty perhaps, or successfully adopting the appearance of someone's darkest nightmares.

My mind was spinning. "So, if someone like, say, an ex-priestess was in the labyrinth," I said carefully, "then Proteus would appear to her as . . . a monster or something?"

"Proteus would appear in whatever form she was most afraid of," confirmed Sisyphus, readying himself to toss the coin.

Hope sprang in my heart like . . . a spring. How could Sibyl get past something that could take the form of her worst fear? Perhaps she was still alive, then? Perhaps she was wandering around the labyrinth now, even as we spoke?

"And say a talking grasshopper was in the labyrinth?" I went on. "It would probably see Proteus as . . . what? A hungry magpie?"

"*What?*"

Sisyphus was so shocked that he flicked the coin much

harder than he'd intended. It sailed up and right over the edge of the balcony, then plummeted down to the battlefield below.

Sisyphus ignored the cry of pain and the angry shouting from below. The grin on his face had curdled into a grimace. He whirled around on me. "What did you say? A grasshopper? TITHONUS! *Tithonus* is in the labyrinth!"

"Yes. You remember little Hoppy, then?"

Sisyphus ran his fingers through his straggly hair. His grin had vanished, leaving in its place just a thin line of worried royal lip. "But . . . if that little bug frees Thanatos, he'll ruin everything! LITERALLY! I must go to the labyrinth!"

Midas and Aurelia watched in bafflement as Sisyphus swept toward the door. One of his guards stepped forward, hand on hilt. "Shall we come, Your Majesty?" he asked.

Sisyphus waved him back. "If I'm in time, I'll need no more than the heel of my sandal to deal with Tithonus. If I'm too late, then all the armies in the world won't be enough."

There was a ball of confusion bouncing around inside my skull. What to do? According to Sibyl, freeing Thanatos was a *good* thing—she believed we had to do it, even if it entailed her own death. But according to Sisyphus, freeing Thanatos was a *bad* thing, something we had to prevent at all costs.

I was sure of just one thing: if there was a chance of finding Sibyl, of making sure she was safe and sound, I had to take it.

I rushed after the king. As we left the throne room, I became aware that the noise from outside had grown in both volume and intensity. Surely the coin hadn't caused that much damage? Perhaps the fighting had resumed? And yet these sounded more like screams than battle cries. *Something* was definitely going on out there.

"Your Majesty!" shouted the lookout at the window. "There's something you should see!" The cries of fear grew louder from the battlefield, but they didn't quite mask the distant boom of approaching footsteps.

The other soldiers in the throne room joined the lookout at the window, crowding around to get a glimpse of what was going on. "Something's coming toward the palace! Something big!" announced the lookout.

But Sisyphus just swept out of the room. What went on in the sunshine was of no concern to him now. The fate of the universe lay in the darkness at the heart of the labyrinth.

BOOK XXVII

Six little legs on the throne of the gods

Sisyphus didn't break into an actual run, but I still had trouble keeping up with his long-legged stride.

"I . . . thought . . . whatever happens . . . is all part . . . of some Cosmic Joke . . . to you!" I panted as I trotted alongside the speeding king.

"Yes, and I would prefer to remain in existence in order to appreciate the joke!" spat Sisyphus.

We had reached the end of a succession of long passageways and flights of marble steps. By the time we were at the threshold of the labyrinth, I was completely out of breath. That's not why I hesitated, however. It was fear.

My head told me coolly that what I'd seen in the labyrinth was not the real cyclops but an impostor—some C-list deity faking it as the dreaded Polyphemus—but this concept hadn't quite reached my heart, the fiery seat of my emotions, which was putting forward its case for not entering the labyrinth by thudding wildly.

But then Sisyphus plunged into the network of tunnels and, if I was to stand a chance of helping Sibyl, I had no choice but to follow him back into the twists and turns of the labyrinth.

"Are you sure this is the right way?" I panted as we plunged for the fifth or sixth time into what was apparently the same stretch of tunnel.

"I'm positive," said Sisyphus. "I have a frescographic memory."*

On we ran. Just as I was wondering whether Sisyphus knew what he was doing, we executed a sharp left and an immediate right, and then we were at the entrance to a broad chamber. This had to be the heart of the labyrinth.

On the far side of the chamber, a set of stone stairs spiraled down into darkness. In the middle of the room stood a thick stone column. It was covered in carved runes, the mystical significance of which we preliterate folk can only guess at. Broken manacles and chains lay scattered around the column's base.

---

* Translator's Note: The modern equivalent of this term is "photographic memory."

"We're too late, then," Sisyphus said numbly. "Thanatos is free."

I was more concerned with *how* he had come to be free. "So Sibyl did it, then. She succeeded," I commented mournfully. "Which means . . ."

"Which means we have to find that cursed insect," Sisyphus blurted out, "and FAST!"

I stared with undisguised contempt at this king who had, so far as I could tell, been largely responsible for this mess. "And how do you expect to find a tiny grasshopper in a labyrinth this big? That'd be like looking for . . . a needle in a haystack . . ."

"Yes."

". . . in the dark . . ."

"*Yes!*"

". . . with a blindfold on . . ."

"YES!"

". . . and boxing gloves . . ."

"YES! I UNDERSTAND!"

But just as Sisyphus finally seemed to comprehend the magnitude of the task, a ghostly voice emerged from one of the chamber's shadow-filled corners.

"The grasshopper hopped down those stairs," intoned Orpheus. "He said he had an appointment on Olympus. Thanatos went down the same stairs, not long after."

While Sisyphus made for the staircase, I ran to where the head lay. "What happened, Orpheus?" I demanded.

The disembodied head blinked mournfully. "We came face-to-face with the guardian of the labyrinth," he said.

"Proteus!" I exclaimed. "What did Sibyl see him as?"

The head's answer stabbed at my heart. "Thanatos," he said. A dreadful image popped into my head of the ex-priestess face-to-face with Thanatos once again — or at least with something that looked exactly like Thanatos.

"Sibyl soon realized it was an impostor," continued the head.

"So how did she get past him?" I asked. "Did she use you? Did she get you to sing?"

Orpheus's eyes slid away from mine. "I . . . played a part. The important thing is, they got past the guardian and released the real Thanatos."

"But what happened to *Sibyl*?"

I thought I could detect a trace of emotion in the head's usual monotone: "When Thanatos was free, he only walked past her. Moments later, she staggered off, clutching her chest."

"Which direction?"

"I don't know," Orpheus replied. "By then, I had been dropped. I rolled into this corner. But I believe King Sisyphus is right. . . . If you really want to help, you must find the grasshopper."

I could feel an immense weight of grief pressing down on me, but for now I had to keep it locked up in the attic of my mind. I grabbed Orpheus by the hair and made for the staircase.

At the bottom of the stairs was a short passageway with one door at either end. I assumed these must be the bathrooms, though I could see no symbols — you know, gods/goddesses, centaurs/nymphs, sons of Ares/daughters of Aphrodite, etc.

A scrabbling noise told me which one Sisyphus was in. I shouldered open the stone door to find him inside another dark chamber. It wasn't a bathroom. In fact, it contained nothing but a few more runes carved into the wall. Sisyphus was studying these by the light of his oil lamp. He didn't attempt to stop us when Orpheus and I entered. He didn't even look up; he just pressed one of the runes with a thumb. The entire symbol slid back into the stone. There was a series of clicks from behind it, and then a rumbling noise. The whole chamber shook, and I realized that it was moving.

"What *is* this place, anyway?" I asked.

"It's a portal," replied Sisyphus. "Hephaestus, Smith of the Gods, designed it. It's a portal between the realms of the Cosmos."

"Oh, yes? And how does that work?" (I must have been out of school the day they covered mystical portals between worlds. Looking back, I suppose I was quite a sickly child.)

Sisyphus furrowed his brow. "Something to do with folding up the fabric of the Cosmos, so that you put two parts together that wouldn't normally be next to each other. The center of this labyrinth was designed to be a kind of knot, scrunching up reality so that several separate parts of the Cosmos get connected."

"Sorry, what? I blanked out for a second there. I was just wondering what we're going to do . . ." My brain completed the sentence for me—*without Sibyl.*

Suddenly the rumble of the hidden mechanism was joined by another sound—a more ethereal, fluting one.

"What's that noise?" I asked.

"The music of the spheres," said Orpheus.

"Well, it's getting on my nerves."

Thankfully, I didn't have to put up with it for long. The noises ended abruptly, and the chamber came to a standstill. Sisyphus pushed open the single door. I looked out and gasped. The doorway no longer led out to the stairwell at the heart of the labyrinth. It now opened into an altogether different place—one I had set hooves in only once before, without ever expecting a return visit.

I was back on Mount Olympus.

The spacious boulevards and gleaming temples of the gods' mountaintop home were the same, and yet the place could not have felt more different. On my first visit here, the Cosmos had just been saved (by ME!) and an atmosphere of relieved excitement had crackled in the rarefied air. Now a cloud of despair and lethargy hung over the whole place. There was no sound of music or laughter or divinely witty conversation. There *was* a steady background noise, but one I couldn't quite identify, other than to say that it sounded somehow *ungodlike*. Downright *animal,* in fact.

Sisyphus and I sped up the luminous marble steps to Zeus's temple. (I let the king carry Orpheus now, seeing as how he was better equipped for the job with two hands.) As we raced across the temple porch and through the golden doors to the Great Hall, the source of the noise revealed itself.

It was the snoring of the gods.

All around us, the Olympian deities slumbered. Some leaned forward onto the long feast tables; others lay stretched out on the marble floor. Zeus was flat on his back with his hands behind his head. Hera, Queen of the Gods, was snoring even louder than her Olympian husband. Ares ground his teeth, probably engaged in some violent fisticuffs in his dreams.

The twelve major gods weren't the only ones snoozing. There were plenty of minor deities — not to mention centaurs and nymphs, satyrs and dryads — all sleeping. Even Hypnos, God of Sleep, was there, fast asleep — and if that isn't irony, I don't know what is. (No, seriously — I *don't* know what irony is.) A lot of the minor deities must have been brought here by Sisyphus's mercenaries, and I knew that Circe the Enchantress was probably one of them. But now was not the time to look for her — not when we had to find Hoppy.

"We'll *never* find him," I whined. "He could be anywhere. . . ."

The imposing thrones of the Big Twelve were still arranged in a semicircle at the top end of the hall. They looked unoccupied, but suddenly a little voice called out from the general direction of the biggest, the one in the middle — Zeus's throne: "I could get quite used to this, actually."

There *was* something on the immense marble throne, something perched right on the seat's edge. Something very very small, with six legs, two antennae, and an irritatingly chirpy attitude.

"Yes indeed, put a cushion or two on it and this would be really quite comfy," said Hoppy the grasshopper.

BOOK XXVIII

Sometimes you sit on the throne, and sometimes the throne sits on you.

"Where's Sibyl?" I demanded, stepping toward the throne of Zeus. "What happened to her?"

"Hello there, Gryllus, Sisyphus," the grasshopper replied amiably. "Be honest now. Bet you never thought it'd end up like this, did you?" The grasshopper let out a little squeaking noise that might have been anything from sob to evil cackle. "To answer your question . . . as far as I know, Sibyl is back in the labyrinth, old chum."

"What happened to her?"

"You mustn't get so hung up on details." The grasshopper let out a little sigh of irritation. "You have to start looking at the BIG picture."

"Oh, yes? And what *is* the big picture, Hoppy?" I fired back. "That you wanted to take over from Zeus? Is that it—*you* want to rule the Cosmos?"

"It's worse than that," said Sisyphus darkly, drawing alongside me.

"Oh, don't be such a drama king, Sisyphus," snapped Hoppy. "Just because our plans didn't work out quite as *you* intended. . . ."

I looked dumbly from king to grasshopper and back again. "OUR plans?"

The resemblance between Sisyphus's face and a tragedy mask

made me long for a return of his irritating grin. "It was Tithonus here who freed me from the Underworld," he explained. "We devised the plan together to get the gods out of the way."

"And it worked brilliantly, too," said Hoppy bitterly. "You really were quite ingenious, Sisyphus. Pity you didn't have the guts to see our task through. If you're going to do something, you must do it properly—with a *proper* ending. What's the point of chaining up Thanatos again and merely prolonging everyone's misery?"

"Er, I don't get what's going on here," I interjected.

"I wanted to let things run their course in the world without intervention of the gods," exclaimed Sisyphus. "I wanted to see what would happen in a world with no death and no deities. I didn't want to *destroy* the entire universe, like you did."

What! Little Hoppy wanted to destroy the Cosmos? If I'd known this, I'd never have carried him around in my ear!

"So . . . *you're* the evil one?" I said to Hoppy.

The grasshopper's eyes glittered darkly. "You say evil; I say brokenhearted. We could debate it until the end of time, only that wouldn't give us very long." The grasshopper glared at Sisyphus. "I'll tell you what happened. Sisyphus got cold feet, that's what. So he went and had me taken away to a far-off island so that I couldn't even see my own plan in action. Very nice!" A crowing note of triumph entered his voice. "Well, it's too late now, Sisyphus. . . . I have won!"

You can only take so much of this sort of talk from a grasshopper. "And what's to stop me from trotting up there

and squashing you, like I should have done when we first met?"
I demanded.

"Because you're a day late and a drachma short," Hoppy
answered. "Because Thanatos is free again and, with the gods
out of action, that means he will do what he will. Even as we
speak, he will be in the Underworld, looking for—"

"GOLD!"

This squawk of pure, joyous greed echoed around the Great
Hall.

I looked back to see Midas and Aurelia at the giant doorway.
The grandeur of the setting made Midas look less royal than
ever. He hung back near the entrance, his little chubby hands
gripping the palace guards' map of the labyrinth.

Aurelia, on the other hand, hardly knew where to start.
The hall was filled with gold: gold candlesticks, gold thrones,
gold cutlery. What's more, the gold on Mount Olympus
made the earthly kind look like candy wrappers. It was
shinier . . . sparklier . . . deeper . . . altogether lovelier.
Olympian gold was somehow . . . *golder.*

The princess with the heart of gold skipped from table to
table, laughing uncontrollably and running her fingers over all
the golden objects as if she might somehow absorb the essence
of their goldness.

"Aurelia, my dear," called Midas, stepping forward nervously,
"I really don't think you should—"

The rest of the king's parental advice was drowned out by
a booming noise. It started off loud enough, but then it built
until we couldn't just hear it; we could *feel* it rumbling through

our chests. All of Olympus rattled and shook around us. The sound was joined by a clatter of lesser noises, as plates smashed, statues toppled off their plinths, and colonnades collapsed like rows of oversize dominoes.

When the rumble had died down, Hoppy spoke softly. "As I said—it's too late now."

Unfortunately, all opportunity for sober reflection as to what had just happened flew out of the window as an alarmed cry rang out from farther back in the Great Hall: "Father!"

It was the Princess Aurelia. I wasn't able to see King Midas. What I *could* see was a plump arm and a chubby, purple-clad leg poking out from under the solid-gold throne that had just fallen on top of the owner of these limbs.

Aurelia knelt by the toppled throne. "Speak to me, Father!" she implored.

A faint groan emerged from underneath it. "Please get this thing off me."

"What?" wailed Aurelia. "I can't hear you, because this thing is on you."

The princess grabbed hold of the throne and attempted to lift it. It didn't budge. After several painful seconds, she gave up and began to wrench the gold bracelets from her arms, casting them angrily aside. Then, with her pale arms now less restricted, she took hold of the throne again. Tears streamed down her face, but they couldn't wash away her look of determination. That look on Aurelia's face wasn't gold; it was solid iron. On the count of three, the princess took a breath and tried once again to deadlift the throne.

It was clear that she no longer considered it to be an

inanimate object. No, it had become a living, breathing thing to her, a deadly foe, and she hated it for its insolent heaviness, for its blunt refusal to hop off her father with a full apology. She despised the gaudy way it glittered and shone with total disregard for the monarch it happened to be squashing.

Perhaps you're a fan of the *Daily Lyre,* as I am—I used to love to hear the town crier read it out. If so, you've surely heard stories of ordinary peasants discovering extraordinary reserves of strength in extreme situations: a frail old granny lifting an oxcart off her infant grandchild, a young girl putting a headlock on a rampaging boar that was going straight for her pet guinea pig.

Now was such a time for Aurelia.

She threw back her head, squeezed her eyes shut with the effort, and grunted, "GET . . . OFF . . . MY DAD . . . YOU STINKING . . . STUPID . . . **GOLD**!"

As she spat out this last word, she heaved upward, shoving the golden throne off the king.

Midas was looking a bit on the pale and squashed side, but he managed a weak smile.

"I . . . didn't think you cared, my precious metal," he gasped.

Aurelia threw her bare arms around her father's neck and hugged him. It was a genuinely touching scene, right up to the moment when she accidentally bumped into Midas's fractured leg, and the king went and spoiled a tender moment by shrieking in agony.

Sisyphus and I just stood and watched (he had his fingers in his ears, but I was denied that luxury). Even Hoppy had jumped down off his throne. However, the insect's attention was not on Aurelia and her father now. He was looking at the figure who lay on the marble floor beyond them.

Eos, Goddess of the Dawn, was as beautiful in sleep as she was in the morning sky (*allegedly*. Sunrise doesn't occur at a convenient time for me). Her robes were the color of the dawn: delicate yellows and pinks, shot through with lines of crimson. Her rosy fingers—the ones that used to sprinkle dewdrops across the waking world—were clasped together over her chest as the goddess slept on.

The shriveled little grasshopper gazed forlornly at the goddess he had once called his girlfriend. After a couple of tentative hops, he stopped. His voice was hoarse.

"This is why I did what I did. . . ." he cried bitterly. "The gods abandoned me. Eos abandoned me . . . left me to become *this*."

The goddess slept on, but part of her slumbering mind must have recognized the grasshopper's voice. "Tithy Withy? Is that you?" she mumbled between the shallow breaths of the long-term dreamer. "I'm so sorry, darling. I really am. It's just, I usually go out with people a little taller . . . and with fewer legs. . . ."

Hoppy's little mandibles quivered.

"It was the only way, darling," the sleeping goddess went on. "It was either that or leave you bedbound, unable to do anything. . . . I thought you'd be happier." Her eyes fluttered behind closed lids. "Of *course* we can still be friends. . . ." she said. "I shall always think of you as a brother . . . a little, six-legged brother. . . ."

The goddess fell silent, but the grasshopper continued to stare at her. Who knew how long it had been since he had looked upon her radiant beauty?

"What have you gone and done, Hoppy?" I demanded.

When the insect spoke at last, his voice had lost its boastful bravado. "I've taken my revenge on Zeus and on Eos and on the entire Cosmos," he said quietly. "I've brought about the end of everything."

The tiny grasshopper did not take his eyes from Eos. He had the look of an insect that had begun to come unglued.

"It's Thanatos," Sisyphus explained. "With Zeus and the rest of the Olympians out of the way, there are no checks and balances. There's nothing to stop Thanatos from going straight to the Underworld."

"So?"

"He's gone to free Typhon, monster of monsters, from its rocky prison," said Sisyphus grimly.

"So?"

"Without Zeus to subdue it, Typhon will be free to complete the task it attempted once before, when the world was young. . . ." Hoppy answered distantly.

"So?"

". . . which was destroying the Cosmos," Sisyphus explained. "That's why Tithonus wanted to get back to Crete. To release my prisoner, so that Thanatos could free the monster that would destroy the entire world."

This was a lot to take in, but it didn't stop me from coming up with an appropriate response:

. . .

. . .

. . .

"Oh."

BOOK XXIX

Enemies reunited

Things weren't looking too hot, then. The noise we had heard, even up here on Olympus, was Thanatos, as he began to wake Typhon, monster of monsters, from its rocky prison deep in the Underworld. I'm not saying that all was lost, but all *was* looking at a map of the future and scratching its head and wondering where it had taken a wrong turn that now seemed to be leading over the edge of a precipice.

But what could we do? The sands of time continued to count down toward the point when there would no longer *be* either sand or time.

Hoppy paid us no attention. His triumphant mood had evaporated, leaving him looking old and confused. Still crouching by Eos's sleeping body, he muttered something that sounded like "Sorry."

Midas couldn't do much either, apart from keep his pained moans to a minimum and wait for Asclepius, God of Medicine, Wearer of the Sacred Stethoscope and Master of the Illegible Scrawl, to wake up and tend to his broken bones.

Orpheus couldn't do much because . . . well, don't make me spell it out for you.

It was left to Sisyphus and Aurelia to sort things out on Olympus.

"Once Typhon is free, the only one who could stop it is Zeus," said Sisyphus. "We have to wake up the gods."

Of course, this was more than just a matter of trotting around shouting, "Wakey, wakey! Up and at 'em!" The gods' slumber was an unnatural one, induced by the potion Sisyphus had put in their nectar. To reverse the potion's effects, Sisyphus would have to mix up a batch of antidote.

Aurelia dashed off to the palace kitchens to get the necessary ingredients.

"What about me?" I asked. "What can I do?"

Sisyphus glanced up hurriedly. "Go to the Underworld as fast as you can. Use the other chamber at the center of the labyrinth. Do everything in your power to delay Thanatos . . . and pray that we are not too late."

I had been thinking more along the lines of cleaning out a bowl for the antidote to go in, and I did consider clarifying this. But then I just nodded and ran silently back across the hall. Apart from the clack of my hooves on the slippery marble surface, the only noise was when I lost control and bumped into Midas.

With the king's howl of pain ringing in my ears, I left the palace of Zeus and raced back toward the portal between realms.

Minutes—and one solo descent in the incredible moving chamber—later, I was pushing open the stone door and stepping once more into the stairwell at the heart of the labyrinth, back in the mortal realm.

I burst out at high speed and . . .

. . . stopped.

Something was blocking my way to the other chamber, the

one that went down to the Underworld. Something not very nice. Something so big it had to stoop to fit in the passageway. The bulky form of the cyclops turned to face me.

Well, strictly speaking, *not* the cyclops, of course—this was the impostor. The fraud, the charlatan, the great pretender—only he wasn't looking all that great. The bogus cyclops.

Proteus.

"HEY! I knows you, pig!" he boomed.

I looked right into that single cyclopean eye, and irritation blazed in my heart. Who did this puffed-up, third-rate deity think he was kidding? Well, I for one didn't have time for this. "And I 'knows' you!" I grunted angrily. "Supposed to be Polyphemus the cyclops, are you?"

"I *is* Polyphemus," replied the pseudo-cyclops, irritatingly staying in character.

I snorted derisively. "Oh really? How nice for you! But right now you'd better step aside, you twerp, because I have important work to do."

Proteus seemed to have trouble following what I was saying. All he could muster was, "Eh?"

I was getting really cross now. "Listen, you crummy faker, I've got it. I know who you really are, so MOVE IT!"

Proteus's brow furrowed in obvious confusion. The uneasy silence was filled by a sound off to the side of us—a low muttering, accompanied by the noise of something being dragged along. It was coming from the stairs.

"Oo is vat?" asked the fake cyclops, unable to see up the stairs from where he stood.

I glanced up to see a small figure around the corner slowly making his way down the last flight of stone steps. He was going backward, dragging something behind him. He continued to mutter under his breath.

"Oo IS it?" the fake cyclops demanded.

Having left his load in the shadows, the figure on the stairs turned for the last few steps. He was an elderly bloke with long gray hair and a straggly beard that seemed to have bits of seaweed here and there.

When he saw me, the old man clamped his hands on his hips and addressed me crossly. "You there! Pig! I thought I told you not to come back. Are you responsible for all the damage up there? There's rubble everywhere!"

He reached the bottom of the stairs and only then became aware of the other occupant of the passageway down here. I don't know if he had heard about Proteus, but the old man didn't seem unduly put out by the apparent sight of a cyclops glowering at him. He glared up at the giant.

"Oh. It was *you,* I suppose. Did Sisyphus send you?"

The fake cyclops let out a bewildered grunt.

"Because you can tell him something from me," the old man continued peevishly. "I did *not* agree to working conditions like these. I've been attacked by insects—well, only one insect, but it was a *talking* one!—I've had actual heads *thrown* at me, the prisoner is gone, and now—to top it all off—I've got this body to dispose of. This is *not* the job I signed up for."

I was uncomfortably aware that we didn't have all the time in the world for this—or rather, we DID have all the time in the world, only that was no longer very much time at all. For all I knew, anyone who had just started boiling an egg was out of luck (and not solely because he or she would miss out on their egg-salad sandwich).

"Who *are* you?" I demanded.

"I am Proteus," answered the gray-bearded figure grandly.

"Oh, yeah? Well, put a sock in it, Proteus! I've got a lot on my plate right now." I glared back at the impostor cyclops. "Right, you—out of the way now, sonny boy, I've got to—"

Er . . .

I looked back at the bearded man. Hadn't Sisyphus said that Proteus was a sea deity of some kind? Maybe all the seaweed in this bloke's beard was just the result of a fondness for health food, coupled with poor hand-eye coordination? Then again . . .

"Hold on . . . if *you're* Proteus, then . . ."—I looked back up at the cyclops, a horrible realization creeping over me like a nasty rash—"you must be . . . ?"

"Gettin' mad," the cyclops confirmed. The real, actual, in-the-horribly-smelly-flesh cyclops! "But first fings first. I is 'ere to get me 'ands on Nobody."

Somewhere in the corner of my terrified brain I recalled the lookout at the window in Sisyphus's throne room. *This* is what he must have seen coming toward the palace. *This* had been the cause of the commotion outside: Polyphemus the cyclops.

"But . . . how did you get here?" I asked, too stunned even to acknowledge my terror.

"I swam," growled the cyclops—*the real cyclops!*—who was clearly not accustomed to engaging in preliminary conversation with potential victims. "Brontes wanted to come wiv me an' all, but he finked salt water might sting 'im up where he 'ad his axy-dint."

Proteus—*the real Proteus!*—still seemed to think that he was in control of this situation. "That's all well and good, but the terms of my agreement include nothing about clearing up rubble, let alone the disposal of mortal bodies—"

Suddenly the obol dropped. Ignoring the deity's babble, I ran past him to the foot of the stairs and peered into the shadows. Proteus had indeed been hauling a body downstairs. My heart almost gave out when I saw whose.

Sibyl.

The arrow still stuck out of her chest, but she no longer looked cross about it—or, indeed, capable of crossness about anything at all now. Her pale face was as cold and lifeless as marble. Those unseeing eyes would flash no more disapproving looks. Those unmoving lips had uttered their last scathing comment.

Oh, gods, must I spell it out for you? *Sibyl was dead.* There. Are you happy now? Because, let me tell you, I wasn't. I thought of all the times that the ex-priestess had saved me. Now I had failed her.

I whirled around and confronted the shape-changing deity.

"Cease and desist from giving me that dirty look," Proteus commanded imperiously. "The girl's death *wasn't* my fault."

But that's not the way I saw it. If Proteus hadn't agreed to go along with the whole scheme in the first place, none of this would have happened: the Cosmos wouldn't be in peril yet again, and Sibyl would still be alive and kicking. So it *was* his fault. Mainly, I suppose, it was his fault because he was *here,* now, right in front of me, and I needed a target for all the pain I was feeling, because I couldn't bear to keep it inside me—there was just too much of it.

A terrible wave of anger rose up in me. It clashed straight into the terrible wave of grief coming the other way, and the result was an explosion of raging despair that crashed down upon me.

In that moment, there was no Gryllus, no me, there was nothing but PIG—and I'm not just talking about a snuffle-around-the-farmyard pig, I'm talking about WILD PIG, a savage boar that, in the face of a threat, knew only to flee or to attack, and now was not the time for fleeing. . . .

I charged.

I was dimly aware of the bellow that filled the labyrinth, but not of the fact that it was coming from me. All I knew was the fear in Proteus's eyes, two little circles of white that marked my target. I might not have tusks, but I knew instinctively to put my head down so that the thickest part of my skull would be the point of contact.

When he realized what was going on, Proteus underwent a rapid series of transformations. First he was a grizzly bear, then a chimera, then a many-headed serpent. I just kept my eyes trained on those little, white, wide-open bull's-eyes. I think Proteus was in mid-transformation—lion to gryphon—when *BAM!*

The force of the head butt lifted him clean off his feet. He landed in human form and immediately started scrabbling away on all fours to escape. No chance. Still swept along on torrents of anger, I prepared to charge again.

"HEY!" roared the cyclops, perhaps unhappy to be in the presence of violence without actually being involved in it.

I whirled around. I no longer saw the one-eyed giant who had once polished off a couple of my crewmates so effortlessly. I no longer saw the creature that had stalked my nightmares ever since that fateful day. All I saw was ENEMY, and there was only one thing to do with ENEMIES.

So I did it.

It was a lot like running into a stone wall, but I didn't care. I must have been on my third or fourth flying head butt when enormous fingers closed around my ribs.

"Vat's enough, lickle pig," a dim and distant part of me heard the cyclops say. He sounded as if he was talking to one of his sheep.

I don't know how long he held me up off the ground, my four legs kicking and flailing like crazy. But gradually the seething waters in my mind subsided, the frenetic tom-tom thudding of my heart slowed, and bit by bit I became *me* again. This was almost too much to bear, because being me meant being aware that Sibyl was gone.

"Wot is you doin', exackerly?" inquired Polyphemus, holding his immense head close to me.

Who can say why the giant had chosen to converse with rather than consume me? It didn't matter, anyway. Sibyl was gone and I knew that once Thanatos had released Typhon from its rocky prison in the Underworld, the rest of the Cosmos would be going the same way.

I didn't flinch under the gaze of that gigantic eye. I knew who I was talking to now, but I no longer cared. What good were a few more minutes of existence?

"It doesn't matter," I said. "Nothing matters. There's no point. . . ."

"Wot? Wot is you talkin ab—"

"Just shut up and *listen*," I ordered the carnivorous giant who had played a leading role in all my worst nightmares. "Thanatos is down in the Underworld right NOW. He's gone there to release Typhon, Monster of All Monsters."

"Yeah? And?"

"And when he does that, nobody will be left alive in the entire Cosmos. Just nobody."

I didn't realize it, but I had just said the magic word for Polyphemus. "Nobody, eh? Ven how does we git ourselves to ve Unda-world?"

BOOK XXX

You don't need a plumber to plumb the depths.

The way to the Underworld was obvious enough. Squeezing an XXL-size cyclops into the portal chamber was another matter entirely—a logistical problem somewhat akin to fitting a great white shark into a sardine tin.

However, Polyphemus surprised me with his use of lateral thinking to solve the problem. Admittedly, most of this lateral thinking involved his sledgehammer fists, which he smashed wildly into the stones around the door. The next stage of his remodeling involved the chamber floor, which he set about demolishing with the heel of his mighty foot.

Before too long we were looking down a shaft that descended into blackness. A huge cable, thicker than a dozen ship's ropes, ran down the shaft.

Polyphemus made to set me on his shoulder.

"Wait!" I said. "I might fall off!"

A thought trickled through the giant's brain like treacle through a sponge. "I can tuck you dahn me loincloff," he suggested.

Of all the terrible events so far that day, this nightmarish prospect topped them all.

"Actually, the shoulder's fine!" I cried. He plopped me onto it, and I sat up there like a pirate's pet parrot (except you wouldn't catch me looking over at Polyphemus and going, "Who's a pretty boy?" for obvious reasons).

The cyclops began to make his way down the shaft, gripping the cable with both fists and spreading his massive legs wide out to the sides to keep us from tumbling down.

"I . . . I'm not sure this is going to work," I said.

But before long that same ethereal noise, the music of the spheres, filled my ears, much louder than before, and the walls of the shaft around us seemed to bend and melt and sway. We must have reached the spot where—how had Sisyphus put it?—different parts of the fabric of the Universe were scrunched up next to each other.

It got worse. Soon it felt as if every little scrap of me, all of those billions of tiny little *whatchamacallits* I was supposedly made up of—atoms!—were exploding simultaneously. This seemed to go on for eons.

But then I heard Polyphemus sigh with relief—his feet had hit the bottom. The cyclops looked back up the shaft to where I had experienced possibly the worst agony of my life.

"Vat felt all tingly," he grunted approvingly.

It took a while for Polyphemus to pummel his way out of the shaft. Finally, we stepped out into the gray gloom of the Underworld. I'd like to say it was nice to be back, but I can't tell porkies*—it was miserable.

As before, the first thing I noticed was the fog. We weren't in the thick of it here, but its white tendrils still crept across the blackened earth.

The last time I had been here, I had returned to my true human form. I looked down now at my pink legs and hooves. That meant I wasn't dead . . . not yet, at least.

"This feels wrong," I muttered, suddenly conscious of the unseemly weight and heft of my body in this place of shadows. "I feel too . . . *corporeal*."

"We isn't even *in* the army," growled Polyphemus impatiently.

"Just pick me back up," I sighed. "We'd better get down to the Punishment Zone of Tartarus."

From my vantage point up high, I was able to look over

* Translator's Note: Cretan rhyming slang for lie: *porky = pork pie = lie*.

the fog and see the rocky walls that loomed around us. The cyclops waded through the black waters of the River Styx. We were nearing the Asphodel Fields now, where the fog was at its densest.

"Keep to the sides," I advised. "Don't go right through the middle of the fog!"

Dear listener, if perchance you've been lucky enough to die and then return anew to this mortal realm (the second part being the *really* lucky thing in that little scenario), then you can probably skip the next part.

The rest of you might be interested to know that the Underworld is modeled on a three-level layout. Polyphemus and I were skirting the middle level—the barren rocks of the Asphodel Fields. If you go there, don't forget an overcoat, because there's *always* a chilly fog in the air. The only problem is that, once there, you *will* forget your coat . . . and pretty much everything else, too. That's because, as the fog seeps into your soul, all the memories of your previous life leak out—until you're left wandering the Fields, trying to recall everything, from whether you turned the oven off to what your name used to be.

Of course, this wasn't the only area of the Underworld I'd been to. I had also visited—briefly—the beautiful Elysian Fields, which I knew were located somewhere above us. This is the resting place for heroes—and so it's the one to pick if you're offered any choice in the matter (though you'd be one lucky stiff if you were).

As we passed the Asphodel Fields now, I looked down into the depths of the billowing grayness. I could make out pale shapes in there, all shambling about aimlessly—the shades of the dead. Their past was lost to them. Whatever status they had held on Earth—tyrant or slave, warrior or poet—none of it mattered now.

Occasionally it was possible to see a blank face or two in patches where the fog had thinned. It was in one of these patches near the outer edges of the fog that I saw a familiar face. It looked dazed and drowsy, but not yet blank like the other shades. It was Sibyl, and she was looking right back at me. Slowly, as if moving underwater, she opened her mouth. Was she calling out to me?

"Stop!" I shouted to Polyphemus. "There's someone I know in there!"

The cyclops slowed and turned to look at the fog of Asphodel.

"Can't do nuffink for 'em now," said the cyclops.

I cried out to Sibyl, but the rolling fog muffled all sounds in this hushed world. And then it wrapped itself around the former priestess—the *former* former priestess—and she was nowhere to be seen.

I closed my eyes, unable to look at that fog any longer. I didn't open them again until Polyphemus came to a sudden halt.

"Tartarus is down 'ere, innit?" he growled.

The main chamber of Asphodel lay behind us. We were standing now at the rim of a huge chasm in the rock. The hole plunged down to blackness like a giant Funnel of Doom.

"Look!" I said. "There's a spiral path around the sides that you can go down."

Something about this observation seemed to anger the cyclops, who apparently had an irrational dislike of the word *spiral* as being inherently namby-pamby. Without warning, he grabbed hold of me and jumped into the pit.

Damp, musty air rushed past my face. We fell for a good few seconds, which I filled by imagining what our splat patterns might look like when we landed. But Polyphemus's luck held—something broke his fall (a jagged outcrop of rock) and he landed on the most expendable part of his anatomy (his cranium). As he struck the ground, I tumbled free of his grip, rolled out of control, and then slammed into a stunted tree.

I looked around anxiously. This was a blasted, terrible place of darkness and crumbling black rock and looming cliffs. The din was terrible—the air rang with the constant sound of earthquake and volcano and unseen thunder, all cracks and booms and horrible bubbling noises that suggested things disappearing under very hot lava.

So this was Tartarus, the infernal abyss in which wrongdoers were punished forever. The darkest pit of the Underworld. The bowels of the universe. The place least likely to feature in the *Daily Lyre*'s annual list of "Top Ten Getaway Destinations to Beat the Winter Blues."

As I picked myself up, a lower branch of the tree that had broken my fall suddenly jerked away from me. I noted with surprise that it bore fruit, despite the lack of sunshine around here. A memory bubbled to the surface of my mind, something Homer had gone on about. This tree must be the one designed for another resident of the Underworld's Punishment Zone,

King Tantalus. Doomed to remain in this spot, every time he reached up for the fruit of the tree, it pulled away, out of his reach. Every time he bent forward to drink from the pool beneath the tree, the water itself shied away from him.* It was a terrible punishment, even if, like me, you weren't all that fond of pomegranates. (Now if it had been a *pie* tree . . .)

I moved away from the tree and its unreachable fruit. We were on a plateau of some kind. The cyclops picked his way forward, across the craggy rocks and alongside the black waters of the now-deserted lake from which the Danaid sisters, convicted murderers all, had been condemned to draw water using nothing but sieves. There was as little sign of them now as there was of King Tantalus.

In front of us rose the ramp that had played such a crucial role in Sisyphus's eternal punishment. The boulder sat menacingly at the bottom. The ramp itself was a huge triangle, carved out of the black rock of Tartarus. Its path snaked up at an alarmingly steep angle. At the top of this, the rock was shaped into a kind of natural bumper: once the boulder hit this, it would begin to roll back down again.

As we passed the ramp, I spied a patch of green and blue over in the distance. I knew instantly that it was the Elysian Fields. (This is where the layout of the Underworld gets complicated. Remember that the Elysian Fields were *above* the Asphodel Fields and Tartarus was *below*? Nevertheless, it was

*Translator's Note: The cruel fate of King Tantalus gives us our English word *tantalizing*. An amusing way of teaching this to a younger brother is to hold his favorite candy bar constantly just out of his reach. If challenged by a parent, explain that you are illustrating a classical allusion, then run to your room and eat the evidence.

still possible for the sufferers in Tartarus to look on the Isle of Blessed, knowing full well that its gates were closed to them forever.)

I joined Polyphemus at the rocky edge where the plateau dropped off suddenly. It was only now that I realized just how big this lowest level of the Underworld truly was. A nightmare landscape was spread out below us, as if we stood at the world's worst scenic lookout point.

The centerpiece of it was an actual mountain, its base ringed by an intricate network of pools and streams of lava. But that wasn't all—there was something *underneath* the mountain, something as big as a small town.

It was Typhon, the monster of monsters, and, from the parts I could see sticking out from under the mountain, Homer's poetic description hadn't come close to doing it justice. The monster's length was immense, from the giant flicking tail to the two sets of front claws that clenched and unclenched slowly. At least twenty or so of its hundred heads were visible. All of the eyes were closed, but the serpent heads stirred restlessly. The terrible mouths gaped open, drooling red-hot pools of lava.

But the scariest thing of all was that in several places the archways of black rock that had pinned the monster down were smashed to rubble. Two of Typhon's vast legs were free, as was its impossibly long tail.

"Vat's Typhon, eh?" snarled Polyphemus.

I looked up at the cyclops and astonished myself by feeling a pang of sympathy. It isn't often you find yourself feeling protective toward a revolting carnivorous giant that on more than one occasion has expressed a desire to eat you. But, in the great Chain of Being, it suddenly seemed that Polyphemus was to Typhon what a chick was to a hydra that had been raised on an exclusive diet of poultry.

"An' oo's vat?"

At first I couldn't see who he meant because Thanatos's black cowl provided perfect camouflage against the black rock. But then I spotted him, moving toward the thick ridge of rock that arched over Typhon's gigantic neck at the point where it separated into its many heads. This was the biggest area to clear, but also the last. Once this was out of the way, the monster would be awake and free—and it was a safe bet that it would be feeling a bit grumpy.

"Vat's—*that's* Thanatos," I said. "Once he frees Typhon, that'll be it . . . curtains for us all."

The cyclops took a few seconds to ponder this. Even by cyclopean standards, he wasn't the sharpest javelin in the Olympics equipment cupboard, and his brain was working overtime to process the information. And all the while the Underworld shook as Thanatos pounded the rock beneath his feet.

The only thing I heard from Polyphemus the cyclops was a sigh. Not a battle cry, not a roar—a resigned sigh. Then, without another word, he hopped over the edge and started to bound down the steep drop. He lost his footing several times, but on each occasion a boulder would halt his out-of-control fall and the giant would get up and carry on.

Finally, he was at the foot of the mountain that pinned the sleeping Typhon. He began to hopscotch across the islands of rock that rose from the lava like floaty toys in the world's most hazardous swimming pool.

The embodiment of Death did not notice the cyclops until Polyphemus was almost upon him. Then he looked up sharply.

Moving fast despite his bulk, Polyphemus trotted out the classic line, beloved of tough guys since time immemorial: "Oo are you lookin' at, pal?"

"I am looking at you—Polyphemus the cyclops," replied Thanatos, revealing the limited and literal nature of his world view.

"Oh, yeah?" replied the cyclops, moving within range. "Well 'ave a look at VIS. It's called Mr. Fist, innit."

The giant's knuckles connected with Thanatos's head with a satisfying sound, like someone biting into a crisp apple. Thanatos collapsed into a raggedy pile of black. He looked like a crow that had been unable to resist just one more nibble of roadkill for breakfast, seconds before the milk wagon rumbled past.

The cyclops stood above Thanatos now, feet planted wide and sledgehammer fist balled. "Want anuvver look, does ya?" he growled.

Thanatos rose calmly. "I do not believe that will be necessary."

Polyphemus's next punch was what is sometimes called a real *haymaker* (although I never knew you could make hay by punching it in the face). This time Thanatos was ready. A pale, bony hand shot out and gripped the cyclops's wrist before the punch could connect. The same thing happened to the giant's left when it attempted to deliver an uppercut.

There was nothing I could do but watch as the two supernatural figures tussled. The amazing thing was, it looked as if Polyphemus was the stronger of the two. The cyclops wasn't much taller than Thanatos, but he was a *lot* beefier. More than that, it was the sheer impact of the giant's life force—his raw animal vitality—that seemed to be winning. He gripped Thanatos's forearms, gasping with titanic effort as he tried to force Death to its knees. Beneath them the dreaded Typhon shifted uneasily in its sleep.

"Go, Polyphemus!" I yelled, hardly aware of the peculiarity of my cheering the dreaded cyclops on.

Another voice by my side joined mine. "You can do it!" It was Homer! "Kick his head in!" he added unpoetically.

The monkeys were here as well—they huddled together nervously in this unpleasant new habitat—and so was King Sisyphus. (Quick update on how this came about: having mixed up the antidote for the gods, Sisyphus had left Aurelia to administer it while he came to help down here. Meanwhile, after long hours of worried waiting, Homer and the monkeys had worked up the nerve to venture into the labyrinth to see what all the noise was about. Eventually they ran into Sisyphus, who had passed on the essential information, then led them to the portal, where the monkeys were obliged to lower the two humans down the shaft by means of a complicated chain of monkeys clinging onto the cable. End of update.)

"Well? Where's Zeus?" I asked Sisyphus. "What about the other Olympians?"

The king shook his head, not taking his eyes off the battle

below. The only thing he had brought from Olympus with him was Orpheus, which seemed like a poor substitute for the thunderbolt-wielding King of the Gods, quite frankly.

"The antidote takes a while to work," Sisyphus said.

"How long is 'a while'?" I asked.

For once, Sisyphus was at a loss for words. "Er . . ."

There was a good reason — something terrible was happening to Polyphemus. As he grappled with Thanatos, the cyclops seemed to be changing. Even from this distance, we could see the giant's flesh beginning to sag and wrinkle. The unruly mop of brown hair on his massive head was becoming an unruly mop of *white* hair, ringing a brand-new bald spot on top. His single eye was looking more and more sunken, and it was acquiring an enormous single bag under it.

Polyphemus was aging in Thanatos's iron grip, the years zipping by in seconds, and the giant's strength was abandoning him. He didn't give up, but he was forced to drop to one knee, wheezing and panting heavily.

Only a village idiot would bet on Polyphemus now. It was clear that Thanatos would win in the end, same as always — it was just a matter of how soon.

The monkeys clung to each other and whimpered piteously, and, as far as I knew, the rest of us joined in. I looked away, blinking back the tears. The Universe had a matter of minutes left to it, and where was I? Not in an all-you-can-eat pie shop, where I belonged! No, I was in the yuckiest corner of the Underworld with a scruffbag of a king, a bodiless head, and a ragtag bunch of moaning monkeys. Could things get any worse?

And then the head began to sing. . . .

BOOK XXXI

Some are born to rock and roll.

Orpheus's song started so softly that you could hardly hear him against the background din, but his voice grew gradually louder. I recognized the tune at once. It was the one I had heard him sing in his sleep, back on the deck of the ship. But now, in the dying moments of the Universe, it sounded different. It no longer seemed just a song of personal regret, though it did still feel intensely personal. At the same time, however, it sounded like a lament for the whole world and all its long-suffering inhabitants.

As I listened to that thing of utmost beauty and sadness in this terrible place, I experienced a rare moment of clarity. For once, for just an instant, I got it. I understood.

Hog's body or not, I was a human, and that meant there were two competing outlooks within me. Sisyphus had been right: on one hand, there was the little piggy that couldn't help but view ME as the very center of this universe of ours. To that part of me, I was the most important thing there ever could be.

But there was something else: the chilling suspicion of just how insignificant I really was — you know, cosmically speaking. In the long run, *did* my life amount to a speck? Or my death? Did anyone's, when you stopped and thought about it? When you looked at the big picture?

But now, as I listened to Orpheus's soundtrack to the end

of existence, this ever-present tension in my mind eased. It loosened and then, just for a moment, it vanished. I felt . . . *unified*. As the last note of the song hung in the air, I wished for only one thing: that there had been time to say good-bye to Sibyl.

I looked up and murmured it anyway . . . and found myself gazing at the top of Sisyphus's ramp. I looked down at the battle below.

Polyphemus was on both knees now. Sensing the end was near, Thanatos released the cyclops's arms, and they dropped limply to his side. The giant sagged and fell forward onto the blackened rock. Immediately Thanatos turned away and calmly resumed the job of freeing the monster that would destroy the Cosmos. I looked up to the top of the ramp one last time, then swung around and ran back to the boulder at the foot of it.

"What are you doing?" called Sisyphus.

No time for explanations. I raced up to the boulder, put my head down, and began to push with all my considerable bulk.

Nothing.

I tried again, grimacing and straining as I shoved. The gigantic rock didn't seem to be even close to moving.

"Has someone left the emergency brake on?" I complained.

"There *is* no emergency brake," said Sisyphus, who had followed me to see what I was up to.

I squeezed my eyes shut, and this time really got into it, slamming my shoulder hard against the rock.

Sisyphus cheered me on with an encouraging "Don't bother."

I ignored him and dug deep into my reserves of strength. To my surprise, I found a little bit more down there. The boulder actually wobbled, and just for a split second it seemed as if it was going to roll forward . . . then it rocked back into its original position. It was almost as if that rock was mocking me for the feebleness of all biological life-forms.

"There's no point," said Sisyphus.

I whirled around angrily. "No! Actually, there IS a point!" I panted. "Look, you might be right. Our lives are little and silly and absurd, but they're still OUR lives. They mean everything to us, even when we know they're insignificant. We keep all of that in our heads and somehow manage not to go bonkers! That's what being human is."

Sisyphus stroked his beard thoughtfully. "But . . . you're *not* human," he said uncertainly.

"Yes, I am! I just look like a pig," I shouted. My mind struggled to regain the clarity it had felt moments earlier during Orpheus's song. "It's just, there are times when it all comes together, when we're at one with ourselves and the world. That's the best we can do. Do you understand?"

Sisyphus stood in silent thought. He was staring hard at the boulder and he looked as if he was looking at it for the first time. He was *really* looking at IT — this rock in all its particularity, its physical being, right here, right now.

He began to nod slowly. "I think maybe I do," he murmured.

"Then roll up your sleeves and get pushing!"

Without the faintest trace of a smirk, Sisyphus set Orpheus down, rolled up his shabby purple sleeves, and joined me at the rock he knew so well. His body assumed the usual position, his hands fell upon well-worn spots, and his flat-eyed gaze fell upon the cursed stone face in front of us.

I counted us in. "A-one . . . a-two . . . a-one, two, three, four . . . PUSH!"

Sisyphus's head dropped low, his body stiffened, his straight arms quivered with the all-too-familiar effort, and . . . the boulder began to roll forward. Grunting with the effort, I put my back into it. Sisyphus, on the other hand . . . he put his *everything* into it.

Slowly, agonizingly, we made our way up the hill, and for the first time I really appreciated the true horror of Sisyphus's punishment. There was no chance to catch our breath, no chance to give our muscles a rest, however much they might scream out for one. If we slacked off for even an instant, the boulder would roll back down again. *How had he kept this up,* I asked myself, *day in, day out?* No, it was worse than that, because there weren't even days and nights in this place, nothing but eternal gloom, lit only by the mood lighting of red-hot lava.

Sisyphus's entire existence had been one endless trek up this hill, followed by an all-too-brief break as the boulder rolled back again. And what kind of a break was that when, with every leaden step back down, you knew what you had to do next, which was roll the boulder *up* the hill again?

And again.

And again.

And again.

And ag—. . . You get the idea. Hard to imagine Sisyphus being very happy with this little setup. No wonder he'd jumped at the chance to break out.

Suddenly more hands joined us at the boulder: little hairy ones, attached to the wiry monkeys who had once been the crew of our ship. Even Homer lent his pale, uncalloused hands to the task. I couldn't tell you what he really added to the overall effort, but it's the thought that counts.

With all of us pushing, the going was much easier. The monkeys' grunts fell into a steady rhythm, and we made good time with the boulder. But then suddenly a noise erupted from the depths of the chasm ahead: rock, shattering and crumbling. This was followed by the worst sound I'd ever heard. It could only have been made by Typhon, as the monster's mind began to swim to the surface of its consciousness. I remembered Homer's poetic description of the beast. He'd been right, it really *did* sound like the hiss of a hundred snakes and the roar of a hundred lions.

Finally we reached the top of the ramp. This was the spot where Sisyphus would normally hop to the flat area on one side and let the boulder roll back down. But that wasn't going to happen this time.

"We've . . . got to . . . lift it . . . up and . . . over!" I grunted.

"We can't!" Sisyphus protested. Rolling the boulder was one thing. Lifting it over the near-vertical bumper at the top of the hill was something altogether different.

But we had to try. The continued existence of the Universe depended on us . . . so no pressure there.

Inch by agonizing inch we rolled the boulder up the sheer rock face. Being the only one without hands, I had to use the top of my head. The pain was unbearable, but we bore it anyway. My muscles quivered; they begged for mercy; they screamed and carried on; they would have tried to bribe me with pies if they could. What they didn't do was give up, and the same was true of us all, monkeys, humans, and pig alike.

At last the boulder was poised on the very pinnacle of the ramp's top section. If we could just give it a tiny extra push, it would go tumbling down the steep side, right onto Thanatos.

But that was an almighty IF. We were spent. It had taken every last scrap of our strength to get the boulder to this point. It was all we could do now to stop it from crashing back down the slope we had just come up.

The monkeys' grunts around me had become ones of distress now, not determination.

"I think I've sprained my wrist," I heard Homer wail. "And it's the hand I write with!"

The boulder wobbled. We couldn't hold on much longer. The sound of Thanatos's pounding was the world's countdown to oblivion. Any second now Typhon would be free. . . .

But then there was another noise, a thin cry that came from the bottom of the slope behind us.

"Hold on! I'm coming!"

At first I couldn't see anything. Then I spotted it—something tiny hopping up the slope toward us.

It was Hoppy—Tithonus, the grasshopper who had spent decades plotting this moment when Typhon would be unleashed! But he didn't seem to be coming to try to stop us. No, he was coming to help, coming as fast as his little back legs would propel him. This wasn't very fast at all. Old age had finally caught up with the once-sprightly insect. Every hop was an effort, but still he kept on coming. It seemed to take an eternity for him to make his weary way up the slope.

At last we were within the aged insect's range. With a final spurt, he leaped up onto my back, using it as a springboard from which he sprang forward, as high as he could, in the direction of the boulder. He struck it head-on.

Hoppy was small enough to fit into the average pocket. He was a grasshopper, after all—he weighed less than one of Aphrodite's lace hankies. And yet . . . the tap he contributed was all we needed. As the insect struck the boulder, there was a brief, wonderful moment when our skin was still in contact with the rock, but we could tell that now we had momentum on our side.

Then the rock began to topple.

I watched it plummet, with Tithonus—little Hoppy the grasshopper!—still clinging to it. The aged insect made no attempt to leap to safety.

Down below, Thanatos stopped hammering and looked up, perhaps alerted by the whistling sound that could only be a very heavy object in free fall. For the first time ever, I glimpsed something other than blackness and void in the darkness of that cowl. It was an eye, and it was wide open.

With fear?

Well, no one likes to have a great big boulder land on his head, not even Death. But Thanatos was flat out of luck. Actually, *first* he was out of luck and *then* he was flat. It was a perfect shot—one moment Thanatos was standing there, looking up helplessly; the next he had been squashed by the plummeting boulder!

Up on top of the ramp, Homer led the monkeys in a rousing cheer. It went on right up to the moment when the boulder pinning Thanatos wobbled. The cheers petered out a bit when the rock shot up into the air. It landed nearby and then rolled away. Thanatos got to his feet. He dusted himself off carefully. Then he raised his scrawny hand, ready to continue the task of freeing Typhon. It would not be long now before the monster was free.

We had failed. This was it, then, the end. . . .

"Hold it right there!" a voice behind us boomed.

Thanatos looked up. He hesitated. Then he dropped his arm in resignation.

I looked back to see the Princess Aurelia racing down the upper slopes of the plateau. She was joined by a towering and well-known figure.

It was Zeus, the King of the Gods, and he was carrying a stack of trusty thunderbolts!

Thanatos was not about to disobey a direct command from the Big Z. He nodded once, straightened himself, and then skulked off into the shadows with as much dignity as he could muster.

We had done it! The Cosmos was safe again and order could be restored. So why did I now have an empty feeling in the pit of my stomach that for once had little to do with the chronic absence of pies?

BOOK XXXII

The King of the Gods is feeling touchy.

Things got pretty busy pretty fast and, before long, the Underworld was crawling with deities. They were all still a bit dazed after their enforced naps up on Olympus, and there was lots of aimless milling about while the Olympians got on with the job of securing Typhon again.

Once Pluto, Lord of the Underworld, had turned up and started barking out orders, things became a bit more organized. We overheard a gang of centaurs moaning about the task they had been given: waking Cerberus, the three-headed hound of Hades, armed with only a squeaky toy.

I heard rumors that a posse was being organized to find both Proteus and Sisyphus, but I knew that neither would be found. The former was able to change into any form he wanted; the latter had shown himself too cunning to be caught a second time by mere deities.

While all the activity continued around us, there wasn't really much a bunch of undead, mixed-species mortals like us could do to help in this cleanup operation. Finally, Aurelia said something about wanting to check up on her father. As she left, the monkeys seized the opportunity to take their panicked leave of the Underworld also.

That left just Homer and me. I wasn't going to budge, not until I had spoken to Zeus. All we could do was watch and stay out of the way as the immortals went about their work of putting the Underworld back in order. I looked on as a group of dryads tended to Polyphemus. The cyclops still looked frail, but he was sitting up and sipping a cup of nectar (extra strong, four sugars). I overheard a snippet of conversation to the effect that Hephaestus, Smith of the Gods, was going to reward his bravery with a cushy job at his forge on Olympus.

"So . . . I suppose Orpheus *was* the NO BODY who let them get past Proteus, then," Homer said thoughtfully.

I frowned. "I don't think so," I said. "When I came across Proteus the second time, I . . . sort of lost it for a moment. I forgot who I was, you might say, and just went wild. In a sense, I was *nobody* then, you know? I imagine that's what the prediction meant."

Homer considered this. "I don't think so," he murmured. "Anyway, I think the Beast in the premonition was referring to Typhon, not Proteus. It was Orpheus's song, wasn't it, that helped you think of rolling the rock up the hill? NO BODY."

I was getting a bit fed up with this. "That's true," I said through gritted teeth. "But it was *me* who started the boulder rolling. And don't forget, back in the cyclops's cave, Polyphemus mistakenly referred to me as Nobody."

Homer considered this for a while. "Well, I don't suppose it matters. I mean, just so long as the Universe got saved in the end, who's going to argue?"

"Nobody," I snapped. "Nobody is going to argue . . . just like Nobody defeated the Beast of the Labyrinth!"

We watched the activity around us for a few minutes.

"So that would be me," I muttered.

"What?"

"Nothing."

We completed the rest of our wait in uneasy silence, and it was a relief when a river god finally came and told us that Zeus was ready to see us.

We were escorted to the Elysian Fields and ushered through the golden gates into that idyllic place of rolling hills, herbaceous borders, and nicely tended lawns. A centaur at the gates pointed out a grove of trees some distance away. Apparently, a throne had been carried down for the King of the Gods and he was set up in there.

As Homer and I made our way to the grove, a couple emerged from the trees ahead of us. I didn't recognize the woman, but you'll never guess who the man was . . . Orpheus! The singer was strolling, hand in hand, with the dark-haired woman. I'll just repeat that, in case you're Boeotian: the singer was STROLLING, HAND IN HAND, with the dark-haired woman. Yes, Orpheus and his body were reunited. What's more, he had some color back in his cheeks!

We rushed forward.

"Gryllus! Homer!" Orpheus enthused. The delighted smile transformed his face into one I hardly recognized, especially now that it had lost his gray-blue pallor. "I'd like you to meet—"

"Eurydice, I assume?" I bowed low and suavely waggled where my eyebrows would be, if I had any. "A pleasure to meet you."

Eurydice leaned down so our eyes were level. "I want to thank you for bringing my husband back to me."

"And for saving the world again, I suppose?" I prompted.

When she smiled, my heart cried out. It wasn't that she bore a close resemblance—Eurydice's hair was long and flowing, and her nose was much more slender and lacking a miniconstellation of freckles. But there was something about her—the flash in the eyes? The quick generosity of the smile?—that reminded me of Sibyl. This thought pierced my heart, despite my brain's reassurances that Zeus would soon be able to put things right for the ex-priestess.

"And for saving the world, too!" Eurydice said, laughing. She was accompanied by a mellifluous sound that was unfamiliar to me: the sound of Orpheus laughing.

I looked up at the greatest singer the world had ever known, paying particular attention to where his head now sat on his neck. "You can't see the seam," I said approvingly.

"Gryllus . . ." Homer hissed, as if I'd put my hoof in it again.

But Orpheus didn't mind. "Gryllus," he said, beaming, "I don't know how to thank you. I'm so happy I could give you a big hug."

"Oh yes? Why don't you?"

The singer's smile faltered a touch. "Er . . . I would. It's just that I'm still getting used to having a body again. I'm not too coordinated yet, and . . ."

"No worries," I said. "It's the thought that counts."

We said our farewells, and the reunited lovers wandered off to spend eternity together in the lush glades and hidden valleys and golf-course-standard greens of the Elysian Fields.

"Orpheus looks completely different now, doesn't he?" Homer commented.

"I think you may have a point." I rolled my eyes. "What is it though? Has he switched his hairstyle to a center part? Trimmed his nose hairs? Or is he perhaps STROLLING AROUND WITH A FULLY EQUIPPED, COMPLETELY WHOLE AND INTACT BODY?"

The thing is, Homer was right. The singer was reunited with his body, but there *was* something else: reunited at last with his true love (the love of his life, not to mention afterlife), Orpheus seemed complete again in every way.

Before they disappeared from view, Orpheus looked back at us and lifted one hand in farewell. It was a brief gesture but an eloquent one, and what it said to me was, "Thanks for everything, Gryllus, and, hey, I guess you were right: you can't switch off, you can't just detach yourself from the business of living life. Because sometimes it *does* all make sense, and being with the person you love has got to be one of those times."

Then again, Homer thought that Orpheus wasn't waving to us at all but was just swatting away a fly. I'll leave you to decide who was right, but consider this: it's not as if the all-powerful gods would go and let a fly into the Elysian Fields, is it?

There was a makeshift sign hanging from a branch outside Zeus's grove.

"No entry until the Father of the Gods summons you," Homer read out.

"Yeah, but obviously that's not for an old friend who's just saved the Universe for the second time in a row," I declared. "You wait here, Homer—I can handle this." I strode in, confident in the knowledge that Zeus would be overjoyed to see me again.

"Who dares intrude?" boomed the King of the Gods, his face royal-purple with Olympian fury. He pounded his fists on the arms of the huge ornate throne that had presumably been lugged here by some unfortunate minor deity. "A PIG?"

"It's me, Gryllus!" I said quickly. "Remember? The pig who saved the world . . . twice now, actually, but who's counting?"—I gave a quick backward glance to where Homer was waiting outside—"Although this second time is subject to debate. You see . . ."

"Enough!" commanded Zeus. Despite our shared history, he remained aloof and stony-faced. "I remember you. And I know what you have come to ask of me. . . . The deity who transformed you into a hog is the only one who can transform you back. The one called Circe is on Olympus still." Zeus stroked his majestic beard. "But the enchantress prefers to keep her own counsel; she is not happy in the company of other deities. She will not remain on Olympus for long. As soon as she wakes, she will ready herself to leave."

The King of the Gods raised one immense, muscular arm and opened his palm. A zigzag light in his eyes flickered, and beyond the grove, there was a flash of lightning, accompanied by an instant boom of thunder. The air suddenly smelled of singed grass.

"Outside this grove, next to the entrance gates to the Elysian Fields, you will find a shortcut to the summit of Olympus," Zeus declared grandly. "Begone now, pig. Go to the enchantress, resume your true form, and bother the

Olympians no more—other than to worship us, as all mortals must."

His gigantic, thunderbolt-chucking hand dismissed me. I got the message loud and clear—my audience with Zeus was at an end.

But I couldn't leave, not yet. I stepped forward nervously. "O mighty Zeus, er, thanks very much . . . but actually, there's something else I wanted to ask you. . . ."

Beneath glowering eyebrows, Zeus's eyes darkened like storm clouds on the horizon.

"It's Sibyl," I pressed on.

Zeus's face was as blank as a slab of marble belonging to a stonemason with writer's block.

"The priestess from Delphi?" I prompted. "When Thanatos was released, she . . ." I could hardly bring myself to say the cruel words. ". . . she *passed on*."

"She passed on WHAT?" Zeus demanded irritably.

"No, I mean she . . ." My voice fell to a whisper. "She *died*."

"Yes? And?" The storm in Zeus's eyes was really raging now. He seemed to have forgotten any lessons he'd learned about the ever-present shadow of mortality. More pressingly, he seemed cross that I was still there. "*Lots* of mortals died when Thanatos was released. That's what *mortals* do! It's what the word *means*."

"Yes, but without Sibyl, the gods would still be sleeping on Olympus. . . . She's the one who went into the labyrinth and freed Thanatos. . . ."

"Then she jeopardized the Cosmos!" roared Zeus, leaping up from his throne. "Thanatos was mere seconds away from freeing Typhon, and if that had happened while we Olympians slept, the monster would have ripped the Cosmos apart! It would have—"

"I know, but—"

"Silence when Zeus is speaking, hog!"

"Sorry, but—"

"I said SILENCE!"

KZZZZZK! There was a sudden blinding flash, and the air was filled with another burning smell—not so much burned grass this time as grilled bacon. I looked in astonishment at the scorched earth right beside me. Another couple of inches and that lightning bolt would have frazzled me to a pork rind.

"So what you're saying is, you *won't* let her return to the Overworld? Because that seems a bit unfair, if you don't mind my say—"

"You test my patience, hog!" roared the Olympian. "Now begone, before it snaps! Zeus has spoken."

The storm was no longer in Zeus's eyes, it had moved directly overhead: a small, tight cluster of churning black cloud. Another lightning bolt sizzled from it—*KZZZZK!*—so close to my back legs that it made me yelp.

"Here, hang on!"

"I said BEGONE!"

KZZZZZK!

"All right, all right, I'm going!"

KZZZZZZZK!

If I hadn't been quick on my hooves, the next bolt would have incinerated me for sure. I raced toward the entrance.

"I can take a hint, you know!"

KZZZZZZZZZZZZKKK!
"BEGONE!"

Homer was waiting at the foot of the hill outside. He gave me a puzzled look when I burst back through the trees and down the slope with plumes of smoke rising from my rear end.

"What did Zeus say?" asked the bewildered poet.

No time to answer, not when I was charging past him and over to a babbling brook, then sticking my bum into its cool waters. It hissed gratefully (the bum, not the brook).

It was only when I opened my eyes that I noticed what had changed in the Elysian Fields. Over near the golden gates, a large gap had appeared. It was as if something had punched a hole between this reality and another. The light inside the hole seemed brighter than the air around it. I could see the first steps of a marble staircase within.

Homer's eyes followed mine. "There was this big flash of lightning, not long after you went into the grove," he said, "and then that hole just appeared."

I approached the opening. That staircase rose up and up, before disappearing into luminous cloud. "It's a shortcut to Olympus," I said. "Zeus made it so I could go and find Circe before she departs." I put one hoof on the bottom step. "She's the only one who can turn me back to my true form."

In my mind danced the familiar daydream of what life could be like if only I were human again. Me, sleeping in a bed again. Me, propping up the bar in my local taverna. Me, wandering into a pie shop without any fear that I might end up featured on the menu. This was a rational biped's world, and there was nothing I wanted more than to take my own two-footed place in it.

It was a nice idea; it really was. All I had to do was waltz up those stairs and make it a reality.

Pity that wasn't possible.

I wheeled around and started toward the gates out of the Elysian Fields.

"Where are you going?" spluttered Homer.

"Up to the Asphodel Fields," I replied, passing through the gates without another look back at the radiant stairway to Olympus. "If we can get to Sibyl before she forgets everything, we might still have a chance of getting her out of there!"

Homer hesitated, barely aware of the fly buzzing around him. Then the epic poet was running, too.

BOOK XXXIII

A certain someone shows a surprisingly soft side.

It's all very well for deities, who can whiz around in all sorts of zappy ways—turning themselves into owls, or riding on the back of giant eagles, or pulling on a pair of winged, flying booties. Meanwhile, poor old mortals like Homer and me have to go on foot.

And let me tell you, it was a long way back—out of Elysium, through the blasted earth of the Punishment Zone, and then up the long spiral path to Asphodel. By the time we were halfway, my four feet were killing me. By the time we were finally nearing Asphodel, I had begun to wish they'd finish the job and put me out of my misery.

"I'm dying," I gasped.

"You're in the right place for it," said Homer unsympathetically.

At last the path began to level off. We stepped out into the giant rocky cavern of the Underworld's central chamber. In front of us swirled the gray fog of Asphodel. We went as close as we could.

"Sibyl!" I shouted. "We've come to get you out of there!"

A few low moans emerged from the fog, but there was no answer.

I tried again, louder. "It's us—Gryllus and Homer!"

But that thick fog just trapped my words and stopped them dead. There was no way Sibyl could hear them.

I took a couple of nervous steps forward, until tendrils of the unearthly fog were creeping and winding around me. Even here, I could feel the numbness of that fog seeping into my mind. I could feel it starting to leech away all the memories.

My voice was frantic now. "SIBYL!"

A gray shape loomed out of the mist. Hope leaped in my heart like a salmon in a stream. It leaped right into the bear's mouth of disappointment as I realized that this wasn't Sibyl, although it *was* someone I knew. Being a recent arrival in this gray land, the shade gazed upon me with a faint glimmer of recognition, a slight, disdainful curl of the lip. It was the priest Hieros, and the reason for his demise was clear. There was a thick golden coin wedged in the top of his skull. He must have been standing under the balcony when Sisyphus dropped his change during the coin toss.

Hieros stumbled back into the fog, but there was still no sign of Sibyl. Worry began to gnaw at me like a worm eating . . . AN APPLE! Yes, that's it—worry began to gnaw at me *like a worm eating an apple,* and definitely not a dead body, which wouldn't be appropriate in this context.

I began to move farther into the fog, but Homer's hand fell on my back.

"You can't, Gryllus!" cried the poet. "You'd never find her in there. Even if you did, you probably wouldn't remember your own name by then, let alone hers." He pulled me back from the deadening fog. "It's over, Gryllus. It's over."

"If . . . there's one thing . . . I've learned . . . in my long life," a small, muffled voice behind us piped up, "it's . . . don't jump . . . to conclusions."

"What was that?" I said, but Homer was already kneeling down.

"Be a sport and . . . pick me up, would you, old chum?" Hoppy puffed.

The little grasshopper was in a bad way, all battered and crumpled. He was Hoppy in name only now, but somehow he had managed to crawl his way up here.

Homer picked the bug up gently in cupped hands. I had to lean in close to hear him now.

"Looking for the girl, are you?" he gasped. "Set me down . . . I'll go and . . . find her for you."

"I don't understand," I said. "Why did you help us? You

wanted Typhon to destroy everything, didn't you? That was your whole plan, right?"

The crumpled insect blinked, apparently with enormous effort. "I thought it was . . . old chum," he managed. "But that was . . . before I saw Eos's face again. You can't go . . . destroying a world with . . . something like that in it . . . can you?"

Homer put the grasshopper back down on the rock floor, and Hoppy began making his slow, painful way into the heart of Asphodel.

"What about the fog?" I asked. "You'll forget everything!"

Hoppy said something in reply, but his voice was getting fainter and fainter. It almost sounded like, "Hope so."

There was nothing we could do but watch him go. Suddenly a dark figure emerged from the mist ahead of him. It was hard to make out, but the figure was too tall to be Sibyl. Too skinny. Too jaw-droppingly terrifying.

Thanatos, God of Death, was walking out of the fog and toward the ancient grasshopper. Hoppy didn't seem to have noticed; he just kept hopping forward with his head down.

I was dimly aware of Homer's shouted warning to the insect, but I knew that Hoppy could do nothing. Of course there were no Olympians around when you needed them. There was nobody but us and Death and the gray, gray fog.

But the funny thing is, I didn't feel panic, more a leaden tiredness all through my bones. What's more, I felt resentful. Did Thanatos have to cast its shadow over every single thing in this life? I thought bitterly.

And then I didn't think anything, because I was moving. Before Homer knew what was going on, I raced forward on a collision course to intercept Thanatos before he reached the grasshopper. The cowl of his tattered black robes continued to point in the insect's direction as I put on a final spurt. I'd just about reached maximum speed when I barreled right into Thanatos's shins. I just had time to register how cold and bony his legs felt, how knobbly his knees were, and then we were both tumbling forward and slamming into the black rock.

A phrase from my childhood bobbed to the surface of my mind. "Enjoy your trip?" I asked Death itself.

Thanatos pointed his cowl in my direction. I was unable to pull my eyes away from that dread blackness, which seemed to extend back infinitely, or at least a lot farther than you'd expect.

"And what were you planning to do next, Gryllus?" asked that uncanny voice.

"I, er, I thought I'd just make it up as I went along."

"I do appreciate . . . the thought, old chum," said a small voice. "But . . . you needn't bother." The little grasshopper looked like a dried-up leaf now, and his voice was no more than the rustle of wind through it. But he was still moving!

"I *wanted* . . . Thanatos to be here," said the insect. "I've had a good run . . . and now it's over."

"But . . . you're immortal," I said.

The spirit of Death reached out a long, pale hand for the grasshopper to hop onto.

Hoppy's voice was the thinnest of whispers now. "Sometimes the gods are strong enough to beat Thanatos," he said. "But not always."

Thanatos lifted the grasshopper and spoke soft words over

him. Instinctively, I lowered my eyes. When I looked back up, Thanatos was setting the insect down again.

The grasshopper blinked his one good eye. "Much appreciated, old chum."

He began to crawl on into the heart of the fog. As he did so, his form seemed to shift and change. With each movement, he seemed to get bigger and bigger, to look more and more like a warm-blooded vertebrate (well, maybe not a warm-blooded one), until finally he was not an insect at all. He rose from his crouching position in human form once more. As Sibyl had said, everything and everybody has its time, and this was Hoppy's/Tithonus's. He didn't look back, and soon the pale outline of his figure was lost in the mist.

It was only when he had completely disappeared from view that I remembered who I was standing next to. An odd idea came to me: in trying to release Typhon, Thanatos had been acting without malice. He was merely doing what he was supposed to do. It wasn't his fault that the usual checks weren't in place.

"About tripping you up . . ." I began. Thanatos, embodiment of Death itself, began to reach one hand toward me. "An honest mistake, that was," I continued hastily, "but I'm sure you'll—"

The hand of Death hovered right in front of me. Its bony fingers clenched into a fist that filled my vision, swaying from side to side like a cobra. Then the cobra struck. Or—for those of you who shy away from the more vividly poetic descriptions—Thanatos whacked me on the head.

Before the blanket of unconsciousness descended, a single thought echoed through my brain: "OW!"

EPILOGUE

I awoke in the Overworld, the land of mortals.

Specifically, I was back on the island of Crete, in the Labyrinth of the palace of Knossos, with Homer by my side.

We were in no shape to navigate the labyrinth—my head was killing me—but luckily we had been deposited near an exit on the outer rim of the giant maze. (Was that mere chance or was it Death being helpful?)

My headache was still raging two days later, despite the medical ministrations of King Midas's top leech-man.

The palace was now the sort of place that gets called a *hive of activity*. With Sisyphus still missing, King Midas—his broken bones now on the mend—had taken over the palace. He intended to stay here in Knossos only until his army's dead were buried and the wounded cared for. After that, he was packing up and going home to Phrygia.

His daughter Aurelia's transformation on Olympus proved to be both genuine and long-lasting. She really was a different kind of royal princess now. She *did* have a heart of gold and not one made from a shiny, heavy metal of high malleability. She informed Homer that she planned to spend the rest of her days devoting herself to good works. To this end, she was going to set up the civilized world's first ever Primate Center for Retired Sailors. I wasn't sure how this would go down with Simios and the rest of the crew, but once they saw the architect's plans—with its clumps of coconut and banana trees and adventure playground, plus two fully equipped tavernas and tattoo parlors—they whooped with undisguised delight.

"Agh, aaagh, aaaggh," commented the captain, gesticulating wildly at me.

"You don't say, Captain!" I replied absently. "How splendid!"

I only wished that I could work up that level of enthusiasm for anything. But for me the day crawled by like an under-achieving snail, and my constant companion through these long hours was the thought that I had failed. I had given up the chance of becoming human again to save Sibyl, and then I had failed to save Sibyl. It all felt wrong. It made no sense that the ex-priestess was no longer here, and that lack of sense rippled out to touch everything.

I was awake the whole night long. I finally gave up on the attempt to sleep when the first rays of light stole into my room. I wearily shuffled outside to the battlements.

It was worth the effort. The sun had not yet appeared, but the sky in the east was the most glorious mix of colors I had ever seen—too beautiful to attempt to describe in words, so I won't try. I wondered if perhaps this dawn was especially beautiful because Eos, Goddess of the Dawn, was giving Tithonus a proper send-off.

As I gazed at the eastern sky, I felt . . . what? Something I wasn't accustomed to, I suppose. For just a few moments, I felt calm.

I knew it wouldn't last. But alone there in the pale light, I realized something. Pondering the meaning of life—even whether it doesn't seem a bit pointless at times—is just a part of what makes us human. It sets us apart from the animals and it sets us apart from the cyclopes and even from the gods—the ability to take a step back and view the world and our place in it objectively.

But this doesn't mean we can just disconnect ourselves from life; we can't look at it objectively and then try to deny the "I" that is doing the looking—Orpheus had attempted that and had failed. We can't hide behind hollow laughter at everything on the grounds that nothing makes sense, that it's all pointless, as Sisyphus had tried.

No, being human meant juggling both beliefs: the fundamental sense of your own importance—all your dreams and hopes and likes and interests—on one hand, with the cold, hard truth of your cosmic insignificance on the other. And if you found yourself struggling to reconcile the two, here's what you should do:

Get a hobby.

Get a hobby, or . . . *whistle a happy song,* or *eat a decent pie,* or *play cards with a friend,* or *get up early and watch Eos do her thing* . . .

These weren't mere distractions, and they certainly couldn't give your life any grand underlying meaning. But sometimes, just sometimes, they could help unite the warring parts of our torn natures, even if just for a while. And maybe that was enough.

I continued along the dark battlements, wondering if I might be able to see the sea from the tower at the corner. I didn't notice the caped figure in the shadows up ahead until a husky voice addressed me.

"Halt! Who goes there?"

I sighed. Was it really necessary to post sentries at a time like this?

"Gryllus," I said.

"Who? You look a bit piggy to me!" Where had this guard been?

"Midas knows all about me," I explained.

The guard didn't respond.

"I'm the pig who saved the world, for gods' sake!" I exclaimed at last. The words sounded hollow to me, but I just wanted to get past this overeager guard with the whispery voice.

"That'll do for me!" declared the guard in her true voice, and she stepped forward out of the shadows, throwing the hood back from her face and beaming at me. "But didn't you have a little help from your friends?"

My heart did a triple somersault. "Sibyl!" I shrieked the obvious: "You're alive!"

The ex-priestess nodded. "They let me back because the books of the dead didn't balance. They had one soul too many down there. . . ." She smiled sadly. "It was Tithonus . . . Hoppy the Grasshopper. So they had to send someone back, and Thanatos picked me . . . thanks to you, Gryllus."

She took a deep breath, savoring the precious sweetness of the early-morning air, even though *I* was in the vicinity. "I can't believe I'm saying this, Gryllus, but I'm so happy I could give you a hug!"

Oh, yes? I'd heard this one before. "Why don't you, then?" I replied.

And get this: she did.

*   *   *

A couple of hours later, Sibyl, Homer, and I were sitting at a table in front of a little taverna outside the palace walls. I'm sure we could have had the full royal banquet with all the ceremonial trimmings from Midas, but somehow this just felt right.

Also, Sibyl was in no mood to wait for fancy feast preparations. Being dead had put an edge on her appetite, and she was currently giving me a run for my money on the breakfast spread in front of us.

Inevitably, it was Homer who raised the topic of what we'd been through in the lower realm.

"So the premonition you had . . . how do you think it actually came true?" The epic poet leaned forward. "*Was* Orpheus the Nobody who defeated the Beast in the Dark?"

Unable to speak through a mouth full of baklava, Sibyl simply shrugged.

"No, it was me, wasn't it?" I jumped in.

Sibyl swallowed. "Who knows? That's the thing about the predictions business. With the benefit of hindsight, you can always come up with some nifty explanation to fit them." She picked up another piece of sticky pastry but hesitated before popping it into her mouth. "Consider this: remember when Zeus arrived and ordered Thanatos to stop? Well . . . did you know that wasn't actually Zeus? The King of the Gods wasn't fully awake by then, but time was running out, so Aurelia ordered Proteus to assume the form of the King of the Gods and pretend to be Zeus."

My mouth hung open in shock. "So you're saying . . . Proteus was the Nobody in the prediction? Why, because he could change his form? He could be *anybody*, and so, in a sense, he was *nobody*. Is that it?"

"Perhaps," said Sibyl blithely. "Then again, consider *this*. Who told Aurelia to find Proteus and have him do it?" She grinned at our blank faces. "It was me! I was already in Asphodel and my memory was beginning to fade. Seeing you, Gryllus, and the cyclops jolted me back to my senses long enough for me to call out to Aurelia when she came down to the Underworld."

"And you were dead at the time? So maybe YOU were the nobody?"

"It doesn't really matter, does it?" Sibyl grinned. "Besides, you're forgetting something *else*—there was a second part of the premonition, wasn't there?"

"'No one will be able to save the Universe,'" said Homer. "Yes, how do you explain that one?"

Of course Sibyl was ready with an answer. "It was when you were rolling the rock of Sisyphus up the hill. No ONE of you could do it; you *all* had to do it, working together."

All this talk of interpreting premonitions was starting to distract me from the serious job of consuming breakfast. The table was almost cleared of food, and I was still hungry. Just one solitary mini-pie sat there, looking lonely.

"Bet you'd like nothing better than that nice hot pie, eh, Homer?" I asked.

"That's true," agreed the poet, who had been too busy listening to eat much.

"Good!" I said. "You can have nothing, then, and I'll have this pie."

I made a dive for it with my snout, and Homer reached for it with his hand. We collided and knocked the pie onto the dusty ground.

"What are we going to do now?" I huffed. I had been talking about breakfast, but as soon as the words left me, they took on new meaning. What *were* we going to do, now that the Cosmos was safe again? The future stretched in front of us, but at that moment it seemed to hold more horrible uncertainty than glorious freedom. What was *I* going to do? Try to find Circe again? I didn't even know for sure that the mysterious enchantress had returned to Aeaea. Was I doomed to remain a pig forever?

"You know, life's a bit like that," I began falteringly. "You try to take something from the Table of Life, but it's snatched from you, and then the Menu of the Future is all smudged with ketchup marks, so you can't—"

Sibyl slapped her hand on the table. "I'll tell you what we're going to do. . . ." she declared. "We're going to order the same again! My treat!"

My anxiety fled, just like that. The future was coming anyway; there would be plenty of time to worry about it.

No, sometimes you just have to enjoy the moment, and if that moment entails good friends and more hot pies on the way, then so much the better.

Afterword

Before we left Knossos, I dictated this second installment of our adventures to Homer. It took several days and copious quantities of pies to complete. Finally, the poet laid down his writing stylus.

"Well, what do you think?" I asked. "Does it need a little more pathos?"

"I don't know," Homer replied with a distant little smirk. "I think it's quite pathetic enough."

Teenage epic poets, eh?

Glossary of Some More Terms for Barbarians Who Still Can't Speak Greek

Asclepius: The God of Medicine and Healing

Asphodel Fields: A part of the Underworld where most deceased mortals go to wander its dark, foggy halls as ghostly shades who remember nothing of their former lives

Circe: Mysterious minor goddess who often turned unsuspecting visitors to her island into animals

cyclopes: Disgusting, carnivorous giants, rarely asked to parties because of poor table manners and recreational farting. See **Polyphemus**.

Elysian Fields: Beautiful part of the Underworld for dead heroes to spend eternity in; has very strict admissions policy

Eos: The Goddess of the Dawn, renowned for her rosy fingers and habit of getting up early

Eurydice: Wife of **Orpheus**; beautiful but very shortsighted (died after stepping on a snake, believing it to be a very thin sock)

Hephaestus: The Blacksmith of the Gods

Labyrinth: The mazelike network of tunnels built to house the **Minotaur** in the Cretan palace at Knossos

Lotus Eaters: Island dwellers who live on a diet of lotus fruit, which makes them forget their home and want nothing more than to stay on the island in their trancelike state

Midas: King who was granted his wish that everything he touched would turn into gold; first realized this ability was in fact a curse when he attempted to eat a bowl of solid-gold Wheato Flakes

Minotaur: Bull-headed, flesh-eating monster who dwelled in the **Labyrinth** at Knossos and was finally defeated by the hero Theseus

obol: A small silver or iron coin used in much of ancient Greece. (In Thebes, the site of the world's first facilities with coin-operated locks, people said that they were "going to spend an obol" when they needed to use the bathroom.)

Olympus: The mountaintop home of the gods

Orpheus: Greatest singer in the ancient world; entered the Underworld itself to bring his dead wife, **Eurydice,** back, but failed. Considered by many to be the ultimate musical performer—even after death, his head continued singing.

Pluto (also known as Hades): Longfaced God of the Underworld and younger brother of **Zeus**

Polyphemus: Cyclops in whose cave Odysseus and several crew members were trapped

Proteus: Minor god of the seas, able to change his form into any shape

sirens: Monsters who lured passing sailors to a watery grave with their irresistible song

Sisyphus: King condemned to spend eternity in **Tartarus** rolling a boulder up a hill

Tartarus: Unpleasant area of the Underworld where the wicked suffer eternal punishment; not recommended for a weekend city break. Also known as the Punishment Zone.

Thanatos: The embodiment of Death. Not really one of the gods. Sometimes referred to as The Great Leveler and The Ultimate Party Pooper.

Tithonus: Young prince who went out with the goddess **Eos** and was granted eternal life but not eternal youth; eventually shrank until he was a grasshopper. Also known as Hoppy the Grasshopper.

Typhon: A terrible monster with a hundred serpents' heads and fiery eyes—so actually, a really *good* monster, then. Consigned to **Tartarus** by **Zeus** after it tried to destroy the world.

Zeus: King of the Olympian gods; also known as The Big Z, Old Man Thunder, and (to his face) "Mighty Zeus, Lord of the Thunderbolts and All-around Diamond Deity"

Note from the Translator

I was alerted to the existence of a second batch of so-called *Pig Scrolls* by a Mrs. Ethel Prendergast of Kickapoo, Wisconsin, who discovered them in her attic. Her son Kenny had brought them back as a souvenir from a Sun 'n' Fun Club cruise to Crete (along with a classically patterned ashtray and a model bull that pees when you squeeze its head).

In my capacity as a freelance expert on the Ancient World, I was able to explain to Mrs. Prendergast that the scrolls were—alas—forgeries and, as such, worthless. I generously offered to take them off her hands for the grand sum of 40 cents.

Subsequent carbon-dating tests revealed that my initial assessment was not entirely accurate; the scrolls *were,* in fact, genuine—and so highly valuable ancient artifacts. In light of this information, I have sent Mrs. Prendergast and Kenny an additional $3.60 (cash), and now consider the matter closed. I should be grateful, therefore, if Mr. Kenneth Prendergast (who is apparently an amateur bodybuilder of some repute in the Great Lakes region) would refrain from texting me messages saying that, unless I return the scrolls (which I bought fair and square), he plans to fly to the U.K. and punch me so hard I will be "orbiting Venus."

Paul Shipton, M.A., M.Phil., Third-Grade Milk Monitor

If you have enjoyed this ancient Greek text, look out for the following titles in Candlewick's Ancient Classics for Modern Kidz series:

The Oresteia by **Aeschylus:** Agamemnon returns from the Trojan War, but everything goes wrong, with hilarious consequences. An uproarious tragedy cycle for the whole family.

Aesop's Fables: Old favorites, such as "The Tortoise and the Hare," and less well-known fables, such as "The Lobster and the Head Louse."

The Odyssey by **Homer:** The exciting adventures of some guy who sailed with Gryllus the Pig. Or try the sequel— *The Odyssey II: This Time It's Personal*—in which Odysseus realizes that he left his toothbrush at Troy and sails back to get it.

Metaphysics by **Aristotle:** If you love *Harry Potter,* try this fascinating treatise in which one of the greatest brains of the ancient world ponders the hierarchy of existence. Or something like that. . . . OK, it isn't packed with terrific characters or magic or an exciting and engaging story in a school setting, but it does have an in-depth philosophical analysis of the distinction between matter and form.
Look, just read it.
No, really.
Please.